BABES and SUCKLINGS

BABES AND
SUCKLINGS

BY PHILIP WYLIE

1 9   2 9

WILDSIDE PRESS

www.wildsidepress.com

For Sally

PART ONE

1

THORNTON never deserted a channel of thought until he had followed it into several branches of association. Blunt, bare ideas discomfited him. In the matter of murders and births, food, clothing, and legislation, as well as in all other matters, he related the theme to a specific case and then to its place in philosophy, in practice, and in the cosmos itself. Thus if someone mentioned the depth of the ocean, he would recall seeing a diver plunge into the muddy harbor water from a dock in Toulon, he would bring to mind figures comparing marine abysses with mountain peaks, and an acute, almost painful consciousness of time and space would occupy him. Nevertheless, he abhorred the effects of such thinking in conversation. It resulted in minute research and hair-splitting.

Moreover, he was introspective. His mind was obsessed with the business of orienting itself and comparing itself with other minds. As he grew, and added to his knowledge, he felt himself becoming more and more aloof, until a sort of solipsism made him both the most self-centered and the most vague person in his experience.

BABES AND SUCKLINGS

Because his vision was broad and because he hated the routine of small talk and often burst it apart out of sheer ennui, he was considered brilliant. He tried to be just about that opinion and admitted only that he was facile-minded to himself. He could not tolerate the easy application of "brilliant" to his mind because he perceived that the word was used in contemporary circles for everyone and everything that excelled mere articulation.

It was a painful state for a young man who had many friends of both sexes, excellent business prospects, a good education in the conventions, a vigorous, intriguing personality, and a thorough grounding in God and the Devil, art, labor, drink, Europe and America, and the cynical piddling of modern society.

If it is true that his attitude was controlled by his glands, then the balances of their secretion were not stable. Occasionally he felt himself so sensitive to the rawnesses of living that he suffered out of sympathy, and frequently he withdrew from the cannonading of circumstance so that the greatest human intimacy was as far beyond his sympathy as a dream. Behind both postures was a professional individual who felt it necessary on all occasions to be disillusioned and critical and facetious.

Sometimes Thornton believed that person was his real ego, and at other times he withered it with the name of defense mechanism, which is an expression spawned prematurely in the midst of mankind and one capable of more havoc than poison.

BABES AND SUCKLINGS

That, briefly, was Thornton as he saw himself. It was rubbish, of course. He was not a dummy stuffed to the neck with processes and empty in the head. The processes were there. But man, the animal, upon whom thought has been suddenly and startlingly superimposed, goes far afield when he considers himself. The knowledge that he is governed by a set of laws depresses him and makes him clever. Thornton, in his struggle to conciliate his body for the outrage of a mind, went through the same fugitive gestures that Socrates and Plato attempted, that Freud commenced to define, and that faint wits from the bosom of mother earth consider sufficient basis for theologies, arts, and lecture tours.

In the end, precisely those homely virtues that have been the bulwark of differentiation of the species, the principle for the breeding of good men or good horses, the teachings of Jesus, and the obvious essence of living, clasped Thornton firmly and set him where only the most insistent of fools would be sad. He recovered from the mental panic that is shaking the tongues of the earth, he relinquished his dogmatic heresies, and yet he managed to avoid being prosaic.

But, because of the original tangle of his consciousness, it was necessary for him to fling headlong at a number of the devices he used to determine himself, lave them in his emotions, batter them with his muscles, and bleed on them. Idiotically enough, that procedure is called growth, adolescence, maturing, developing, by the very people who believe that the fittest survive. Instead, it usually leads to enfeeblement, perversion, and

5

dwarfishness. Intellectual and physical obstacles should be removed from the route of progress, rather than cast into it; otherwise, *reductio ad absurdum,* it would be wise to blind all poets with the purpose of producing Miltons. Thornton was aware of the dilemma confronting him, but the popular attitude made any escape impossible.

2

Dawn was near. Thornton sensed the odor of it, rather than its ghostly, visible presence. His knees were tremulous as he bent them to descend the brownstone steps. Sarah's window grated and he looked up at the yellow oblong of light that streamed from it. She blew a kiss and he waved his cane. Her bare shoulders leaned out and she watched his casual disappearance into dark and distance. She was exhilarated. Men original enough to rise and dress in the clammy hours of a night that had once been loving were valuable, she thought. They appreciated the nuances of life; they felt the fustiness of breakfast together. If he had stayed, she would have liked him for the romance of his presence at her matutinal table.

Thornton, moving noisily through the early mornings, realized that her emotions no longer had a place in his compassion. He was through. Opening the window and leaning out had determined that. It lent to the whole *affaire* a taint of assignation, of departure upon the receipt of value. He passed a news-stand where a figure stood holding outstretched fingers over the embers in a rusty ash-can and singing aimless "do-deo-do's."

Thornton halted and returned. "Morning *World*," he said.

The man stopped singing and extricated a paper from the piles waiting for the subway riders. Thornton paid his nickel and listened while an iron worm rumbled down Seventh Avenue and passed beneath his feet, shaking the sidewalk.

"Who's gonna win?" the man asked.

"Win what?" It was like being wakened from a doze.

"Hell." Just "Hell"—a pointed and logical comment on the obliviousness of his customer. Thornton felt rebuked.

"Dempsey."

The man laughed. His disgust was audible as Thornton retreated. Then a truck, rolling ponderously over the cobble-stones, drowned it. He held his breath, crossed the street, rounded a corner out of sight of the newsdealer, exhaled, and walked to his apartment.

He was sleepy and dimly distraught. The alarm-clock indicated four. He wound it and set it at ten. Then he undressed, climbed into bed, and thought about Sarah and the news-man and Dempsey until he slept. A cloudy light fell on the disorder of his flimsy, yellow hair and the swift, straight lines of his jaw and brow.

7

BABES AND SUCKLINGS

3

Cynthia stood in the awful grandeur of the Pennsylvania Station and drank it thirstily. She opened her pigskin pocket-book, took out a baggage check, stared at it absently, and returned her gaze to the colossal columns that towered above the little people everywhere on the floor. Then she sighed as if she were executing something in her soul. She wanted to desert her post at the information booth and to run up the broad stairs, two at a time, so that she could absorb the full sweep of the architecture. The small restraint stabilized her reflections, which were running dizzily hither and thither through faces and clipped conversations.

"Oh—here you are, Mrs. Sherman!"

Perry Breck identified himself in the multitude, hurried to her side, lifted her valise, and commenced a smooth, integrated chatter, as if he had discovered her in an embarrassing predicament and wished to relieve her of discomfiture. His urbanity only served to confuse her. A cab lifted them to the tornado of sound in Seventh Avenue and moved impatiently through the traffic.

In the space of an hour she had been thrust up to a room in her hotel, she had bathed, she had been brought abruptly into a quiet restaurant, where she suddenly relaxed and realized that she was very hungry. Perry Breck timed his interrogation so well that she knew beforehand what courses would be cleared away and what would remain when he asked his first question. With the ice he said: "When your wire came, I realized that I had been expecting it ever since I met you in California. One becomes a little—ah—disillusioned in New York. It is a great help to the insight."

With the coffee: "Tell me—is it final?"

Cynthia nodded. "Yes. I couldn't go back. Funny—but I don't hate my husband. He was dull and I think he will be sorry I left him—sorry and surprised, because he really thought that as long as he had money, no woman could ask for more."

"And you found that was not true?"

Cynthia lifted her eyebrows in mild surprise. "Why—yes."

He laughed lightly. "You're under thirty, my dear. Under thirty. Well— I don't wish myself that misfortune. What will you do?"

"I don't know."

"Sue him, of course. The California courts will award you plenty of alimony. That's the first step."

"But I don't want his money. I thought I'd get a job."

His airy laughter was uttered again. It was pleasant laughter. "My dear child, are you fitted for anything?"

"I'm not a moron."

"Of course not. So you will not get a job, as you say. I want you to believe what I am going to tell you. I have lived in New York all my life. Any serious

9

discussion of business women is mere piffle. There are girl stenographers and girl clerks, manikins and show girls, and every last one is working because work introduces her to men. Men mean money, or, at least, idleness—which is their goal. The only other sort of working-woman is one whose sex is useless to her and who works merely to keep alive for something that has already lost its purpose. Find me a girl at work who hasn't a man in the background, and I'll buy Brooklyn Bridge for you. Unless, of course, she is the type who will never have a man in the background."

"I can't be expected to believe that."

Perry Breck repeated his affable, empty chuckle. "Not yet. But I can eliminate the middleman for you—the employer. And I can make it unnecessary for you to undergo the disagreeable mummery that wage-earning entails. By introducing you to my friends."

"What do I do then? Marry one of them?"

"Oh, dear," Perry Breck said. "Oh, dear."

4

Geraldine McGrath, of Columbia, of Great Neck, of the *Evening Record*, and Donald Shaw, of Dean and Payson, Advertising, opened their doors simultaneously and stood face to face in the hall. They scanned each other and he followed her downstairs, opening the front door by half-encircling her with an awkward gesture. She said: "Thank you."

She was careful not to be totally impersonal.
"Subway?" he asked.
"Yes. Down town. I'm a reporter on the *Record.*"
"Are you? I'm with Dean and Payson."
"Have you lived here long?"
"No. I just moved in."
"Me, too."
"Here we are. I go up."
"I go down."
"Good-bye."
"—bye. See you—"
"—later."

5

Michael Palidini finished his caricature, called the telegraph-office, and asked for a boy, whom he dispatched to the *Record* with the fruit of his labor. It was Saturday afternoon and early spring. A reluctant twilight dipped the streets in constantly deeper greys. The air that rilled through the open windows and the balcony door made the room more a part of the afternoon than of the apartment building. He breathed it with that satisfaction which is brought in the hint of summer and the ease of work completed.

Then he procured a large crock from the kitchenette, poured into it half a gallon of alcohol, an equal amount of water, a spoonful of juniper extract, a jug of cider, and the juice and slices of a large bowl of fruit. He stirred the punch thoroughly, tasted it with a wooden spoon, fetched a glass, and drank a deep draught. On second thought he added a dash of pepper to the contents of the crock.

His door-bell rang. Michael pressed the button and waited. Thornton appeared.

Michael greeted him vehemently. His eyes shone, his hand was held out warmly, his mouth smiled. Thornton became instantly happy in his company. A tedium slipped from him like a monody moved out of ear-shot. He dipped out a glass of punch, tasted it, and then drank thirstily while Michael watched with a grin half compassionate, half amused.

The liking the two men held for each other would have been pathetic or absurd to an outsider. It sprang from mutual esteem and the mutual protection of something precious shared between them. Michael, while only ten years Thornton's senior, looked twice his age. One, perhaps, was a young man who seemed still younger, and the other matured beyond his right. They commenced a second drink standing and smiling at one another, not talking.

They were, in fact, friends of an older and more noble school than exists in common practice. Human relationship was seldom more complete. The friends of Michael and Thornton were occasionally forced to a bitter and distasteful defense of the friendship against the assaults of the Freudian-minded and the feeble-minded. But the two men involved either blinked

sardonically at such insinuations, or were so careless of
conventional reputation as to ignore them.

Michael said: "There's going to be whoopee made
tonight."

"Mmmmm. Will there be a new girl for me?"

The artist set his empty glass on the long table.
"Am I my brother's procurer?"

"One gets to rely on your parties."

"And Sarah?"

Thornton settled himself in a chair. "Sarah leaned
too far out of a window—and fell."

"And broke a blood-vessel?"

"—that was nowhere near her heart."

"She'll probably come over here tonight."

"Cock-eyed. Whereupon I shall pass out."

"And she will leave in tears."

"In someone else's car."

The two drinks burned in Thornton's vitals. The
fieryness made him perversely complacent and specula-
tive. "It's a dirty world."

"Sure," Michael agreed.

"I amble about New York all day and half the
night, and I can't find one person who is leading what
you would call a pure and earnest life. So-and-so is
looking for a divorce on such-and-such nasty grounds.
Bill is chorine-crazy and his wife loves the landlord. I
fall for a movie actress's face and meet her at a night
club, listen to three jokes, and go home in purple laughter. I like the way an actress acts, and the best she can
do on examination is to be a dope-fiend and everybody's

friend. I run up to the open country for an early week-end, and a farmer seventy-two years old is being run out of town by the parents of the twins. I then amble out to a prim suburb, and the latest dirt is pumped into me like serum: the good boy in my class in college has run off with the bank's ready cash; so-and-so has killed three people driving while intoxicated; and a distant relative has gone off his nut and poisoned his wife and three children. It's hard for an unattached bachelor to do wrong, but I tremble every time I move from my flat. A little psychoanalysis shows you what virtue there is in the people who advertise that they are trying to be virtuous by joining churches and the like. Your work is all rotten. I'm being pushed out of my job by a hu-man puff-ball and I'm too disgusted even to resent it. And yet all the world is yammering about the good old things and the better new ones. Why, this world is the lousiest, most obscene, stinking pig-pen that was ever constructed and the reek itself is so strong it hides the carrion until your foot is in it."

"I've often felt that way."

"Of course you have. And what do they do when you toss the morsel at them? They settle on their dig-nities and say: 'Ah! Outrageous young man! Reform-ing the universe! Isn't that just too cute? Come here, little boy, and I'll show you a comfort for your dilem-ma. I am Lilith and I am old John Moneybags.' Pat, pat, pat. Rebel? I'm not rebellious. I'm milk and honey. They say: 'Tut-tut. This is Father Time speaking and he wishes to say that in a few more scythe swings your

14

growing pains will vanish.' Thornton threw his cigarette stub at the fireplace, where it exploded into sparks. 'Goodness gracious!' "

Michael laughed heartily. "Bravo! I like it. A Tolstoy come to throw back slang in their faces. Shouldering the moral responsibility of the universe and bearing it dripping and alone. I've felt that way."

"Then you got a girl, grew older, earned money. Come to my arms, O friendly routine of solaces! A drink, by God. Raw alcohol for a raw world. Aged in the gullet. That's progress. That's America."

"You're stealing my stuff."

"Sure, Michael. Old man Invective. Old man Invective. He don't say nothin', but he must mean somethin'—it doesn't fit the tune. We are drunk enough to appear in public and live. Let's eat."

They went out.

6

Later in the evening, before the guests had commenced to arrive for Michael's regular Saturday night party, Perry Breck called and asked permission to bring a "knock-out" with him, and Geraldine, from the offices of the *Record*, proudly bragged of a new "boy-friend" whom she wished to introduce to the circle.

So they arrived and became acquainted with each other: Thornton, who was young and bitter, Cynthia, who had left a husband in California, Gerry, the lady

15

reporter of parts, Don, of the advertising profession, and Michael, host and artist. Before midnight they were very drunk. At four the survivors went to an all-night restaurant for bacon and eggs. Ten or a dozen, maudlin, noisy, sleepy. Then they drove home with humming heads and hammering arteries.

7

Three years and more before that evening, Thornton had fled from an old and celebrated university in a fit of irritation and despair. That flight, however, was executed without melodrama. The world in his head was filled with sharp colors and vigorous astonishments, but the world that surrounded him was prosaic and tawdry. He had long since relinquished certain expectations for reality, not without his quests and not without postponements of hope. Stripped entirely of a belief in the pageantry of life, Thornton would have preferred not to live.

For a year he had worked as an ordinary seaman on a tramp freighter and lopped the tops of trees in British Columbia with a lumber gang. His peacefulness and diplomacy usually saved his person. The world of hard-boiled men was not a part of his understanding, even after that. True, he could recall standing outside the door of a bunk-house while knives were thrown and chairs were smashed on skulls, and he had explored the horrible Asiatic alley in Marseilles. Two or three times

16

his own fists had smacked on human flesh. But none of it was glorious, and very little was picturesque. He was satisfied to settle in New York surrounded by comfortable furniture, a glittering bath, and French windows. His tastes were literary and his mind was facile, and in a short time he was drawing an adult salary from an advertising agency.

He had met Michael at an early period in his life in New York. Michael, like Thornton, had come in from the sea—a self-taught artist, a man of esoteric culture and natural talent. To Michael, Thornton seemed at once the embodiment of the intrinsic human principles that made what he considered a creative person and the essence of the romantic and paradoxically cynical tradition of his generation.

It was Michael who made the first advance. Listening to the younger man at a lunch that had been undertaken for business purposes, he selected him at once from the many persons he had met.

"Come down for supper," he said.

Thornton came rather shyly. Michael talked and refilled his glass. Both men lied a little, boasted, understood each other. A friendship was commenced.

8

When Michael was alone, he dreamed. And so poignant were the thoughts that made shadows in his mind that he did not like to be alone. The world in which he

17

found himself at birth was wholly explicable to him. That understanding was not of the common, matter-of-fact breed that makes our Babbitts. Michael was half Irish and half Italian, and enough passionate imagination had gone into him to make any but a strong man insane. Perhaps he was insane; to have etched in over his artistic sensitivity an impersonal, profound logic might have made him so out of the conflict of wish and reason.

It seemed to him that he was like God, and God was merely growing. With a hand on his stomach and one on the arm of his chair, with his pipe between his teeth, he could revolve the world before his eyes, knowing it intimately and knowing it from a telescopic perspective. He could draw a line around the world and see all its people: barbaric islanders in the Pacific, savages, Hindus, Turks, Spaniards—and so on. From that majestic vision he could rush back to his room and see the face of one guest, just departed, fitting that face into its little sphere, prying into the convolutions of the brain behind it, and making slides of its motives for microscopic examination. The greatest and the smallest were one to his research. Vice and suffering, society as a group, antiquity, racial objectives, science, were evident and simple. He was a man who could be completely conscious of any fact or situation.

Michael perceived the effect of his personality on Thornton, who had the same capacious sight and sympathy. He worried about the youth and occasionally thrust a delicate finger into his mechanism to make fine adjustments. He did it knowing that Thornton was perfectly aware of the object of the act, just as he had been aware of punishment when his father had whipped him, and reward when the reward had been given. Thornton was one of the few persons in whom he was sufficiently interested to take corrective measures. That feeling about Thornton stood in all his reveries as the one honest and hopeful indication he could discover: it represented hope to his idealism, and hope for the race. For himself, he could be called cynical, stoical, even satanic—but for his ideas he sought another name and longed vainly to hear it applied by the world.

He had built himself in his obvious world along giant lines. His body was tall and strong and had never been ill. His choice of the sea for fifteen years was deliberate: how otherwise would he be able to live and to study? How otherwise could he examine the facets of the earth? He became an artist through inevitability. When he selected the brush instead of the pen, a great writer was lost. With his passionate soul to feel and his meticulous mind to explain, he was sure of achievement.

Pondering in solitude, he saw himself thus: Rhodes, standing at the gates of the world, superman, genius, God. But there was no more pride in him than in a tree. He lacked vanity as some lack curiosity, and others ambition. Pride would have made him intolerable.

And yet Michael had realized none of his capacities. He died without realizing them. He was blamed for it and tormented by it. The truth was flung into his face by his glittering friends: he was a mighty poem blowing into the sea page by page; he was Mona Lisa jeering, Don Quixote refusing to ride forth, Casanova hiding in a monastery.

It occurred to few that he suffered at his own hands for that failure of himself. Most of his critics were less complicated. Their motives were visible, their promptings assayable; and they could not understand a great man who refused to do great things for any other reasons than drink, a woman, laziness, or the easy reward for mediocrity.

Even Thornton could not understand why his friend who could paint so well was suddenly satisfied to exhaust his talent on stocking-advertisements, on flattering portraits, on simple illustrations that thumbed their noses at Michael from open magazines, books, buses, and newspapers wherever he went. But he did not attribute it to laziness or women or drink. He found it instead another reason for resenting the city. He thought that Michael, coming from the sea, from a life of animal freedom and animal desire, had been subjugated by the walls and towers of Manhattan and by the littleness of the people who lived inside them.

There was foundation for that theory. Whenever Michael was given the proper stimulus, he poured out such a stream of abuse upon the institutions of the city that they would surely have perished if rhetoric had physical power. He was a catalyst. The elements he resolved often merited his wordy hate. To hate a thing or a device made Michael witty. So, when his audiences wanted to listen, they gave him the chance to speak about the tabloid newspapers, the parlor socialists, the skyscrapers, or any other metropolitan heritage—then they listened to such artistic flagellation as they had never heard. And, often enough, Michael did not wait for an opening, but leaped to his feet when a subject was mentioned and flayed it to the bone.

But it was not Michael's godlike aloofness, or a cosmic sense of frustration, or an intense, cynical destructiveness that caused the atrophy of his genius. Those things he had, undoubtedly. The real reason was so subtle as to defy most explanation, all understanding. Spite would not be the word for it; sadism is inadequate. It was composed of the knowledge that he was born a splendid being into a world inadequate for his demand, of the discovery that, whatever his triumph, it would be art and not reality, of the witnessing of disintegration in everything existing. It was as if he had wanted to live a million years in the future and, failing that want, could accept no compromise. To a few friendships he remained true during his life—but his death in some recondite manner shattered even that fidelity. To the world he was always a liar for profit, an actor for bread, a malicious preceptor.

He painted what would give him the most money for the least work. He said what he thought and never tried to sell those words. He loved and was loved—less well, and better. The place where he had been was scratched out when he died. He left only the consciousness of the passing of a locked secret, a forgotten

21

enchantment, an untranslatable rune that might have spelled the answer to all questions.

9

How Thornton and Cynthia came to love each other as an isolated incident gives undue pre-eminence to a single case. To tell of a man's love for a certain woman, it would be advisable to mention all other fanfares in the hearts of both, as well as the infidelities of their friends and neighbors, the behavior of their parents, the amount of deliberate experiment which each had made, and to add thereto the random selections of several historical loves by way of rounding out the single example. Thereby love would be set in a perspective and its particular degree, direction, cause, and motive could be shown forth with accuracy and candor. Thus, if Romeo and Juliet were the only love-story in the world, love would be regarded differently from the way in which it would be regarded if Helen's immortal history were unique. Fortunately Geraldine and Don announced almost simultaneously that their relations were mutually involved and the courses of four persons who were acquainted became, in a deceitful way, parallel.

The human mind, if it ever sets about the business, can conceive nothing so intricate and imponderable as the course two intelligent persons must follow in this muddled era in order to attain and continue the attitude of love towards each other. On the Sunday that followed his party Michael investigated that opinion.

He and Thornton were eating breakfast together at a restaurant where they ultimately expected others whom they knew, guests of the night before, bringing headaches and queasy stomachs to a doubtful meal.

"Familiar as I am," Michael began, "with the mechanisms of all that has to do with progress, I am still astonished by it. There is something very hypocritical and abominable about America. For instance, on the stage and in the magazines, in the movies and in most of the popular novels, the women are dressed and behave in such a way as to stimulate the desire of men to the highest point. But the philosophy of the books and magazines and theaters is conservation and purity on the part of the woman. People want that—to be tantalized out of their senses. But gratification? That is horrible, wrong, unthinkable. Nice country."

Thornton yawned. His head ached slightly. It annoyed him to think that Michael never had a hang-over, never, apparently, suffered from any indulgence of his senses. "That—" he yawned again—"hypocrisy permeates everything."

"First complication of the mechanism. The second is psychoanalysis. My God!"

"Why?"

"Because it is so harmful and stupid and purposeless. They make a medical profession out of a science that is about as far developed as—as—numerology."

"As what?"

"Well—as far developed as the transmutation of metals. Then they use it as cure. Cure! Hell. It is a pastime for neurotic, stupid people and about as harmless as juggling Mills bombs with the pins out."

Thornton called the waiter and ordered an omelet. His appetite was returning. Michael halted for an instant, ran his hands through his red hair, and began again.

"A layman is as well qualified to be a pschoanalyst as an M.D. at the present state. Look at the mistakes psychoanalysis has made. Look at the invention of the subconscious mind."

Thornton raised his eyes from his plate as if he expected to look at it in all its false and heinous monstrousness. "Yes," he said. But he was startled, as he was often startled by Michael. The subconscious mind was a thing that he had accepted without question and given a place in his catalogue of ideas.

His companion swallowed with haste. "The subconscious is merely a characteristic of the feeble mind, and not worth attention as anything else. The idea that we have a secondary set of wits is absurd. The notion that most people never put into words what they see and think is, on the other hand, quite correct. But a mind worth its salt is altogether conscious. If it has an undue desire for the person of a member of the family, it knows that. If it has impulses to steal, it can trace those impulses to its repressions. It knows its own dark businesses. All that is alleged to be subconscious is merely a lie born of vanity, and fat women like to have

24

those lies wheedled out of them because it feeds their selfish interests. Take a sensitive, delicate, untaught mind and start to wheedle and you soon bring about a permanent calamity."

"It sounds reasonable. I think you're right. Why doesn't someone say so?"

"Why doesn't someone say that Christianity is ruining mankind? Why doesn't someone say that New York is inordinately ugly?"

"Let's," Thornton said, and Michael laughed.

"What I was getting at is the second complication of progress and its relation to men and women. Psychoanalysis. It worries them a hundred times as much as it helps. It reacts on their tantalizing complex, makes it boil, leaves it frozen. The third complication is law. So many laws. You step outside them very day, and if you are trapped once or twice, lo, a new fear and worry. Honestly, how do you dare approach a girl these days?"

"How do you?"

Michael laughed again. "I never do. They come to me."

"That's a boast."

"It's a shameful admission. But I asked you. What do you do?"

Thornton shook his head. "The same things we have always done."

"With the current vogue for teasing—moral teasing? And with every girl aware of her complexes? And with police ready to snatch you for violations at any moment?"

"Sure. Get 'em in the dark and kiss 'em," Thornton said.

Michael suddenly bowed to someone behind Thornton and whispered: "See! They come to me."

It was Cynthia, but her attention to Michael was only casual and friendly, while to Thornton it was nervous, almost petulant. The artist watched them with rather sad eyes. In her gladness and his awkwardness he read sorrow. It meant a great deal to Michael. He was sure they would be in love before the week was ended. He was sure of it when he had seen Cynthia on Perry Breck's arm, surer when he had turned to Thornton to see how he witnessed the arrival of a new Eve from California. Thornton had forgotten to smoke his cigarette. So had others of his male guests. But—and there his mind rambled—Thornton had that which he, Michael, lacked. An unconquerable wish to win. An indefatiguable illusion concerning the value and rewards of victory. And he was honest. If he wanted Cynthia enough to forget his cigarette when he saw her, to forget himself even, to become silent and watchful—and then, if Cynthia wanted him—she could make the terms. Well—she was a strange girl. Good-looking was less than half of a definition. She was beautiful in a calm, voluptuous way. She could make him work for money. She could forbid him to see himself, Michael. She could love him and go on in that impeturbable dignity, never showing that she was hurt by going. What such a girl could accomplish with Thornton appalled Michael. Then he wondered about his own words. "See! They come to me." Had he said them because he wanted to inspire the active conquest of jealousy in Thornton? Did he want Thornton to love her? Or did he hope that she was really looking for him? How did his subconscious mind articulate itself on that problem? Both were true, he decided, and grew less noble in his own eyes. He listened while they talked and then, on leaving the restaurant, Thornton whispered: "Last night at your party —I got her in the dark and kissed her."

10

The night before, Perry Breck had escorted Cynthia from Michael's party at two o'clock and ordered the driver to tour the park before he turned through the gloomy streets to her hotel.

Cynthia, breathing fresh air and regarding the quiet dark after hours in the smoky, turbulent apartment, had been very quiet for the first few blocks of the drive.

"Well," Perry Breck said, "what did you think of them?"

"I loved it!"

The banker reflected that such a passion would lose her beauty for a time to the uses for which he thought it was intended. He had asked her opinion of the people and she had answered with approval of the atmosphere.

"It isn't like that—in the day-time. And Michael

27

Palidini is unusual. Most of those people are rotters of one sort or another."

She smiled. "If you had been brought up in California, hungry for the tiniest thing that was intelligent, or even skeptical—if everyone you met knew all he or she cared to know—shouldn't you like to meet some people who thought, or tried to think?"

"Certainly. Besides, we're all entitled to amusement."

"I suppose that is why you associate with them?"

"Of course. They're clever. Some of them are real. Kids like Thornton. Every year a few graduate into the class that earns money. Write books and plays. Give exhibitions. Succeed."

Cynthia nodded. "That's your criterion."

"And there is no other." He took her hand. "Nice in the park, isn't it? Are you in a hurry to retire?"

"I am now."

He leaned forward and spoke to the driver with faint annoyance in each careful syllable. "Hotel Wilcomb."

Cynthia sat on the edge of her bed. She kicked her slippers to the floor and maneuvered her dress over her head. Then she leaned back, lit a cigarette, and thought about the party. Her process was almost diametrically opposed to Thornton's. He went from a detail to the cosmos. She drew an infinitude of details out of a kaleidoscopic blur. Yet their assay was usually the same.

First, Perry Breck. He had taken her because he wanted to shock her. He knew that, by watching, he could discern the precise amount of her clinical sophistication. If she failed to laugh at the right point, he could say to himself: "She doesn't know about that!" and he would derive a paternal and anticipatory satisfaction from the discovery. He could hug his smug self and think: "I'll tell her about it. It will be a lead. . . ." She believed she had deceived Perry. Intuition, she thought, had obscured the blank places in her education. She failed in her estimation of his shrewdness. Perhaps she exaggerated her own skill at dissimilation.

Then—a room full of people. When Cynthia was dressed well, when the future depended on her resources, she entered a room filled with people like a clever gladiator. She was flushed, stimulated, confident. She knew the inherent power of her beauty. She had not learned its limits. And her confidence had been shocked by the banal, unillusioned manner in which Perry had evaluated it. Nevertheless, she walked into Michael's with proud sureness. Other women had scoffed noisily during the evening. Cynthia ignored other women who scoffed. She was undoubtedly as crude as the man who had said that beauty was a financial asset. But she was younger than he and it gave her an advantage.

She had attracted Michael's attention at once. But she noticed also the men who held their cigarettes in fixed fingers and stared.

"This little girl," Perry said, "has come from California to see the circus."

Michael glanced at Breck and bowed graciously to her. "How do you do?"

29

Her mind wrote rapidly: this Michael is so superior to Perry that he can afford to be insulted by him with no other emotion than an amusement so slight as to escape its target.

She liked Michael. "He wants me," she thought.

Then Geraldine.

"This is Gerry. She writes all the love diaries for the *Record*. A sob sister."

"If you're ever indiscreet," Gerry said, "telephone me."

Cynthia wondered what that meant. Gerry was wedging a young man towards her. A man who was neither blond nor dark, tall nor short, fascinating nor dull. "Don. The boy-friend. Private. Keep off."

Laughter. Did they greet all strangers so warmly? she wondered. Cynthia thought not. She shook hands with Don. Names followed. A squat, dark man who was a poet. A colorless person whose name leaped at her from the bill-boards of a thousand motion-picture theaters as soon as she heard it. She stared. Yes. It was his face, his figure. He said: "All the way from California, eh? Well, well, well! The old stamping-grounds. Yes, sir."

"And—" Michael's voice reached her—"this is Thornton, who is quite drunk, but does not yet know it, who is a genius and will tell us all so when he has had another drink; and he is also quite tame—unless aroused."

"How do you do, Mr. Thornton?"

"Thornton—first name. Pleased. Captivated. Have a drink for you."

He extended a cup of punch, which she accepted. They looked at each other. She wondered what he would say next. He did not keep her waiting.

"All the way from California, eh? Well, well, well! The old stamping-grounds. Yes, sir!"

The actor could not avoid hearing him. She gasped at the grotesque caricature of his imitation. A volume of laughter in which the star joined saved her from imminent embarrassment.

"Ha!" Thornton said.

Tears rolled down Michael's cheek. She thought they must be very drunk.

Someone was prodding her shoulder. "Dance?"

Cynthia moved away from the group. An hour later Gerry wrapped her in a drunken arm. "I think we're going to be fast friends. Very fast."

"I hope so."

"Where's your conquest?"

"Who?"

"Thornton. Don't pretend. I'll tell you what I'll do. I'll find him for you. I'll get a lantern and look for him. If there is an honest man, it will turn out to be Thornton—or Michael. He won't have anything to do with me."

"Who won't?"

"Both of them." Gerry evidently considered that consummate wit. She walked away shouting: "Get me a lantern!"

BABES AND SUCKLINGS

A pale young man rushed towards her. "What's the matter? Found an excavation?"

"No. Neither have you."

Then Thornton had seen Cynthia go out on the balcony and followed, closing the windows behind them.

"Well," he said, "it's dull."

"I thought it was very exciting."

He shrugged. "It is not. It is dull. These are stupid people—with the exception of Michael. I'm glad I'm going to pass out."

"You sound like a college boy."

"So does everyone else."

"Look!" he said suddenly. "Look way down there to the street, where all the little people go walking, walking, walking, with nowhere to go and no reason for it at all—only going because they must rise at seven and work to keep themselves rising at seven." His voice was very deep and moving. Words came that did not make sense to her. But Cynthia's scalp crept and tingled. He went on with hot emotion. "I see the rainbows coming out of the clouds all red and blue and yellow and people in ragged clothes poking around in the dirt looking for a pot of gold they will never find. And the limousines rushing by on the street stuffed full of fat and jewelry that left a dirty past in an apartment in Chelsea where it was kept and pummeled by equally fat fingers thirty years ago today." He staggered and caught the rail. "I see Jesus, Jesus, looking from his golden throne with a crafty smile on his face and no heaven at his feet. I see Perry Brecks piling up gilt-edged securities and steering through a perfumed world on the strength of a rat in their eyes, and derby hats full of bogus brains all ramming towards a counterpane. It's poetry. But what poetry! It doesn't rhyme, it hasn't a meter. It tells you nothing and leaves you with your mouth wide open and a sick feeling down in your abdomen that is half a regret and half a wish and no glory anywhere, nor any love, nor any handiwork of God. Kiss me!"

Then, quickly, he seized her, placing a passionate kiss harshly on her parted lips, after which he slipped through the door and was incredibly gone from the high, cool balcony.

Her mind undertook the declension of that incident. It was absurd and it was heroic. It was picturesque and vain. It was part of a pose and conjured in her a desire to pose, to caress her person with voluptuous, appreciative gestures and to consider it, too, as an instrument over which fine emotions played. Cynthia did not feel that Thornton had amazed her nearly as much as she felt that he had justified taking an attitude towards herself. But, presently, that vanity fell before a small self-consciousness and a clearer understanding, gained through steadier thought.

She smiled, without priding herself in being wise and maternal. Thornton, in his fashion, had done her homage. He had paid a compliment that was intricate, but equally spontaneous. She realized that the inhabitants of her new background—or some of them—were far more complicated than any men she had ever known.

The women she did not include. She knew that they would be identical.

In the darkened room she drew a soft quilt to her chin. It was exhilarating, romantic, and pleasantly dangerous. She admitted the latter casually, because all things seemed dangerous to her. The sentiments of delight were born of a considerable self-assurance. California, marriage, desertion, Perry Breck were bases for an intelligent and an alluring woman. In 1880 a woman a trifle less direct than Cynthia would have said: "Heigh-ho!"

A rendezvous for late breakfast had been mentioned. She decided to go there in the morning. Then she slept. Through the anæsthesia of sleep rose the *confus murmure* of *L'Extase*, but from the city and not the sea. She could detect no difference. Her fingers curled. Dawn seeped through the heavy curtains. Clamor rose with the rising sun. Cynthia continued to breathe gently in the motionless room.

11

They were different at breakfast. And she was in many ways dissimilar to them. First impressions recoiled upon new findings. Thornton made a physical catalogue of her and saw that she was as tall as he. Michael noticed a number of things that varied from his original conception of her. She was a little more proud of her beauty than he had thought at first. That was noticeable when he complimented her and she refused to accept his praise with quick insistence. Cynthia found that they resembled other men more closely than she had thought.

On leaving the restaurant they went to Michael's "Casa." A Negro maid was busy removing the last traces of the party. Her swishing broom tainted the air with the smell of dust. Broken glass clinked into the ash-can. The fire was rejuvenated in the grate. Michael himself went about that business thinking how life made stage-hands of its dramatic personæ, forcing them to set the props for every occasion: a fire for becoming acquainted, a bed and pillows and soft music for loving, trees for the soul, and so on, to a hole for a coffin. He said nothing about that, however. It ran through his mind and was put away for a time when he could dissertate upon it.

Cynthia wondered what would happen. She was glad that Perry Breck was not with her. He was embarrassing among those people. Elsewhere she might easily be proud of him. The arrangements were at last complete. She finished her tour of the drawings that covered his walls and addressed Michael.

"I never dreamed that an artist would be as domestic as you—or half as civilized."

"Probably I should be ashamed of it."

She was nonplussed. Did they have no casual conversation? Did everything said mean something? Was he serious?

"Oh, no," she answered. "You should be proud."

Thornton came uneasily to her aid. "He is proud. He's like an old woman about his home—paints cabinets and actually keeps a huge supply of tools on hand."

"That's true."

What had she done? Had her remark been trite? Was it rude to discuss another person's house? She felt a constraint she did not understand. She could not know that she had lifted a little corner of Michael's discontent or that Thornton, in hurrying to her defense, had said to his friend: "This is my woman, and you must not rebuke her."

It quieted a slight unrest in so far as she was concerned. She was glad Thornton had spoken. Both men, however, grudgingly accepted the trifling impasse as a pattern for their future conversation. Cynthia was to be included in it always, Michael was not to solicit openings for attack in what she said, or to take advantage of any she made. Thornton was her champion.

All that happened in less than a minute and over practically nothing. Both Michael and Thornton were oppressed by the amount of possible disagreement that lay in the future. They saw that it might separate them. They probably fretted against the conventions of behavior which would make such accidents possible. She felt that the words had represented an engagement of some sort, but she was not sufficiently acquainted with them or their habits to appreciate its purport. Later she could have avoided it.

That evening, when Cynthia and Thornton had gone, Michael said to another guest: "People are becoming so complicated that the barest, simplest exchange of facts is filled with dire consequences."

"What do you mean by that exactly?"

Michael did not reply. He had articulated his thought upon the subject and it was closed thereafter.

Thornton, at the same time, said to Cynthia: "Michael hates to have people suggest that he's too urbane or civilized."

"Why?"

"He does—that's all."

"You're referring to what I said about his apartment and artists?"

"You are perceptive, aren't you?"

"I think he's worse than a woman."

Thornton smiled. "He has that advantage of the opposite sex. But you'll find that he is principally male."

"I never dreamed that anyone could make so much of such a trifle."

"Did we?"

"You both glared at me, and what I said was really only a compliment. You are ridiculously sensitive. And a little bit silly."

"I suppose so."

At the moment, however, the subject was dropped. Cynthia sat in a chair, lit a cigarette, and moved candid eyes from one to the other. She was then a comparatively strange and very attractive girl who had been invited to Michael's apartment on a lazy afternoon.

"How do you happen to know Perry Breck?" Michael asked.

BABES AND SUCKLINGS

She knew that they would want to learn all they could about her. The afternoon would be spent on something like a witness-stand. Probably they would corroborate what she told them afterwards.

"I met him in California. He was involved in a business deal with my husband."

The fact that she was married, of course, was news to them. She indicated it rather bluntly, as a sort of retribution for their attitude towards her first innocent statement. Michael took it quite impersonally. She saw that he looked immediately at Thornton, who was fumbling in a pocket for a fresh cigarette.

"So," he said, "you're married." The cigarette came out and fell on the floor. He moved to disregard it and procure another, changed his mind, picked it up, and tapped it on the edge of his chair arm.

"Yes. I'm married."

The cigarette was lighted. "I thought so."

Michael turned to her with an expression of very faint contempt. For an instant she realized that he understood her manner and its motive. Another woman would certainly have been annoyed and persisted. But Cynthia said: "It was a silly marriage and I've left my husband for good in California. He's too indolent to bother me. We—we fought constantly."

"I see." Thornton made an unnecessary trip to the ash-tray with his cigarette and then threw it into the fireplace. "I see."

Michael must have considered that she had made

amends. His tone was thoroughly friendly. "We're all glad you did leave him. His bereavement is our gain."

"And mine."

"I don't like Perry Breck," Thornton said.

"Helen of Troy couldn't have inspired jealousy more quickly, Mrs. Sherman."

"Cynthia."

"Cynthia, then." Michael had avenged Thornton's defense of her. He said angrily to himself that he wished to high heaven someone else would call and that he had never been in a stickier or more nonsensical situation and that love was a sport for butchers and maniacs, but not for well-meaning human beings.

"Of course I'm jealous. And not a little fearful."

"Of what?" she asked.

"His money, his looks, his social position, his general reputation."

Michael, reiterating his thoughts on the gentler relations of the sexes, restrained a desire to shout some short, awful, obscene word and leave the room. The door-bell rang.

"Aurelius Goodney!" Michael said.

"Who's he?"

Michael spoke as he walked to the door, pushed the lock button, and waited for Aurelius. "He's really the most remarkable person I know. The last of the romanticists. He's supposed to be the hero of a dozen books—and if half of what he says is true—he is. Tell him a story of blood and danger and he'll tell one a thousand times as horrid and terrible—about himself.

Thornton thinks he's a Munchausen. Nobody ever figured him out."

A pleasant voice issued from the hall. Aurelius entered. He was short and slight. His blue eyes sparkled like a many-faceted stone. His first motion, a bow upon the mention of Cynthia's name, was so full of energy that she compared him at once to a jack-in-the-box. He sat down energetically, lit a pipe energetically, after filling it from a pouch with the greatest show of energy. It was almost exhausting to watch him live, because he managed to convey a sense of skill and force into the very business of breathing.

"I've just had the devil's own time," he said rapidly.

"What happened?" The corners of Michael's mouth turned up. It was as if he had anticipated the fact. As if Aurelius could come from nothing but the devil's own time. Thornton grinned openly. Cynthia perceived it with a feeling of sympathy for Aurelius. The atmosphere had changed. They who had been pained and groping actors were transformed into an audience.

"The damnedest thing I ever saw," Aurelius continued. "I was just getting off the ferry—"

"The ferry!" Thornton repeated.

Aurelius hesitated. It was patent that his words had overleaped his thoughts. "Why, yes. I often take a ferry-ride on pleasant Sunday afternoons. Always, in fact. Just as I was getting off on the New York side, I saw a crowd collecting up a street. I ran, of course. The crowd dispersed as fast as it had gathered. Faster. And out of the middle of it came a bull. A full-grown, black bull. I've seen them in the ring in Spain a hundred times. Mean ones, those black bulls. It had escaped from a slaughter-house, apparently. I was for it the minute I saw it. Of course, I know a good deal about bullfighting and bull tactics." He stopped and gazed at his hearers with a pleased expression.

"Of course," Michael prompted.

"So I whipped off my coat. It came straight for me. I led it on and then turned it at the crucial moment—just as the toreador turns it. What a picture! In the heart of New York City—a bullfight. Six times it came and six times I turned it. Then they got ropes. The first man missed and the bull tossed him. He landed and didn't get up. The crowd hollered as such crowds always do."

The smile that she had seen on the faces of Michael and Thornton now asserted itself on Cynthia's. The little man was too outrageous to be given polite credulity. He did not seem to be the least bit offended.

"Then you rushed in—" Thornton commenced.

Aurelius looked at him with a vexed frown. "Not at all. That was the damnedest part of it. Suddenly the bull, seeming to tire of me, wheeled and charged straight up West Street. I, on the jump as usual, clambered on the running-board of a passing cab. 'Follow that bull!' I said. The driver nodded. The chase began."

As he spoke, he had risen to his feet. He jumped on an imaginary running-board. He pointed to an imaginary bull. His face took on an alarmed and concentrated expression.

"The bull rushed up the street. Its haunches steamed. Its little eyes gleamed angrily. Street after street was passed. Its feet clattered on the cobble-stones. Then it veered up a side-street. At that point I heard shooting. A policeman stood in its path, revolver drawn, feet spread. He was about as accurate as a New York policeman usually is when excited. Out of six shots, he hit once—a glancing tear on the bull's side. But the bullets sang around me. That certainly was a good cab-driver. He didn't stop for the shots at all. Straight ahead we plunged. I caught a glimpse of the cop flying through the air. I knew there would be another patient at Bellevue. On we went. People fled screaming on every side. Once the bull stopped."

He was nearing the climax of his tale. He acted every word, hastily assembling chairs to make a relief map of the drama. "I tried to attract his attention. Nothing doing. He charged through a dozen ash-cans. The noise seemed to frighten him. He went on through a milk-wagon and fetched up on a brick wall. That stunned him. He backed away, pawing and lashing his tail. Then he came about, and on we went."

"'Pass him!' I shouted to the driver. Pass we did and the bull took after us, snorting and bellowing. We had almost reached the park—we were going up Twenty-third Street—when I noticed an alley-way between two buildings. I told the driver to stop there. Someone caught my idea and opened a gate. Then I went out in the street, stopped the bull, brought him around, and headed him into the alley. In he went and bang went the gate. Fortunately it was a blind alley. The bull was penned."

No one spoke for a moment. Aurelius peered from one face to another. "There was a nigger in that alley," he said, as if to satisfy our silence with excuse for compliment. "I had to hop in afterwards and yank him out. Close quarters for that sort of thing. The bull was under me when I went over the gate. Believe me, I wasn't quartered at Seville for nothing."

Thornton rose then and shook his hand with solemnity. "That was mighty brave. I wish to thank you on behalf of the public."

Aurelius grinned happily. "It wasn't much. But I thought for a minute that there was going to be hell to pay."

Cynthia could not speak. She bit her handkerchief and stared at the fire. Michael left the room and returned with an armful of logs.

"I'm still in a lather," Aurelius said. "Mind if I take off my coat?"

"Not a bit."

"Just telling that story as you did would be enough," Thornton said absently. But Aurelius did not even cast a suspicious glance at him. Instead he resumed his pipe, which had gone out, and sat down with vehemence.

"It reminds me of a day in Manilla—"

But he got no further. Cynthia rose. "I must be going. I—I have some letters to write."

"I'll see you to a cab," Thornton said.

Michael expressed disappointment that they were leaving so soon, but he did not press them to stay. Aurelius bade them good-bye cheerfully.

After they had gone, he said: "Who's the girl, Michael?"

"That's the girl who is going to make or break Thornton. A girl who has just left an unpleasant California marriage."

Aurelius's airy good nature had vanished. Instead a reflective, wistful person sat in the chair. "As serious as that?"

"I think so."

"We'll watch out for them—or, rather, you will."

"We'll try."

Aurelius nodded to his inward thoughts. "They didn't believe my yarn, did they?"

"Why the deuce do you tell them like that?"

"I think I have a perverse nature. But it was the devil's own time and I'll swear that was an Andalusian bull. There's some sort of funny business going on in the back yards of the rich."

12

"Where are we going?" Cynthia asked when Thornton took her arm in his determined possession.

"My house."

She knew that he would regard any objection on

44

her part as old-fashioned and perhaps even insulting. She had never been in a man's apartment alone. It was easy to be natural.

"All right. I thought that if that Goodney person told another story, I'd be so rude he couldn't help noticing it."

"But didn't you half believe it?"

"No!"

"I did. He's a mighty queer person—one of the sort to whom things like that happen all the time."

"Are there people like that?"

"There aren't. But there are, just the same."

He was glad she had agreed to go to his apartment without demur. Conventions, he felt, were for other people. Especially conventions like that. He was capable of being both charming and proper under such circumstances. "This is it," he said presently. They stood in front of a long row of brownstone façades.

His apartment was pretty. She thought that it was, perhaps, too pretty for a man. But she was not used to men who had studied architecture and color harmony, who knew the names of materials and the principles of decoration. Besides, the efforts of a maid, who evidently tended it daily, had not erased a distinct carelessness that was consolingly masculine to her.

The grate was littered with cigarette stubs. A half-written sheet of paper invited her eyes from the roller of his typewriter. He withdrew it before she had an opportunity to read it. Then he took her coat and hat, hung them in a closet, offered a chair, and sprawled on the day-bed in the alcove.

"I like your house," she said. "May I be permitted to like yours if not Michael's?"

"I want you to like it."

She used the ensuing hiatus in conversation to inspect it quite completely.

"That door goes to the bath and that one to the kitchenette," he offered when he saw that she was questioning them.

"I see. Do you cook?"

"Sometimes. But it's mostly a bar. Would you like a drink, by the way?"

"Not now. After supper."

Then she was going to stay for supper with him. He liked her for that. He had shown his house, and it had given her a feeling of intimacy, of comfort, and of security. In a moment the tenseness between them had evaporated. They both attributed it to Michael. He crossed the room, took a guitar from the closet, and sprawled on the bed again. She did not speak. He began to sing. His voice was surprisingly good. Accurate, mellow, sentimental, perfectly suited to the instrument.

He began by singing "Water Boy," and from the first plaintive call to the last, she was entranced.

"That's lovely," she said.

"I like to sing. I wanted to be a singer—once."

"Do you know—" she hesitated. The song which she wanted him to sing was not altogether proper. It was a cowboy song and it contained cowboy words. She

46

had heard it one night in Salinas during the rodeo. And never again, afterwards, had she heard that song. Its melody was lonely and pessimistic. It had made her unforgettably sad. It was like the cold stars and wind on the plains and night. She wished very much he would sing it, but she could not tell him.

"Do I know what?"

"I guess I'd better not ask. You'll think I'm—"

"What is it?"

"Ten thousand—cattle?"

He thrummed the guitar. Instantly she was in Salinas in the room that looked over the valley, with the night and a voice for company. He knew the song. He would know that song.

> Ten thousand God-damned cattle,
> They left my ranch and rambled away,
> Sons of bitches
> Is what I say.
> Now I'm lone man, dead broke today.
> My girl she left me strayin,'
> She left my ranch and rambled away
> With a son of a bitch
> From Ioway.
> Now I'm lone man, dead broke today.
> Lone man—
> Ten thousand cattle strayin'
> Lone man
> In gamblin' hell delayin'—
> My girl she left me, ramblin,'

BABES AND SUCKLINGS

And I'm lone man,
Dead broke
Today.

A lump choked her. She saw Thornton through a mist. He was being what he sang—alone in a far land, his girl gone, his cattle lost, his life shattered. The smell of cattle country came back to her, and the emotion of that ineffable night. He began again.

Thrum-thrum-thrum-thrum. "Lone man in gamblin' hell delayin.' My girl she left me ramblin.' Now I'm lone man, dead broke today." It was like seeing through Thornton into the depths of his heart where the music dwelt. It was more, because it was part of something beautiful she had forgotten. He understood. He felt with her. She wanted to be kissed until she was weak. She wanted her heart to be broken. She cried. The last note of the guitar whispered through the room and was lost.

After a long time she said: "You know how I feel about that, don't you?"

"Mmmm."

"Sing it again."

"Some day."

"I think I've been a little bit foolish."

"I'm glad. It makes me feel that the world isn't quite so harsh and dull."

"All you people—you're terribly afraid of dull things, aren't you?"

He put down the guitar. "Are we?"

"Where I was born and educated, you're supposed to be sensation-seekers." The last vestige of her emotion was gone. "I've read lots of books about you."

"About us?"

"Certainly. It's about you people here that everyone writes. But you're a hundred times as human as I thought you'd be."

He was embarrassed. "We're not different. We think differently, that's all."

"I'm not even so sure of that. You and Michael and Aurelius are a little unusual. But there are girls like that Gerry everywhere. And Don's a type. And that movie actor last night was absolutely common."

"Stupid."

"The thing you fear. But don't you get tired trying to be clever? I'm sure the women do."

"Because they have to try so much harder?"

"There!" she said. "That's just what I mean. You have your little patents and formulas, and off they come like—like—"

"Undershirts—"

"You're teasing me. All right. Do. I'm not a wit and I'll never be a wit. I don't like wit. It's insincere."

Thornton pondered the insincerity of wit in general and his own particular sort of wit. "I suppose it is."

"Of course it is."

"What are we to do, then?"

"Be as dull as possible. It's the only way to be happy."

"If you're talking about happiness—"

"—it's absolutely out of the question," she finished for him. "I have read about that, too. But I don't believe it."

"These people who are creative are bound to be more or less wretched."

"They do it on purpose."

"Wait till you know them better."

"I'm not sure that I want to."

He had brought her to sudden and unexpected wrath. He understood that she was trying to express a point of view. But points of view had become abstractions to him—largely because he regarded any that were foreign to his own as unsound. It was precisely that conceit which hurt her. In trying to reflect it to him she had merely been bogged in argument. He apologized hastily.

"I didn't mean to be annoying."

"Well, you were."

"I'm sorry."

"You're not half sorry enough."

He frowned. She had regained her poise and was being intentionally stubborn and unforgiving to impress him against possible repetition of those circumstances. He thought she was merely feminine and he had a predilection to consider femininity synonymous with inanity. But, because he did not know her well, and because of a desire for her that he admitted was increasing, he remained good-humored.

"Then I'm more than twice as sorry as I was— which ought to be exactly sorry enough."

"Very well. I won't go. But you must behave."

"Shall we have no debates in our long life together?"

"None. What makes you think our life will be long
and together?"

"My horoscope."

"You're a very nice boy, really."

"And you're a dear little old lady."

If they had been sitting side by side with their
arms wound around each other and dirty smears under
their eyes, they would have been no more like children
making up after a quarrel. Each thought that the other
was very immature, and to each came a sentiment of
mingled superiority and responsibility. They did not
consider that the afternoon had been in any way casual
or ordinary. Theirs was not a blowing about in the easy
wind of new friendship. Every puff of air was significant; every word the index to a new volume that must
be opened and read with as much care and as much as-
sumption of ease as was possible.

With the coming of darkness Thornton lighted the
lamps in his house. It was extraordinarily easy for them
to talk, once they had mastered the process of avoiding
differences. So they told many truths about themselves
and some lies until the mantel clock struck seven and
Thornton asked her to go to dinner with him. Then she
said that she had been hoping for that for a full hour.
They laughed. She went into the bath and he stood ad-
miring her coat in his closet and thinking it a considerable delicacy to have such a garment among his own,

to have her voice come from the adjacent door in trivial talk—thinking, too, that it was of such rubbish that romance was made and the whole idea was naïve and that he was behaving in a decidedly young way, which he could scarcely correct by any polite means.

13

When Cynthia had gone to her hotel, alone in a cab after Thornton had bickered chivalrously and with dwindling point against that late solitude, he walked back to his house with adagio footsteps punctuated by an impatient cane. She had gone. She wouldn't let him take her. Was she afraid that he would cross the lobby, enter the elevator, go into her room? He was there on the street, slightly fuzzy with wine, melancholy, unamiable. What was the matter?

Supper had been successful and pleasant. During it they had fitted in segments from their pasts so that each had a notion of the other's history that was like an unfinished cross-word puzzle with the easy words supplied and the more difficult ones left for struggle or abandonment at a future time. He felt that he knew her better. A tall blonde girl with a slumberous volcanic quality that is more readily identifiable in brunettes. An irrationally frank person. One who had possibly commenced to be candid as a facetious slap at stupid society and continued out of inertia until her frankness was likely to be considered an extravagant virtue.

52

Certainly it was no longer a pose. But he doubted that it was a virtue.

During the twelve hours that had intervened between then and the time of Michael's explosion of the theory of a subconscious mind Thornton had meditated on what he had heard. He had tested the theory on Cynthia with fair success, and now he felt that it should be applied to himself.

"If I finish a supper with a striking blonde and she goes home and I then find myself in a detestable humor that I cannot explain, Michael must be wrong." With that premise he cajoled himself into a stretch of introspection which took him to his door. He decided that he had anticipated an easy conquest of Cynthia from the attempt of which he had refrained because he was a little tired of conquest, a little annoyed by her candor, and because he wished to bait himself to increase his appetite. Having thus reduced his situation to a wholly tangible and not very worthy set of motives, he became reconciled to it and retired.

Cynthia moulded her opinions more simply. Her marriage gave her a certain pinnacle of maturity from which she saw Thornton as a charming, unusual boy. She tinkered with the notion that he was a desirable male. Because the corporeal form of her husband had been older and larger, that notion amused her. She was annoyed at Thornton's insight and attributed it to a femininity of character—an attribution over which the most erudite of psychologists might have come to academic blows. But, as she had never known a human being quite so imaginative, she determined to traffic with him socially for her own pleasure. New York bore fascinating fruit.

14

Thornton awoke knowing that he would be more or less oblivious of life that day. He wondered constantly just how much he liked or disliked a given thing. His job was a particular problem to him. Often he surprised himself by the fervor with which he railed against it. At other times he was roused to such a pitch of interest that he was constrained to set work—any work—as the highest point of human achievement. Thereby he judged himself an extremist.

But, on that particular morning, he knew that sling or arrow would meet with armor. He shaved his fragile beard, brushed down the yellowish hair that was so lightly rooted in his head, and made coffee. As its aroma rose in the room, he began to sing. He remembered that it was bad luck to sing before breakfast and stopped. Then, scorning his weakness, he sang more lustily than before. His mind was full of Cynthia. He had dreamed a dream about her which left in his wakened soul a desire to see her at once.

In the actual matter of his employment Thornton was unfortunately situated. He had started in New York as a reporter. Six weeks afterwards he had changed to publicity. Finally, through the effort of a friend, he found a place in an advertising agency. He had gleaned a fair technical knowledge of advertising in a time so short that it would have brought indignant denial from any of the chiefs or patrons of that profession. His easy effort was equal to the diligences of most of his con- freres. He earned, at that time, a hundred dollars a week.

His immediate superior, however, was a man who had been put in that position a year after Thornton's arrival. Thornton, who detested subordination of any sort, had taken an instant and personal dislike to Arn- stein almost against his will. Arnstein was pulpy and bulbous. His eyes protuded. He claimed to be an intel- lectual and an artist-dilettante. His pretense of liking Thornton was vacuous and gave rise only to distrust. He was older than Thornton. He patronized out of what Thornton found to be a complete inferiority.

And, as Thornton had indicated to Michael, Arn- stein was soon engaged in the process of ousting him. The method was subtle and sure in the long run. Arn- stein merely disapproved of everything Thornton did. For a year he had been praised. Suddenly praise was supplanted by Arnstein's sad, sympathetic criticism. The younger man felt that he was being engulfed in a senti- mental treachery. But there was no redress. Arnstein was his superior. To become enraged would be to pro- cure his own dismissal. To go over Arnstein's head was to court a situation in which Arnstein could, by being hurt and surprised, make him seem an ingrate and a devious fool.

BABES AND SUCKLINGS

The cancerous predicament grew. Thornton found himself forced into the ignominious position of rewriting a few simple lines of copy ten and twenty times. Yet Arnstein greeted each re-edition with pale, apologetic negation.

"Your mind isn't on your work, Thornton," he would say. And: "Take a day off tomorrow. Then see if you can't do better." Or, more definitely objective: "Really, that's simple. I don't see how you can go wrong on it. It ought not to require so much redoing. The firm doesn't like that sort of thing. And you're late with it already."

Thornton, knowing in his heart that the copy was excellent and that its lateness was due to the machinations of Arnstein, would shut his firm jaw and try again. He pitted his patience against Arnstein's dogged policy. But he knew he was losing. After four months the head of the firm sent a reprimand to him. A tally for Arnstein, he thought. It was the first reprimand he had ever received. His impulse was to resign at once. But, when he thought of the sly, squid-like smile Arnstein would permit himself at the news of that resignation, he bent over his desk and worked with diabolic fury.

As time passed, he found himself speculating on which of Arnstein's friends or relatives would occupy his place when he was gone. It made him more than a little cynical in his attitude towards business and its ideals. He had accumulated plenty of evidence to support that cynicism. Business was no more decent than any other motivated intrigue. A poor liar had no chance in it. Of course, a good liar might still be stupid enough not to perceive his own lies.

But, on that morning, he was oblivious. The whole panorama of business was remote. He worked for a living, and if he lost one position, he would find another. The subway riders were fools because they did not have that attitude. Next to their souls they held dear their jobs. To lose a job was to die utterly. Any indignity rather than that. Day-laborers were better, moving placidly and unexcitedly from one place to another with sufficient experience, if not sufficient imagination, to know that very few people actually starve to death in this civilization and that one bit of menial work is often advantageously exchangeable for another.

He even wondered, as he sat among the subway riders and deplored them, how Michael could be aroused to such savagery over such men as Arnstein and the heads of his and Arnstein's firm. But Michael loved excoriation.

Thornton remembered him on the subject of Boyce Boynton, an advertiser of means and reputation whose extra-issue was the Babbittization of the Bible. "A Macfadden," he said. "A Macfadden for God who has taken a holy and illustrious work that was apt to have been forgotten in the hurly-burly of modern hocus-pocus—whatever that means—and revitalized it with the newest methods. To St. Paul he has given salesmanship. To John the Baptist, high pressure. To the Gospels, billboards and car-cards. And now you and I can drink at this new reservoir of undiluted God because it has been

57

visualized by a mighty name, laid out by an artist, and set up in bold-face upper case. Think of what it must mean to the Churches to have a man like that rush in —trained and ready, high-powered, high-geared, and high-paid—just as sales were falling off and distribution was getting poor. God! Just to meet him once, face to face, with a bushel of his own metaphors and a free right hand! I could die happy!"

Thornton smiled at that point. Then, abruptly, he left his wandering thoughts and intruded his person into the crowd on the station platform. A man with a hideous sore on his face jolted him. Thornton recoiled, beat angrily on the heels of those ahead, reached the street, and drew a deep breath of reasonably clear air. He strode off towards a tall office-building.

It was fortunate for him, or, perhaps, for Arnstein, that Thornton was immersed in obliviousness that day. Otherwise the unpleasantnesses that descended on him rather suddenly, shaking his routine of life to its foundations, might have been received differently.

Thornton was late. He was always late. It made him feel guilty to slide into his desk as unobtrusively as possible at ten o'clock. But he felt equally guilty to arrive at nine with the stenographers and to chatter in the early hours until the executives took their places like teachers in a school. His sentiment of guilt was at a minimum, however. His mood had no relation to conscience. He opened the door of his office (which he shared with six others) by a carefree if not jaunty gesture.

He sat. One of the secretaries approached. Thornton could not be expected to know that her walk mimicked a favorite motion-picture actress.

"Hurt yourself?" he asked absently.

"What do you mean?"

"Thought you were limping. Made a polite inquiry."

So obscure is the justice of human interbehavior that, out of her pique, Thornton was forewarned. What she said was: "Limping! Gee! Don't you know anything about poise and posture? Listen, big boy"—her voice was confidential and delightedly malicious—"Arnstein an' the boss are waiting for you and what I know about what's going to happen to you is nobody's business."

From that he inferred with a sickening emptiness of feeling that he was going to be fired. "They sore?"

"Sore? They ache all over."

"And belly-ache," Thornton said, as if in rebuttal. That impressed him as funny, almost heroic. It would be miserable to be fired, particularly in the presence of Arnstein. But he would do it well. It was more miserable to continue. He noticed that all the people in the room were looking at him. He was sorry that he had been flippant. It prevented any loftiness in the walk to the door. To hell with it all. In that queasy and uncertain mood he stood and moved forward, looking neither to the right nor to the left, and eyes followed him as eyes follow a form on an ambulance stretcher.

The head of the firm regarded Thornton uncompassionately. His name was Flint. He seemed to have all the properties suggested by that substance. He said: "Sit down."

Thornton turned his gaze towards Arnstein. In his too lucid dark irises something between laughter and contempt and partaking of both made Thornton tighten the muscles across his abdomen. Arnstein was being inscrutable—but not quite inscrutable. It was typical of him. Within the law and yet unethical.

"For some time,"Mr. Flint commenced, "I have had unfavorable reports of you. Disappointingly unfavorable. I must say they surprised me. When you came here, your work was excellent. Since then it has been falling off. Mr. Arnstein"—he turned appropriately—"has been bearing the brunt of your laxness. He has borne it, I must say, admirably. Not until recently, and then not through him, I began to hear about your change of attitude towards your work. Yesterday I spoke to Mr. Arnstein, and I must say that what he told me has been rather—ah—damaging to your prestige. Have you any explanation to make?"

"You must say, you must say, you must say," Thornton repeated to himself. "I expect he must." He wavered. Suppose—just as a gesture—he should spill the whole intrigue against him? What would they say, Flint and Arnstein? The former so intent upon the pursuit of business ideals (and millions) as to be unaware of it, and the latter so clever as to leave no clue. What would they say?

"I have no explanation." Thornton heard his voice speak.

"What!"

"None. As far as I can see, my work—or what of it I have been able to do—" he allowed himself to glance at Arnstein, who sat impassively—"has been at an even level."

"But you admit that you have not been able, as you put it, to do all the work assigned to you."

"I admit it gladly and without caution."

Mr. Flint was puzzled. He pinched the loose skin on the back of one hand. He thumbed his nose pensively. "In that case I am afraid we will have to dispense with your services." He could not tolerate even the suspicion of facetiousness.

Thornton no longer suffered from emptiness and nausea. His morning obliviousness had been magically recalled. Soon he would get his hat and stick, his few personal letters, a pencil for which he had a fancy, and depart from those offices forever. He might even be in time to reach Michael for breakfast. Or Cynthia. His new allegiance uttered itself. Mr. Flint's voice called him sharply to focus again.

"—two weeks' salary from the cashier. And I must say that I am really sorry you have been delinquent. This is a magnificent institution. A young man could have no better opening. It is not a thing to be thrust aside lightly. I trust you will appreciate the gravity of your error in the course of time to come. We of this company all—"

For the last time he listened. Flint was swelling under his hymn to himself. Thornton wished he would hurry. Cynthia. His mind touched another idea. He would ask. Flint was intruding on his time. Thornton interrupted him in the midst of his rhapsody.

"Excuse me, but I doubt that I can be interested in that from now on. Nevertheless, I should like to ask one question."

"What is that?" Mr. Flint realized that he was possibly wasting seed on barren soil.

"I have a friend" (Thornton's friend was imaginary—the device of inspiration) "a friend who has recently come to the city. He is far more able than I ever was. I wonder if you would consider him as an applicant for my position?"

Arnstein uncrossed his legs, recrossed them the other way, and leaned forward, spilling over his own thighs.

"The position is already filled," Mr. Flint answerer crisply.

"May I ask by whom?"

Arnstein opened his mouth, but Mr. Flint, caught in the flow of his own words, replied: "Why, a Mr. Solomon, the nephew of Mr. Arnstein, happened to be available and we are going to try him in—"

For the second time Thornton found the courage to interrupt his senior and erstwhile superior. "I understand," he said softly and turned to Arnstein, "perfectly."

He did it deftly, obviously. It was more effective than an avalanche of explanation. The two men froze. What Thornton intended to convey was patent to Mr.

Flint. He looked like a man who has suddenly come upon a rattlesnake. Arnstein puffed pallid with inarticulate spleen. Thornton went out, closing the door carefully.

15

In the elevator he lit a cigarette. A fit of trembling seized him. He dropped his match. At the eighth floor, exhaling a voluminous cloud of smoke, he drew his salary. The sleeves under his arms were clammy. His knees were weak. Once, on the way to the street, he giggled. He was wondering what Flint and Arnstein were saying to each other. He walked three blocks without noticing the streets or the directions. Then, in a drug-store, he drank a cup of coffee. After that he called Cynthia.

"I've lost my job."

"What!"

"Fired this morning."

"What for?"

"Somebody's nephew. Want to hear about it?"

"Of course."

"I'll come up. Put on some sort of haberdashery and wait in the lobby."

It was he, however, who waited in the lobby. Cynthia came out of the elevator. Her hat was blue. Her dress was blue. Blue like water. It made her eyes seem blue instead of gray. They walked to Schraffts.

He told her the story, making the most of his dramatic dénouement.

"I think that's the rottenest deal I ever heard of," she said, "and if I were you, I'd do something about it. I wouldn't let them walk over me—not even a little bit."

"I don't feel that I've been walked over."

"You should."

"Arnstein did me a favor."

"You'll get a better job, of course. But you ought not to take anything from him."

"I don't mean I'll get a better job. I mean I'll stop working for good."

"Why—how can you?"

"Art. I'll be an artist from now on."

"I didn't know you could draw."

"I can't. But this is what I've been thinking. Every time you pass a news-stand there's a new magazine. Altogether there must be several hundred of them. I've sold short stories. I'll write a lot. Some of those two hundred magazines ought to use what I write. And if they don't like fiction, I'll interview successful men— like Flint and Arnstein."

"That's not much of a career. You'll fray at the hems and shine at the seat and let your hair grow and drink too much—" Cynthia had expected to comfort a torn and depressed human being. Instead she found an independent and stimulated young man who had already dismissed his entire official past.

"I'll write a book at the same time—"

"That would be different. If you will write one."

"Of course I will. We'll hitch our prodigal wagon to the proverbial star—"

"We?"

"Editorially, if you insist. Let's go somewhere, Cynthia. Let's do something. Celebrate. Let's have a day. Three—four hundred I've wasted in that office looking out at a wall of windows, doddering out of a needful bed for it, staggering home tired from it, shaping my life to it, and now I'm through. Free! It—it's almost too much—"

"Don't be sentimental."

"I'm not." He withdrew his self-exultation. "But I want to celebrate. Let's get a drink."

His eyes flashed. His cheeks were flushed. The recklessness of that mood thawed her resentment. It was certain that he was different. She perceived that it was better to thrill over the loss of a job than to grieve. It would, at the least, buoy him up in the search for another. "All right, let's go."

She had never taken a drink in the middle of the morning. It lifted her mightily above the perplexed residue of sleep. It colored the bustling thunder of traffic and made it glamorous. It sang in her and invited a second and a third. But Thornton was quieted. When he had finished the third pink cocktail, he paused, changed his order to a high-ball, and began to talk. She was eager to listen.

"I lose a job," he said solemnly, "and that's that. Thwick! Done. Where am I? Nowhere. What have I done? Nothing. I've seen a snatch of the newspaper world, the theatrical world, the publishing and the advertising world. But that is not part of me. It has nothing to do with me. It is like the adding machine to the clerk. Day after day he beats upon it until it is of the same substance as his arm or leg. It requires no thought, no attention; it assists him to live. It does not teach him. It gives him no moods, no pleasure, no pain. It does not even expose him to the risk of pleasure or pain. I sound like Michael. Excuse me. But I think I have something to say. What I mean is that I could continue it for fifty years and die and have had nothing more of life than my leg has. It feels. It moves. Things happen to it. But the leg does not change or care. I had more life, more consciousness, if you see what I mean, when I was chopping wood up in the north country. I told you about that. Or when I was scraping decks in the Pacific. I could sit and think. I could enjoy. Good food tasted good. I did not eat because it was time to eat and for no other reason. And everything was that way. Has been this way. Am I confusing?"

"No. Don't stop."

"Women. I have theories about women." He knew he was fatuous, but he had had too many drinks to check himself. "Happy life with a woman is vitally necessary. But, per se, it is nothing. Only when we lack a felicitous sex-life, do we realize how important it is. Women are like men. They have—I forget how many less cubic centimeters of brain capacity—but they are like men with that reduction. They can't imagine. They can't yearn. Yearn. That's the most promising emotion in man. Yearn. I want to yearn—and I've almost forgotten how. I wan't to want things. I want to hear a slow waltz played by a French orchestra across a bay on the Riviera. I want to—crazy words, crazy tune—" he sang.

Cynthia became anxious. He had slipped beyond her province into one she considered worthless or drunken or both. At the door of the speakeasy a man stood grinning. He had been listening for some time. "Let's get out of here," she said. "I'm suffocating."

"Me too."

He wondered why she was suffocating. She took his arm and he loosed himself confidently. The effort threw him off balance. "Maybe you better," he said contritely, and offered his elbow. She did not take it.

There was a tea-room across the street. Thornton looked at his watch. "Combination of ideas—association," he said. "Yonder a restaurant. Here, the lunch hour. *Ita*. Let's lunch."

She was surprised when they were seated again. His intoxication had vanished. He seemed to sense that he had frustrated her jubilant beginnings and he set out to retrieve himself. She responded quickly. For a short time she thought that it would be she who would require air and motion.

"Food is better," he said, reading her symptoms. "Quicker. We eat, then we take one high-ball. Then we fare forth. One trouble with vice is that it's embarrassingly physical. Always regretted that we couldn't

67

pervert the soul for pleasure instead of the body. That's the best argument I know against its existence. We always pervert the wit for profit and the body for fun. Wonder why the other scheme isn't tried? That doesn't sound very consistent, but I think it would in the hands of an able rhetorician. Or do I bore you?"

"I think you flatter me—or my condition."

"Try another tack. Shouldn't be morbid in the presence of the ill. Shaw. Let's talk about Shaw. Personally, I never read Shaw. But I'd like to. And I'd undertake to discuss him at any time. Shaw, Wells, and Kipling. The big three of literature where it can be called literature. The crafty old Irish cynic, the lofty Welshman, the old empiricist. That means something else. The question that is usually brought up is, will Shaw survive and be addled and cozened by posterity. Addled and cozened. I like those words. Some day I will look them up. My feeling is, no. No. Decidedly no. Shaw will not survive. We fail to foresee posterity in the right light. We fail to see the present day in the right light. Too many little syllable-picklers painfully toiling night and day overy every single sentence. Nobody notices and nobody reads. Next posterity will be a machine posterity. No use for Shaw. Shavian itself. On the other hand, we might talk about Picasso. Never look at pictures. But I can talk about Picasso, too."

"Please don't."

"Do you feel better?"

"Much. Are you like that often?"

"Never except in the case of extreme paleness."

BABES AND SUCKLINGS

She looked down into the willow-ware bowl of soup that had been set before her. Its contents appeared to be rotating queasily. With a numb hand she lifted a spoonful. They ate without exchanging many words. When the coffee arrived, Cynthia was in command of herself again. They walked into the broad daylight, crossed the street, sat at one of the small tables in the speakasy parlor, drank a high-ball meditatively, and went to Fifth Avenue.

A bus took them down town. The sun was warm and enervating. People flowed along the sidewalk like a bright hall carpet. Traffic towers winked their jeweled eyes. At Tenth Street they clambered down from the lurching platform.

"It was nice," she said, and he agreed.

Michael answered his bell and admitted them.

"We're cock-eyed," Thornton said.

"Have you had lunch?"

"Yes."

They divested themselves of their wraps. Michael stood before them with a musing expression on his face. His hands were muddy with paint. He was wearing a shirt torn at the shoulder. A clot of tan muscle showed through the hole. Canvas stretched on his easel blocked out a square of the wide windows in the adjacent room. He was worried. Unless they had a good reason for drinking in the morning, it was a procedure of unpleasant possibilities.

"How come you hunted out scamper-juice at dawn?"

69

"I forgot." A grin overspread Thornton's face. "I was fired this morning. Utterly and with trimmings. I called Cynthia and asked her to joint the labor depression. Hence the binge."

Michael was relieved. Cynthia, watching him closely and to advantage because he was off his guard, understood for the first time his feeling towards Thornton. It raised the level of Thornton's importance in her estimation.

"That's fine," Michael said.

"I think so. I've had some difficulty in convincing Cynthia. She is all for the eight-hour day."

"I was—but I'm not."

Michael looked then at her. All that he had predicted was about to be fulfilled. "In that case, I'll join the party as soon as I wash."

"Have you eaten?"

"Not a thing."

"Then we'll have to have lunch again. Mustn't try to drink without it. We did. It made Thornton talk about life."

"Not to mention Shaw and Wells and Kipling and Picasso."

Michael disappeared. His mind seethed with its own rumors. Were they already in love? He could not tell by looking at them. What would Thornton do without his job, with Cynthia to investigate? Was it good or bad or just meaningless for them to be together, for them to react in that manner to Thornton's deposition?

While Michael ate breakfast, they drank coffee.

BABES AND SUCKLINGS

A number of ideas for entertainment during the afternoon were discussed. At last, however, after giving them up one by one, they were persuaded to return to Michael's house. They drank several high-balls there and talked endlessly. Sometimes that talk was feverish and excited. At others it was slow and pleasant.

At last Michael said: "I have a date for supper, but I'll see you afterwards, if you like."

Cynthia nodded. Usually so much drinking had been accompanied by dancing, by driving from one country club to another, by swimming, perhaps. But New York was not California. Instead of making her gay, it made her somber and thoughtful. But, in its background, a dramatic desire grew steadily and sensuously. It was unfamiliar to her. She and Thornton rose. Their eyes glittered. Their cheeks flamed. But they were quite self-possessed.

Through the three or four hours that followed, Michael sat in his apartment alone. He had had no engagement for dinner. He had sent them away because he hated temporizing and he recognized a proper instant. The young man for whom he cared so much and the young woman who was so beautiful were drunk beyond embarrassing inhibitions. It was safer for them in consequence. A little civilization cast aside might make their future very nearly sacred. He bent his head into his hands and was silent. Occasionally he rose to fill his glass. Too bad, the working of the world. He wished that there were no women in it. Only men, honest, brave, intelligent. At last he fell asleep.

71

BABES AND SUCKLINGS

Cynthia and Thornton walked out on the street. The amber light of late afternoon touched the tops of buildings. They walked smiling. He held her arm in a close embrace. Through the slow passage of day she had reached certain conclusions about herself and him that fitted to her desire. His arm made them articulate.

"We're going to your house, aren't we?"

"Yes." If Thornton had been sober, he would have said: "If you wish" and thereby damaged the spell.

A duskiness as if the air were tinted hushed the apartment. They hesitated on the threshold; their entrance had a universal significance. She removed her hat and coat. He hung them in the closet carefully with his own. When he came out, he saw that she was sitting on the day-bed and not in a chair. He was touched by a diffused warmth, and when he took his place beside her, kissing her fragrant hair, he was tempted to do no more than contemplate the ecstasy of the moment. With a slow caress, she absolved him of that temptation and replaced it with one infinitely stronger. So they yielded quietly, gently. He kissed her lips and her clothes. Then, past all thought, looking down into her eyes, he smiled. Her smile, misty, delirious, was an answer. And some time after that, half-dressed, locked in each other's arms, they fell asleep.

16

So Cynthia had come to town and in a short week had found herself a lover. It was very perplexing. By all the tenets of her half-mythical instruction, it should have been different. She did not think of marrying Thornton and he had not mentioned marriage. Perhaps he felt it would be indelicate because she then had no divorce. But, certainly, he took her very seriously and their love was very serious to him. On the train from California, with the ties between a dead life and a new life broken, she had pictured herself having *affaires*— light, charming *affaires* with important men who had passed youth and attained the goals of maturity. She had seen a worldly Cynthia in a glittering universe of dinner clothes and smart restaurants, theaters and concerts. Not married. The mistress of a great man, perhaps. Love would enter only as a pleasant physical factor about which she would be quite disillusioned and entirely selfish.

Thornton was undergoing a similar redistribution of ideas. His reasons for seducing Cynthia—an antique word which caused both of them to smile—apart from the sensuous instincts of the moment, were various. It flattered his vanity to know that he was successful where Breck had failed. That, in turn, increased his opinion of her, because he felt that he was better than Perry Breck. The dramatic sequence of living made it necessary to follow up the kiss he had given her on the balcony with a pyrotechnical verification of all it implied. But, when it was done, he began to consider her as a human being, and that necessarily had numerous disturbing corollaries.

For one thing, she took charge of his thoughts. He commenced to speculate on the merits of a permanent arrangement, if not actual wedlock. That was foreign to determinations he had already made, among which predominated the economic and epicurean advantages of grazing through a world of diverse females, as well as the ego-centric adversion to fidelity and its consequences.

It was a shock to him to realize the force with which he resented any notion of Cynthia allied to another man. That notion, taking him in the dark of the night after he had loved her, was graphic in detail and it launched him into an hour of perspiring wakefulness. To refute it he tried at once to remember all the reflections of Michael on that subject and thereby to acquire an attitude he considered "European." When he was utterly unable to accomplish that by intellectual effort, when his emotions still clamored for the end of that picture of Cynthia, he was outraged again. Abruptly he saw that any such lapse on his own part held no terrors to him. That, of course, was not right. So he lay sweltering and produced a legion of disparagements against himself which he recognized as vain.

The period that followed was one of pleasure in which they accomplished very little adjustment to each other. Thornton was not compelled to work every day. Cynthia had nothing to do. They sat up until dawn on scores of evenings. They played bridge. They drank. They became a temporary and subsidiary part of Michael's household, and, at the same time, Cynthia gradually moved to Thornton's apartment by degrees so minute that neither of them were conscious of it until she paid a hotel bill for a week during which she had never entered the hotel except for her mail.

That infiltration of her impedimenta and person was undertaken for convenience and completed for economy. With a feminine practicality that she disguised as sentiment, she brought to his house an overnight bag filled with perfumes and cosmetics and sleazy pyjamas. A dress followed. Two more dresses. Then her clothes came back with his laundry. It amused him. To her it was comfortable good sense.

Thornton accompanied her when she paid the unnecessary bill. He said afterwards: "Why don't you give up the hotel?"

Cynthia had already decided to do that if he was enthusiastic. She could not be sure by his tone. "What should I do then?"

"Live with me."

She felt a quaint pang over the passing of an old treasure. Two months ago that statement would have brought insulted response. Then it seemed quite normal. She knew already that no one she had met in New York would object, or look askance, or even remember that there was a proper subterfuge of two apartments as an alternative. "You'd be bored," Cynthia said after a moment.

"Don't be an egg. I'd like it."

"Really?"

"Of course."

"Well— I might try—for a week."

So the week was passed and extended. The vast majority of people whose unimportant lives are ordered by routine could conceive of that period in the lives of Thornton and Cynthia (if they had the power of conception) only as a sort of daring and indecent vacation. But it was not a vacation of any kind. It was a reality, a fixed scheme. It was their life. It is not because they are artists and authors that artists and authors intrigue the small wits of the public, but because their means of earning a livelihood leaves them independent of schedules, of locations, of particular dictates. The average man cannot imagine what it requires to paint a picture. But he is able, through the beneficent generosity of evolution, to perceive the advantages and pleasures of leisure. Leisure is enviable. That is the foundation of the urge to make vast sums of money and the urge to practice an art.

Through the hot summer they lived in idleness. Vast and painless discussions were held over the subject of Thornton's future, in which he was to become rich and celebrated. But the discussions themselves exhausted the impulse to work. Besides, each of them possessed a sufficient capital for present needs.

So peaceful was their integration that Michael and

Aurelius were awed by it. The former said one day: "When I saw Thornton look at Cynthia, I thought that the devil was out. And behold them—as settled and organized as two Babbitts—and just as happy."

Aurelius frowned. "So far. But they still have money—and nothing has happened to them to make things otherwise. Thornton has lost his intensity for the moment—which is normal and biological. And nobody knows just what Cynthia will do—least of all herself. There hasn't been any digestion. He accepts her and that's that. She is living under such new circumstances that sheer novelty will carry her for a time. I can imagine the California husband. A native son. Think what it must mean to her to live with a man—or, say, a boy —who doesn't wake up with a sour breath and vocabulary, who is considered witty by people whom she admires sometimes against her better judgment, who never grumbles, who goes where she wants to go when she wants to go there, who has enough imagination to anticipate her wants and to understand them—the little ones that have appeared. If marriage were as simple as that—most marriages would be successful."

"They aren't married. That's part of the secret."

"It is now. Later on, it will be a problem."

Michael knocked out a pipe and grinned. "That is precisely what I have thought. Only—I took the opposite side to hear you say it. When Thornton wants to work, when another man desires her ardently—well, God help them."

BABES AND SUCKLINGS

17

Don, in his own fashion, was a gentleman. Gerry was not a lady. All the other mathematical combinations of that proposition were demonstrable. Don, brought up in a middle-class family, of middle height and medium coloring. Of fair education. Don left Columbia and moved to a rooming-house. One day he walked out into the hall and bumped fairly into Gerry. During the three previous months while he had worked in an advertising agency, he had wondered vaguely about love and marriage, which, he assumed, would supplant proms and petting in his later life. In the evenings, when he had washed after work, gone out to the street, sat in a marble-topped restaurant over his paper, and returned with an apple and a bar of chocolate for late consumption, a vague disturbance in his corporeal self led him into fancies of no great complexity.

He was earning forty dollars each week and his prospects for increase were good. It enabled him to consider marriage as a present solution. He liked girls. He considered himself sophisticated where they were concerned. He was embarrassed by knowing no likely girl in New York. But after meeting Gerry he spent a day of pleasurable anticipation. "She lives across the hall," he repeated to himself. Maybe— So, that night, he rapped on her door and was admitted.

Three hours later, in his own apartment, he grinned

at his reflection in the bureau mirror. He also said: "Hot dog!" and executed a series of amiable movements that would have seemed very funny to an unsuspected observer. Gerry had kissed him good-night—on the first night. And she was a wonderful girl. Intelligent. Popular. Clever. All that a man's wife ought to be. He had many of the sentiments of grandeur and much of the benign acceptance that Thornton had exhibited under similar circumstances.

Gerry, behind her opposing door, combed out her long, black hair and she, too, confessed to her mirror. She was gratified at the accessibility of Don. She perceived that he was nice. Four years of extension courses had made her vain and cautious in so far as males were concerned. Three months in a newspaper office produced another resultant. She did not like the men there. She classed them as conceited and vulgar. The truth was that, in a few days of close association, they had seen through her so utterly as to make her every word a further definition of her character. Newspaper men did not like that sort of woman, being kindly and widely experienced. They had a word for her.

For Gerry was a very slight exaggeration of what most women either are from birth or become in life. She was a definition of the female profession. Gerry was extremely attractive. Her long, Stygian hair was aphrodisiac. Her black eyes, red lips, slender, curved torso, pale limbs and arms were like Lilith's. Gerry could be, and usually was in the company of men, a gay child of romance and fortune who could mysteriously turn into a universal mother and a receiver of all love. Gerry accepted no information (with the single exception of scandal) because her knowledge was already so great as to make any contribution an affront. She was convinced that she was the dominant species—ruling by brains alone, master of emotion, destined and predestined.

Occasionally insinuations of the truth were brought to her ears, and the bearer lost his standing in her estimation so swiftly as to leave him (it was usually her) floundering and indignant. Such insinuations ran the whole gamut of disparagement. She was selfish and vain and a liar. She was ignorant, and one of the most hypocritical people alive. Gerry justified Gerry's behavior. Her sophistication was a pretense based on no experience. She made her past virtuous or wicked according to the needs of the moment.

Gerry, as are thousands and tens of thousands of her sisters, was frigid. Those who understand that condition are divided. Half of them, upon hearing it, clamp their mouths and say: "Through her own fault." The other and more discerning half is moved to a vague but none the less acrimonious condemnation of society. But few enough people understand it at all, and, of them, it would be better that the majority did not.

There are probably ten times as many women like Gerry in America as in any other country. It was not her fault to be born there. She did not know she was frigid. Her mother would have lapsed into something between nauseated regurgitation and ferocious hysteria at the exposition of it. The blight is as monstrous as would be a general atrophy of the eyesight through deliberate disuse, although it is rooted in a behavior different from disuse.

She was typical. In such cases it is not necessary to etch in a background of prohibitions. Her parents, naturally, desired her to be chaste, and so, by true and false suggestion, by command, by example, reiteration, rebuke, the production of abnormal fear, by induced ignorance, spying, exhaustion, by substitution, superstition, and as many other means as their feverish souls could summon, they saw to it that she was chaste. Perhaps, so invidious was their scheme, if they could have known that she would go to her grave unsatisfied and in that sense still virginal, they would have preferred it to the pleasant association with some man not her husband—which was certainly the thing they dreaded. Probably they looked upon that side of life as unpleasant. At least, for women.

So Gerry at fourteen overcame the hideous fear sufficiently to let herself be kissed. At sixteen she permitted a continuous kissing, progressing through the whole infantile ritual to maturity, when a certain amount of tampering was allowed with her greater passions— which were never passions at all because it was inflexibly foreordained that the very thought of consummation was taboo.

In Don's stratum of society, that was precisely what one expected to find in a girl of twenty. He had heard rumors of its harmfulness. But he was able to live and die without investigating the rumors. So was Gerry. Once to admit that her imperfection existed would be to admit its attributes: jealousy of other women, hatred, spite, envy, meanness in defense, circumlocutions of living, hysterical conduct, insatiable lust. Of course, the possibility of that admission did not arise until she discovered the fact. And her discovery of the fact was made, naturally enough, in terms of the deficiency of others. Which, in turn, led her to court disaster elsewhere. It was a vicious ring of retroactive evils.

Michael always laughed when he thought of her. "There is one of your American sisters," he would say to Thornton or Aurelius. "Isn't she wonderful! Beautiful as a dream and passionate as an ice-box. Sweet as honey outside and wolverene inside. A dirty dowager in the larva stage. Less woman than—" whereat he would become obscene. Gerry made him want to be obscene, offensive, to laugh in her face.

But Don and Gerry carried on their romance in tranquil conventions. A zest was added to it by the fact that they lived independently and alone. When they had spent half of the summer together, Don was unexpectedly moved up to a copy-writer's position in his agency and his salary was doubled. At about the same time. Gerry discovered that he was a direct descendant of Aaron Burr, and that he had played left half on the second team at college.

It was not her plan to write sob stories for the *Record* all her days. Furthermore, the men at the office understood her so completely that they were able to devise unique torture for her. Most of it missed fire because of her self-assurance, but that which struck its target was insufferable. Once, for example, she had arrived at the office slightly intoxicated. She believed herself a masterful drinker. But the reporters and rewrite men noticed it at once. Somewhat to her surprise, they were very nice to her. They made her talk about herself, which was easy for Gerry. She told them a great deal. She made a date. They praised her beauty.

And then, to her undying regret, she undertook a discussion of her hair. The alcohol and the unanticipated compliments had done their work. She spoke in that intriguing and distinctly naughty manner which she reserved for the elect of her affections. "Yes, I do think I'm lucky to have the hair I have. But it's just luck, you know. It covers me like a bathing-suit. Just like a bathing-suit." She reached the vehement line that had once insured her a summer-long engagement. "And —it's a secret—but they match. All black."

The uproar that followed and the diversity of jests, not at all kind or particularly decent, which occupied the ensuing days were almost more than she could bear. But she did bear it. Gerry was tough—a compensation for indignities already borne.

The upward drift of Don and the growing certainty that the newspaper microcosm did not understand her as she deserved to be understood pulled her intentions in one direction. Cynthia heard a great deal of it, pro and con, during August. Gerry liked to confide in her because she passed over fatuity and patronage with innocent mien and because she never disagreed.

Thornton could not understand the relationship. He was sure that Cynthia detested Gerry—although Cynthia had said very little about any of his friends. It occurred to him that she might have considered Gerry a rival at first and instituted their friendship purely as a system of open defense. That was flattery to his vanity, as he perceived, but there was no other evident reason. Both he and Cynthia agreed that they liked Don. He knew that Gerry hated Cynthia—although he did not know why. Gerry in private had been too mocking about their liaison, too saccharinely well-behaved to Cynthia in public. And Gerry was indirectly responsible for their first quarrel.

18

In August Thornton began to write and the August conversations were usually held in Gerry's room while he was at work. Cynthia insisted on leaving him alone during the greater part of the day-time, despite his protest that he liked to have her near when he wrote. She found that, each time she stayed at home and attempted to read, the sound of his typewriter was exasperating, and even more so was his abstracted look of inquiry that followed any interruption. She hated Gerry quite sincerely, but with a hate that she almost liked to indulge. Gerry's sham was a window through which she looked with repelled fascination. And, superficially, Gerry was good, if transparent, company.

On one such day Gerry sighed with measured melancholy. "Do you really think Don and I are suited to each other?"

Cynthia, with a certainty that any definite answer would involve her falsely, said: "Don't you?"

"I'm not sure. Don is the plodding type. And I'm not a plodder. I was made for the whole emotional gauntlet. I'm not cool and poised like you. I have too much temperament, I suppose."

"I see."

"I feel things he doesn't feel. I know things he will never know." She extinguished her cigarette emotionally. "And yet—he seems such a logical person to marry."

"Do you love him?"

"In what sense?"

Cynthia frowned as if she were considering gravely. "In every sense?"

"How can a woman of today be expected to love anyone in every sense? That's a ridiculous statement. I suppose you love Thornton in every sense?"

"No. I don't."

"How do you think he would like to hear that?"

Cynthia ignored Gerry's inconsistency. "I've told him."

"What did he say?"

"Nothing. He always says a lot that means nothing

85

—or else he never says a word—when he really feels or thinks."

Gerry noted for her own information that Cynthia was tricking Thornton into a pathetic masculine generosity. The idea that Cynthia was telling the truth never occurred to her. "Well, perhaps Don is strong and silent, too. But tell me, do you think he'll amount to a great deal?"

"With your assistance and—guidance," Cynthia said, "he will have to amount to a great deal."

It was a dubious compliment, but Gerry did not exactly distrust it. She thought Cynthia much too naïve to be subtle. "Thanks. Then, I suppose you're for it?"

"For what?"

"Don's and my marriage."

"I didn't say that—precisely. Why don't you try the same makeshift for companionate marriage that Thornton and I are trying?"

That was against Gerry's instinct and her training. She could be unconventional where unconventionality was condoned, but to be so openly before the whole world was unthinkable. Anger that Cynthia should suggest such a thing reddened her face. So she described it to herself. But the anger rose, actually, from an inner knowledge that she would be wholly unable to try such an arrangement.

"Don wouldn't do it."

"If you wanted him to, he would."

To deny that would be to deny her power over men. To admit it would be to make herself responsible

86

for refusing the trial. She found herself, for the first time, struggling against a superiority in Cynthia.

"I'll ask him."

Cynthia was quite aware of the form of rhetoric that request would take—such a form as could have but one answer. That was, of course, provided she asked Don at all. She felt keenly sorry for Don.

"Why don't you? It's so simple. You can play house—the way we play house. Then, if you like the game, you can make it a business."

"Goodness," Gerry said. "I've got to go to the office. It's four o'clock."

19

Cynthia went home with a definite irritation. She had given herself away to Gerry in some manner which she could not describe, but which made her annoyed. She found Thornton sitting disconsolately at his typewriter. For the first time that she had noticed, he did not rise and kiss her. He smiled vacantly and looked back at his work.

The cumulative effect of her mood was a shock to her. Before she had weighed the words, she said: "I think I'll call up Perry Breck and ask him to take me out."

She had no sooner spoken than she was sorry. What she had intended was something—anything that would be a rebuke to Thornton for his neglect and a

87

small retaliation for the afternoon's ignominy. If Cynthia had been a little less human, she might have seen that she had told Gerry one or two truths she had no intention of telling anyone—truths that made her feel treacherous towards Thornton. Now, as she stood with her hat on the back of her head, her mouth open, a pettish frown on her brows, she still hoped to hear a counter suggestion from Thornton.

But he, remembering simultaneously that for weeks they had scarcely been out of each other's company, believing her wish to see Perry Breck was genuine, swallowed his jealousy and said: "All right. If you want to do that, go ahead."

Cynthia was proud. It was a moment for weakness, but she managed only to temporize. "It's so fearfully hot, I don't know what I'm doing."

Thornton wrote three clattering words to finish a sentence. When he looked up, she had pulled her hat over her eyes again.

"See you later," she said. Her voice grated. The door slammed. He rose, hesitated on half-bent knees, and sat down again. Cynthia was angry. Ten minutes later she called and said that she was going to meet Perry for supper and that she did not know when she would be in that evening.

Weakness seized him. He sat on the bed. Such a thing had never broken their lyric life together. For a half-hour he sat. He decided that she was unreasonable and that he was cruel and stupid. He believed that such things would not occur if they were married.

BABES AND SUCKLINGS

The phone rang again. He leaped up, thinking that it was she.

"Hello, Thornton? This is Don."

His voice sank as he answered. "How are you?"

"What's the matter? You sound the way I feel."

"Nothing."

"What are you doing for supper?"

"Nothing."

"Want to eat with me?"

Thornton had decided, temporarily, to call Michael. But he answered: "All right. Whenever you say."

"I'll be over soon."

Some time later Don arrived. He found Thornton seated at his typewriter. He had progressed but one line on the work he was doing. In a brown paper bundle Don carried two bottles of gin.

"Brought you a present."

"Good. A drink is what I need."

They made cocktails, using a shaker that held a quart. Then, without further ado or any but random conversation, they drank one of the bottles of gin. The process consumed an hour. Don sat in a chair with his feet on the bed. When he emptied his glass, he refilled both his and Thornton's. Thornton played two records on the Victrola that he and Cynthia had bought. The music disturbed the vast tranquility that was gradually descending upon him.

"Well," Don said, "I feel better."

"So do I."

"Shall we eat?"

"Let's have another."

They had another out of the second bottle. Then, arm in arm, they walked out of the house in search of a restaurant. In a muggy Italian place that smelled of garlic and steamy food, they took a table. Don ordered wine. A carafe filled with a yellow, flat-tasting liquid was supplied to them. They munched antipasto.

"Where's Cynthia?"

Thornton marveled at that. He had waited for a question that seemed never to be forthcoming.

"She has gone out."

"Gerry, too." Don eyed his companion glassily. "All women are like that. I'm going to marry Gerry." He inserted it as irrelevant martyrdom. "Wish I'd seen Cynthia first."

"Thanks."

"You're welcome." Don bowed very seriously. "What do you think about Gerry."

"Nice girl."

"She likes you."

"In—in a what-do-you-call-it—Platonic way."

"I suppose so. Well—you have to marry some-one."

"Ought to be in love."

"I am. She is. We are."

"That," Thornton said swiftly, "amounts to con-jugation."

Don scowled. "Don't quite get it."

"Never mind."

"Of course not. Don't mind. Nothing personal."

"Seldom is."

"Is that funny?"

"I couldn't say."

Don pushed back his plate ponderously and put his elbows on the table. "You're a cynic, aren't you?"

"No."

"Well—compared to me you are, anyway."

Thornton admitted it.

"Well," Don said, "in that case, don't you get good and sick of everything once in a while?"

"I never know when I'm sick of anything. Not till years later. And just now I'm not sick of anything. I'm only sore and hurt because Cynthia ran out on me— which isn't a very cynical attitude, is it?"

"No. And Gerry went to dinner. She's probably home now. But I haven't the nerve to call her up."

"I'll call her."

"Will you?" Don smiled wistfully.

Thornton left the table, stepped forward, hit another table, ricocheted, turned the corner, and caught the telephone. He called his own number in a thick, unnatural voice. He heard it ring for some time. Then, hanging up, he called Gerry. She was at home. She would like to see him. Oh. He was with Don. Well—it would be all right. They were tight? Then they should bring something for her.

He reported the conversation to Don, leaving out the eagerness in her words when he gave his name. Don listened, his chin on his chest, his eyes closed.

"Hey!" Thornton shook him.

"I heard you. Just resting. Need a little rest."

"What's the matter with you, anyway?"

"Don't exhort me. Don't exhort. Things aren't the way they ought to be." Don shook his head and stood up painfully. "M' lift's all mixed up. Gerry's a good girl. Let's go!"

"Brought you a present," he said to Gerry when they finally reached the house. "Brought Thornton one and got one for you."

She mixed the gin with ginger-ale. The faces of his two friends were indistinct to Thornton. Gerry smiled at him and he smiled back. Don waggled his finger at them. "None of that!"

He slumped back in the deep chair he had taken. "I suppose so—but you must doubt it."

That seemed inordinately amusing to Thornton. "Catch up," he invited Gerry.

"Watch me." She drank her gin without dilution, a drink that would have sent most men groping and choking in search of water. Another followed. Together they examined Don. He was totally oblivious. A moment later he snored. They carried him to a day-bed.

"And that," Gerry said, "is the end of the boy-friend."

"He brought it on—or in himself."

She giggled. "I wish he said things like that."

Thornton made a slow negative motion with his head. "I'm sure, if I were sober, I wouldn't even consider saying that—wouldn't even admit I had thought of it."

The room was dimmer. He perceived with mild surprise that Gerry was sitting close to him. He gulped his drink. The light did not change. It was a poisonous illumination, like the rays of the sun in the afternoon of a black thunderstorm.

"You're a nice boy," she heard him say, "and I don't think its fair of you to waste yourself on out-of-town girls."

"No?" He tried to settle his pale hair and succeeded only in increasing its disarray.

"Or—are you partial to blondes? I never thought so. And I never thought any woman would get such a hold over you. Yon don't mind my saying that, do you?"

"What?"

"Are you drunk as that?"

"It's inconceivable."

"You like me, don't you?"

"Say," he said sharply, "which one of us is drunk?"

"Please!" She nodded towards the supine form of Don. "He's out of the picture."

"I have to go."

"And leave me all alone?"

"Yes."

"You'd be glad you stayed."

He lunged towards his hat, put it on backwards, and opened the door. Perspiration pricked through his forehead. "Good-night."

Don opened his eyes suddenly. " 'Night, old timer."

He shut the door again on the astonished Gerry.

The street was filled with people. He dodged through them. He walked by leaning forward until his balance was lost and then stepping to regain it. That sort of walking, he found, was very fast and as easy as floating. By and by he reached more desolate streets and finally he stood in the center of a cobble-stone pavement between two dark, lofty buildings. The stars twinkled and swirled in the cleft above him. The monody of Manhattan rolled from the distant thoroughfares.

"Here I am," he said aloud.

"Here I am," he repeated. "Love is a lonesome harlot, there isn't any God, and work is buffoonery. Here I am. That's all there is. Me, me, me, me, me. The wind and me. The wind coming up the river full of tug whistles. The rain at night. The smell of smoke and wet bricks. The hush of night. The wind and me. Me, and my love is far away, becoming a ghost." Tears filled his eyes. "Here in this dark, vasty silence is me —am I. Nowhere, with nothing for tomorrow, and yesterday become nothing. No one really cares. No one really knows. The people are bad little dreams. And love is a lonesome tart." He began to sing "Ten Thousand Cattle." He sat on a curb, his head in his hands, looking into his bitter heart.

Then he walked home. Once, for a few minutes, he was lost. He asked directions from a policeman, who laughed in his face. In return he insulted the policeman caustically and pointedly. The officer threatened to arrest him. Thornton staggered away at a tangent.

There was a light in his apartment. He stared at it,

trying to remember whether or not he had left it on. He decided that Cynthia had come home, and went upstairs. He was very tired. He would lie down and sleep immediately.

Cynthia sat in his apartment talking to Perry Breck. He opened the door and regarded them with dumb surprise. She spoke cheerfully: "Hello, darling."

Her cheer wounded him. He didn't want Breck to be there. He was not suspicious of the circumstances, but he was outraged. "Hello."

Breck stood and smiled. Thornton thought he saw malice in that smile. And Breck, if he had known, was not unmalicious. Unwitting, he considered himself polite. "Howdy, Thornton. Don't mind my dropping into your place, do you?"

For several unpleasant seconds Thornton stood still. They, too, had been drinking. Breck held an almost empty glass in his hand.

"Of course I do," Thornton said abruptly.

"Please, darling, lie down and rest. You're not yourself." Cynthia, anxious, piteous, kissed him. Internally she was furious. But Thornton never knew that.

"I'll sit up with—with your guest," he said.

"I'm running right along."

Thornton turned to Breck. "Don't linger." He had retaliated for his hurt. Breck left.

Cynthia spoke to Thornton. "I'm so ashamed I could cry."

"Of me?"

"Yes."

Thornton shrugged. "I don't want that shifty-eyed lady-killer fooling around here. He's no good. An errant ass."

Cynthia slapped him. She slapped him so hard that her hand was printed on his face. He felt no pain. He never remembered the instant that followed. He only knew that, a moment later, Perry Breck was in the room bending over Cynthia. And Cynthia was sobbing hysterically, lying on the floor, her cheek rapidly swelling where his fist had left a dark bruise.

"As for you—" Breck wheeled towards him. Thornton's fist stung. He saw Perry reel. Then everything ended.

20

He woke in a world of unspeakable suffering. His head was pillowed on a cold, wet towel. Cynthia was making coffee. He did not dare to speak. She ignored him, as if she knew he was awake. Shame and horror and headache and nausea and nervous misery ate to the pith of his bones. He caught her eyes, his own expressing animal sorrow. But hers were adamant.

She brought coffee. He drank some of it and was sick. She paid no attention to him. Hours passed. She packed her bags, went out, brought back sandwiches, and averted her head while he ate. Twice, then, he tried to speak to her, but she only sighed without replying. He focused burning eyes on the ceiling.

"I'm going," she said.

He looked. She was wearing her hat.

"Don't."

He said no more. He was incapable of saying more. Then she came to him. He heard her crying. He felt her hands on his face. All afternoon she sat there, reading and looking through the window. Darkness descended. She brought supper and cooked it. Later in the night she opened a bag, undressed, lay beside him.

"I don't know why it is I stay with you," she whispered.

Thornton took her in his arms and trembled.

21

On the following day she intercepted a letter for herself from California. It was signed by a firm of lawyers and indicated her husband's intentions of obtaining a divorce. Cynthia stood in the hall and read it slowly. Then she walked down the street. She and Thornton did not have sufficient money for the steps the letter suggested. But that was less important than another factor. If he knew that she was free, he would wonder incessantly why she did not marry him. She was not sure of the reason herself; she knew that she did not want to marry Thornton at that time.

She went to Michael's house. "My husband's lawyers have written that he wants a divorce."

"Well?"

"I'd like it. But I don't want Thornton to know I am divorced. Can you understand that? I scarcely can."

"Yes. I can understand it. Your guarantee is not high enough."

"And that's selfish?"

"Of course. But—a person who was really unselfish would die—in a day." He seated himself. "I suppose it requires some time—for communications and all that?"

"It will be rather nasty. I'll have to be caught in a jam—or something. But I shan't have to appear."

"Suppose—" Michael's brow furrowed—"suppose you leave a note for Thornton—tell him you've gone out of town—any excuse. Then you and I will have dinner together—and be found in a hotel together—and then you remain in seclusion for the two or three days you'll need for papers. Or—should you rather have a stranger?"

"Of course not, Michael. But I can't afford it. We can't."

"I can." He smiled. "The miracle is—that you stay with him."

"I like Thornton."

22

"Now what in hell did she do that for?" Thornton frowned with a truculence assumed to bolster up his fidgety soul. "We had a fight and I behaved like a dog.

But I thought it was made up—and then—she goes away." He moved uncomfortably in his chair. "Wants to think things over. I wish I were older—I have a feeling I'd understand it better."

"You would," Michael answered.

"I must love her—or I shouldn't feel as I do."

"Yes."

"Do you think it's—safe—for her to go away?"

"I do. And I think you ought to appreciate her more afterwards."

Thornton left with a feeling that he had been justly rebuked. He called on Gerry against his own intuition. When he had gone, Michael dialed a number on the phone. "Hello, Cynthia," he said. "I'll be up for you at seven. You say they'll be ready to catch us at nine? What a rotten pretender the law is—isn't it? Feel all right? . . . Yes. He was here. Worried, of course. Did you ever see him when he wasn't worried? Oh—I'll take care of him. . . . No—he's not angry. He's puzzled. Believes you had a right to go away for a few days and wonders why he made it necessary. It's all very normal. Seven, then?"

23

"I hear your girl-friend has deserted you. Alone?" Gerry asked.

Thornton banished a surly retort. "Yes."

"When will she be back?"

"In two or three days, according to her note."

"Oh. She left a note?" Gerry pondered that circumstance. "I suppose you've heard the news?"

"What news?"

"Don and I are engaged."

"I'm glad. When are you going to be married?"

"Soon. I don't believe in long engagements."

"Oh."

"Won't you be a little bit sorry?"

"Is this an assault, or is it roguishness?" Thornton asked listlessly.

"Whichever you please."

"I choose to call you a flirt, then."

"Thornton, sometimes I think you're downright dumb."

"So do I." The company of Gerry was as unsatisfactory as he had known it would be.

"Are you happy with Cynthia?"

"Very."

"Then why do you go around like a fish out of water half the time?"

"Maybe that's a sympton of happiness."

"Don acts that way—but it's like Don. It isn't like you. And you don't deny you behave that way, I notice."

"I think—" he hesitated— "It's because I'm not interested in anything else but Cynthia."

"Huh!"

24

Thornton went back to his home and wrote all day, between moments of melancholy thinking. He had believed that he and Cynthia were too intimately associated to permit the occurrence of such a thing as her unannounced departure to the country. Yet, because of his treatment of her, she was justified in any such action she might care to take. Late in the afternoon Perry Breck called him and invited him to supper. Thornton was astonished. It relieved him of a suspicion he had refused staunchly to admit to his articulate thoughts. He grew sentimental over the magnanimity of the older and more worldly man, and at the same time he was ashamed of his own folly.

"You and I got off on the wrong foot," Perry Breck said.

"It was my fault."

"I thought maybe you'd like to take dinner with me."

"I don't see how you can ask me." His abnegation was complete.

"Forget that."

So he dined with Breck. They had numerous drinks. They laughed. They were witty. At last, turned serious, they discussed Cynthia in terms only of praise. After that dinner, when Thornton had gone back to the unusual loneliness of his apartment, he wondered about

Breck. He wondered, too, about his drunken violence. Had Cynthia forgiven him and Breck befriended him because, in the last analysis it was a pure, explicable, barbaric emotion expressed in its simplest form—an emotion that could be understood by its beholders, that even aroused their admiration? He decided that, whether or not so unconventional an analysis was true, it would never do to test it a second time. Wife-beating and general, malevolent pugnacity were scarcely achievements, even in an anthropoidal sense. Besides, both Cynthia and Breck might have felt nothing but pity for him. And both of them might have shown him a noble side of their characters and no more. So, feeling safer in his mind about Cynthia than he had ever felt, he waited for the end of her absence calmly.

25

The aftermath of her journey, which was made to Ninety-fifth Street, and not to the country, passed between Michael and Cynthia in silent regard and very little speech.

She said, one day when they were alone: "You know, Michael, there is a godlike quality about you. I'm not trying to thank you. I know that what you have done for me, in a way, gives you pleasure. But you did it so beautifully."

"I thought we'd agreed—"

"To say no more? A woman can never say no

more. What her lips refuse, her eyes always proclaim. True of a man, too, usually. But I met Perry Breck today, and he told me you'd called him and sent him to see Thornton."

"I told him that you were away and Thornton was cut to bits. He was reluctant. But he agreed to take him to dinner."

"I'm glad you're not a woman," Cynthia said.

Michael looked at her very suddenly—so suddenly that she blushed at the implications that were summoned to her mind. "That," he said quietly, "was as subtle a remark as I expect ever to hear."

Nothing more passed between them. It would have been superfluous.

26

"A woman always goes to the country," Gerry said to Cynthia, "for one of two reasons. Which was yours?"

"Supposing I said a third?"

"I shouldn't believe you." She looked at Cynthia as if to fathom her secret. Then she offered her a cigarette. "I suppose Thornton told you about Don and me?"

"He did."

"Last night, after dinner or before?"

"During. Why?"

"If it had been after dinner," Gerry said speculatively, "I think the world would change for some people."

"Are you trying to be deep?"

"After dinner," Gerry repeated, blowing languid smoke, "when he had brought you from the station" (that was part of Cynthia's ruse) "and eaten, and when he was thinking about certain things rather purposefully—"

"I see."

"I wonder if you do," Gerry said. "Where is he now?"

"Working."

"Has he sold anything yet?"

"No."

"He will."

"Of course he will," Cynthia agreed.

When she started towards home, Cynthia wondered just how jealous of Gerry she was. The knowledge that Gerry had cost her any jealousy whatever was nearly insupportable. She attacked Thornton obliquely.

"I went to Michael's and then Gerry's."

"Did you have a good time?"

"Yes. Gerry is an admirer of you—in case she hasn't made it plain." Was that vituperative? she wondered.

"She has made it boringly plain."

"And—"

"Geraldine is a fake. You aren't annoyed?" His eyes were clear, and there was masculine amusement in their depths. They were magnificent eyes when they were clear and amused.

"I hope not." That was all right. Everything was

all right. Thornton loved her. In Michael she had an incredible friend. Aurelius was good company. Perry Breck brought occasional fluxes of the wealthy world to their door-step. Don and Gerry were interesting. It was a much nicer world than any microcosm she had observed in California.

27

Don and Gerry were married. The elaborations Gerry had planned in her day-dreams were discarded by her middle-class family in Great Neck. One automobile carried Thornton, Cynthia, Aurelius, and Michael to the wedding on Long Island. It brought them back to the supper in the new apartment which the bride had prepared for herself and her husband. None of Don's relatives was present. Gerry's were left at home. Five or six youths of indifferent appearance and demeanor who, the others assumed, were Gerry's unfortunate suitors, and a half-dozen girls of college acquaintance stayed for the party and stood, most of the time, drinking cocktails and chattering.

The only notable event, to the minds of Thornton and Cynthia, was Aurelius's discovery of an old friend among the six girls. She was one of the bridesmaids. And, as Aurelius saw her in the temporary aisle of the McGrath house, his explosive nature violated the sacred moment with such force that he said: "My God!" in a loud voice. The girl turned, recognized him; and, thereafter, Michael, Cynthia, and Thornton shared Aurelius's visible impatience at the length of the ceremony. The reunion of Aurelius and Nadine furnished a contra-tone for an otherwise monotonous afternoon. Who she was, or how she had known Aurelius, did not appear at that time, however.

Riding back to New York with Nadine in the party, each of the five expressed opinions of Gerry which would have been decidedly disturbing to Don, at least, if they had been overheard.

"Why didn't someone stop it?" Nadine asked. "I would have if I had been here in time. Anyone married to her is on the Via Dolorosa for a fare-you-well."

"I thought it was a joke until the last minute," Michael said with mock surprise.

"She intends to make money with him," Cynthia contributed.

Thornton was taken aback by such candor. He thought that Nadine had instituted it, and that everyone was exaggerating for effect. Don was his friend. He was optimistic about the marriage. Gerry was skilful and she had ambitions. She could manage and prod Don to his own advantage. And because he was sure he could rouse a passionate sort of love in Gerry himself, he thought that Don could accomplish the same thing.

The others were not so sure. "That girl will be in the hands of a psychoanalyst in a year," Aurelius said.

"And Don in a sanitarium."

"You people don't talk about Cynthia and me like that, by any chance, do you?" Thornton inquired.

BABES AND SUCKLINGS

Michael turned curiously. "We talk—but not like that."

Thornton did not respond. With a shock he realized that other people talked about him and about Cynthia. That other people entered into the intimacies of their lives and dissected them as casually as he did the same thing. That realization was typical of Thornton. It represented an incompleteness in his mental equipment and it definied him. It had never occurred to him before that other people talked about him in his absence, that his name was brought up, and that he was described as the names of others were brought up and considered by him. The realization was devastating.

They had been carried through the heavy traffic towards the city. All of the occupants of the car noticed Thornton's preoccupation, and Michael guessed its subject. One of the things he had liked about Thornton was his naïve unawareness of the fact that he was the focal point of considerable hypothetical and actual discussion. He felt that the practical and discerning mind of Cynthia had made Thornton open to the new sophistication. Then his stream of thought was switched back to Don and Gerry and he disregarded Thornton except for occasional covert glances of silent amazement at the concentration with which the young man's mind worked and its specialized fury of attack.

They drew up at the brick apartment building and were escorted to the bridal suite by a grinning elevator-boy. The business of the supper began, with chattering bridesmaids and indolent young men trying to be at

ease. Gerry, of course, outchattered everyone and outshone everyone. At a wedding the path for such a performance, no matter how abnormal it may be, is made
psychologically clear for the bride. The famous and the
fair sink quietly into oblivion as a gracious gesture.
Thus Nadine and Cynthia, as well as the men, who
were being brotherly to Don, made no concerted move
toward any sort of activity.

Thornton, sitting compartively alone with the single cocktail to which he had promised Cynthia to con-
fine himself, was still in the mood of analysis into which
he had been thrown. Here were his friends being married. Here was his mistress, charming and delighted, deriving a secret pleasure he could see and not feel. Michael, standing aloof and smiling. Aurelius busy with
Nadine.

Here was a spread table and the dressy henchmen
of the caterer. Music from behind palm-trees of slightly
funereal aspect. Lights, dancing, noise, living caught at
a particular high point decreed by society. His body
was heavy. His mind did not belong in that room or to
those people. Its solemn isolation terrified him. He held
his drink until it was warm, detaching himself from everything near him, without volition or aim. He was a remote entity to which nothing was quite familiar and
everything preordained. He remembered being in that
state. He contemplated its recurrence with awe. The
wedding eddied and rippled into hilarity. Cynthia's
smiling face stood out and then vanished. Everything
was reduced to nothing save her name. Perhaps, he

thought, he was going insane. He took Cynthia home in
the gray morning. She was still volubly objective. But
the mood had not left him.

28

The same gray light, falling through recalcitrant
window-panes on the littered apartment, announced to
Don and Gerry that it was time to retire. The instant
of discovery towards which she had been directed for
twenty years and more found Gerry tired, hollow-eyed,
distressed. She delayed it by a score of invented compli-
cations. The familiarity of Don's lips and hands did not
anæsthetize her eventual fear. Fear and unwonted distaste. Even Don, gentle and clumsy, frightened her.

Icy hands, icy feet. "Don't," she whispered passionately.

Too late, then, to resist. Don had a wife and she
was no less a woman. Blind Don, joking, caressing, pal-
pitating with a physique suddenly abhorrent. He mastered her that one time because her fear and her lessons
and her shattered lust had discomposed her.

She lay awake with clenched fists until the hot sun
poured into her eyes and long afterwards, while he
lumbered through a distraught sleep. When he woke, a
different woman would be waiting for him. The gauntlet that his wedding-guests had predicted was to be run.
"The answer," Michael had once said dreadfully, "to
a maiden's prayer."

BABES AND SUCKLINGS

29

At the same hour Thornton and Cynthia, naked as they were born, slept calmly on opposite sides of his wide couch. In its untenanted center, where the first sun came, they held hands tightly.

30

At that hour Aurelius and Nadine looked at each other and recalled a passion impetuously disrupted years ago in a little café off a busy Parisian boulevard. A passion unforgettable and hesitantly renewed. And at that hour Michael, walking firmly along the empty streets at the river-front, perceiving all those things as if by second sight, spun his cane until it sang and wondered why this happened, why that happened, and what absurd gods would answer his prayer if he relented enough to pray.

31

There was no particular and immediate reason for Michael to be walking through the hours of darkness. He knew the limits of what could take place so well that, in a manner almost childlike, he would deliberately undo as many conventions as he could with a hope that something out of the ordinary would follow. It is true that life holds very little to a man who is aware of its limits and his own. His own bounds were made by himself. And of his many acquaintances (among whom Thornton was nearest to the fact) none comprehended that.

Michael was always ready and eager to tell others what he thought of the sun and the moon, of God, art, publishing, patriotism, politics, war, or anything else under the sun except himself. No one ever remembered hearing Michael talk about Michael's dreams, or his ideals, or his life before he came to New York. Naturally, scraps of that career were brought to light by him, but it was never a topic in the way that topics were made of Thornton's father, who was a Baptist and a librarian, or Cynthia's husband in California, or Gerry's invented early sex-life, or Don's business, or Aurelius's battle against the dope habit over which he became victorious by a narrow margin.

Michael certainly delighted in confounding the staid and proper. But he was equally ready to contribute funds or energy to a cause that interested him. Such causes were invariably personal. Those who were victims of circumstance moved his giant pity. Those who fell through the stupidity of their own devices, on the other hand, aroused only his scorn. But he made his own definitions of circumstance and stupidity.

When Cynthia came to him in anxious need, she did not have to call upon the loyalty of his friendship.

111

In his eyes, she was doing a very noble and valuable thing. He wanted passionately to help.

Gerry, on the contrary, although she was victimized by her family, was vain and boisterous and hypocritical. Whatever he might have accomplished for her, he refused. If she had come to him terrified and helpless, confessing the reason of her fear, he would have found a philosophy for her. Because, next to his understanding of human sham, he understood human weakness best.

He was the feudal lord of his community, bishop of its thought, open-handed provider of its pleasures, confessor of its tribulations. No one who had Michael for a friend could have taken his own life, or left his mate, or sunk to any level of blank despair, unless it was with his permission. And, occasionally, he "permitted" such a thing. Like a biologist, he saw disease in the unfit and was undismayed by its course. Then he would make no move to enhearten, to weed out, to reform or assist.

It was that clear sight which made him unhappy. The perfection which he could imagine for himself was beyond his attainment. Too fecund, too versatile, too skeptical for great art. Lacking the long clinical training for writing, and disparaging that branch of expression partly on account of his own unfitness, knowing why he disparaged it, positive that music was the triumphant form and unable to compose, scornful of musicians. A better critic than creator. That was part of Michael.

BABES AND SUCKLINGS

He had the skill of a Michelangelo and the soul of a Jonathan Swift. His *métier* conflicted with his belief. When he tightened up the screws of his tall easel, it was to produce a smooth-lined, empty picture that would sell to advertisers for a thousand dollars. No time and no effort went into that work. The junks putting out to sea, the water-colors of Bo-Peep, the portraits of Javanese women and a hundred other women, were piled in a closet. Instead his posters and advertisements occupied a public place. Magazines wrote articles about him. He was given awards. The academies of design looked upon him as a talented illustrator.

When he grew weary of flattery, he turned to caricature. Acid, redolent lines etched the sneers and vanities and biles of his subjects. Newspapers bought them and were sued for libel unfruitfully—because a picture may be an insult, but there is no proof for twelve doltish men. On one occasion his temperate stocking-advertisements brought a member of the clergy to his house. That visit was a distinct triumph for Michael—and yet a triumph gained out of nothing.

The righteous man, a pastor of a popular metropolitan parish whose celestial wisdom, dolled out in the Fairfax fashion, vibrated in one of the evening dailies, had been sufficiently sensitive to hate Michael's stockinged girls just as Michael himself hated them—although his reason was different.

"You are Mr. Palidini, I presume?" the black-coated gentleman inquired.

Michael was a forbidding figure. His hands were

113

paint-daubed. His red hair was disheveled. His sleeves, rolled above his elbows, revealed the livid scar on his wrist. In his smouldering eyes there was a lack of courtesy, an unveiled, dangerous dislike of the clergyman. For, when Michael had seen the cut of his collar and the choking area of his black vest, he had known that the errand would be critical. He stood with his hands on his hips, his feet apart, huge and inimical. "I am."

"May I come in? I have been delegated by morality, shall we say, to call on you."

Michael moved aside and the minister entered his apartment with the same caution he would have used in an alley where, at any moment, a foe might leap upon him. He stared vapidly at the paintings on the wall, the bottle of whisky, the divan, the fireplace spattered with corpses of cigarettes, the easel, and the brushes.

"Hum, hum," he said, "this is, indeed, the sort of thing I expected."

Michael would have thrown him bodily down the stairs save for a caprice which banished his wrath at the intrusion. "I don't suppose I can offer you a drink?"

The legate of God removed his pince-nez. "I fear you do not realize that I am Reverend John Aramis Potter."

"Ah," Michael said. "Sit down."

The man sat angularly. "I have come to—ah—to express an opinion and ask a favor."

"Two difficult enterprises, I don't doubt."

"Beg your pardon? But to the facts. Recently,

114

through no fault of my own—I have two cars at my disposal—I rode on the subway. There, to my great consternation, displayed so that everyone could see, was the—ah—portrait of a young lady in her—ah— underthings." He bit his lip and reset his glasses. "The thing insinuated sex—positively reeked with sex, I may say."

"Goodness," Michael said. He frowned thoughtfully. "That is unfortunate. Very unfortunate."

"I supposed you would be facetious. I seldom find that the so-called intelligentsia are anything but facetious."

"Perhaps you are unable to draw them out."

The minister was somewhat bewildered. "Such work has a bad effect on the womanhood of the nation; the Church decries it, our more sane—" he swallowed —"and devout citizens abjure it. Such things should have no place in the public mind."

"What about love?"

The man leaned forward. "Brother, what can you know about love? It is a holy thing. A thing not of the flesh. And you, in this pagan and dissolute environment—"

"Love has nothing to do with the differences between the sexes?" Michael asked innocently. "Then homosexuality is as fine and fair a thing as marriage."

"That, of course, is ridiculous."

"Not at all. It is a conclusion far more logical than most of your own religious conclusions. Think about it. Pray over it. Who knows? In a year or two you may see the light and move to Columbus Circle. I painted a normal, healthy, rather pretty female in her chemise. It was a nice picture. The girl was calculated to rouse normal, healthy emotions. To insinuate that the stockings she wore would arouse the same emotions. I'll venture to bet that half of your congregation are wearing my stockings—and partly because of that girl. I dare you to take a census. Woman want to be charming. Why? Because it is the difference between the sexes that makes love, that necessitates it."

"My dear man—"

"My dear man yourself. You came in here uninvited, not to criticize me, but to criticize the morals of humanity. I am a servant—as you claim to be. I would paint the girl in a diver's suit for the same price. And, if you wish to criticize humanity, learn something about it first. You believe the world is good and bad. It is neither. I can tell you things about your own congregation—why—in this morning's paper—"

"Very lamentable."

"Exactly. I could tell you things about yourself. Your personal habits. Don't go. I won't. Instead—"

Michael began to quote the Bible. His pronunciation, his memory were perfect. Ruth, Ezekiel, the Song of Solomon, Psalms, and passages from the Gospels ran from his tongue with a familiarity that the minister would have envied if he had not been inarticulate. Michael had an astonishing knowledge of the Bible. He was among the few who had come upon it in maturity and recognized it as splendid literature.

116

BABES AND SUCKLINGS

"To my mind—and it is a purely personal conclusion—the Scribes and the Pharisees are in the pulpit
—where they have always been. Talking about things
of which they know nothing. Sinning behind closed
doors—as you do. Stupid braggarts. Oh, I'm tired of
thinking about you. Get out."

"May God have mercy on your soul," the minister
said, rising.

"And make me seamy and testy and a busy-body.
If you come back here, I shall break your neck."

Michael slammed his door. The minister did not
recover from that interview for weeks. But he was so
badly frightened for his own security that he did not
take any of the malicious steps against Michael which
his revengeful nature suggested. "I must be compassionate," he decided. "The man is a demon. God rest
his spirit."

When he had gone, Michael rested in a chair. He
was ashamed of his baiting. Ashamed to have drawn
such absurd criticism on himself. His head fell in his
hands, and the colors on them mingled with strands of
his hair. So prostituted was his art as to involve him in
bickerings with the clergy. He wished he had thrown
the man downstairs and made an end of it. None of his
friends would have understood him. He would ·have
hidden that mood from them. Later, he knew, he would
recount the episode and laugh.

A few days afterwards, still smarting under the
same obscure sore, he had embodied his superficially
sarcastic creed in the most outrageous subject that

presented itself and poured it into Thorton's ears. The younger man never knew that he was listening to a bitter reprisal. To him it was only Michael playing Gargantua—the part of all parts best suited to him.

Cynthia and Thornton had called. While she was absent from the room, he commenced his diatribe spontaneously.

"There's a thing that ought to take its place in philosophy. If I had a mission, it would be to recall ceaselessly to the minds of the world that small but generally disregarded fact that, in so far as it has yet discovered, man is nothing but blood, bone, muscle, tissue, and chemicals. In his sublime impertinence he overlooks that from the day he is born. He makes a convention of it and expects to escape. Only when a sarcoma eats out his days does it occur to him to admit that skin is more than the drapery of an eternal and spiritual entity removed from everything except a vague sublimity.

"I'd do it by that very thing: evacuating the organs of the body. And if I were a writer, I would consecrate my pen to the subject. I would do it in the most classical of veins. For, after all, what has survived the ages in a more intact state than that ancient habit? Besides, in the omnivorous digestion of new topics, this one has been sadly overlooked. Rabelais and Boccaccio were aware of it. But subsequently it has become the property of doctors and quacks who treat it with a Spartan eye and an unimaginative tongue.

"Consider it from the view-point of its importance.

BABES AND SUCKLINGS

Each day ten minutes of a lifetime are frittered away in a purely physical employment. In a week, allowing one day for constipation, one loses an hour. In a year four whole working-days are consumed. Think of it! Solitary confinement for four days every year, sunrise to sunset, uninterrupted (except, perhaps, by the twiddling of a door-handle or a plaintive and importunate voice), alone, tranquil. If one lived to a ripe old age, he would have thrown a whole, active year into the sewer. In a year children are conceived and brought into being, empires are toppled, cities are founded, philosophies are invented. And yet there are no great poets of the cabinet, nor is there a record of its inspirations.

"Who knows what Napoleon may have dreamed while launching his luncheon towards the Seine?"

Michael strode across the room. A grin overspread his features. Thornton listened, enthralled by his eloquence.

"Shelley may have originated his most honeyed phrases—phrases that made man seem trebly ethereal —while he sat red-faced and pop-eyed. However disgraceful such a notion may seem to some, it remains the truth. And its very truth justifies its utterance. For the greatest discoveries are made often in what man has disregarded. Assuredly where a man spends a year, he must do some thinking.

"Yes, it is a shamefully neglected study. In America, where only the infirm are privileged to be possessed of bowels, there has grown up a science of euphemism and camouflage like that which surrounds sex.

BABES AND SUCKLINGS

"Although an inordinate care for them is prescribed by all parents and drubbed into children, the fact itself is avoided. The roads of our broad land are dotted with 'comfort stations.' One 'washes one's hands.' One 'powders one's nose.' But the routine exhaustion of the descending colon never enters into conversation. There are even no common expressions for the invaluable process. At least, the use of those which exist subcutaneously would insure ostracism. In everyday parlance, one may be seasick, one may vomit—a vastly more sordid business—but small children are guiltily shushed from the admission of evacuatory propensities.

"Thus does man at a single step become both a hypocrite and a liar. If, perchance, the overcoating of religion has strengthened his bodily emancipation and his consequent self-deceits, the lie is doubly assertive. It would be nice amusement to undertake with such a person a metaphysical argument based on the presence of toilets in churches."

He thought of the Reverend Mr. Potter, smiled, and went on. "The babe is taught that it may hunger, thirst, or beg its pillow in public. Other needs equally normal must be whispered. So the child is started on its road to perjury and it slips from infancy into a world where it is not difficult to compromise the intelligence a few steps further by the identical process and become a thief or a murderer.

"For the moment, I pass over the social aspects of the question. Let us consider the purely physical. Nature has impartially provided its necessities with pleasure of performance or penalty for non-performance. Thus it happens that it is more enjoyable to indulge in sexual intercourse than it is painful to refrain, and in the matter of breathing, similarly. The fact that I use the word 'indulge' shows that my own life has not been wholly uncorrupted.

"The ten minutes a day (which might, in our inimitable American manner, be happily combined with one of our nationally advertised courses in educational reading) if satisfactorily utilized, may not produce an active pleasure, yet they yield the same sort of comfort that follows the ingestion of an excellent meal. On the other hand, they are prolific of pain and grief for the negligent.

"And now consider the social facets. The babe is an amateur. The child an experimenter. The adult, his interest dulled and his ganglia fatigued, merely an actor who goes through the business without intentional gusto or ritual of any sort. As in many other things, science has fettered him. No longer does he saunter candidly into the thicket, to brush away his earthy cares with moosewood or bass. The symbolism has gone. Gone, too, the quaint and provincial house that once decked a million back yards, whence father and mother issued as unashamedly as Eve. It has toppled upon its pedigree of meals. Even in his intimate duties man harnesses himself to a machine in this latter day. A machine (in the most modern instances) with a moderate-temperatured, rainbow-hued seat and a hydraulic force that banishes the thing he will one day wholly become, before that philosophic thought can occur to him.

"Yet, in the face of innovation, the bowels still require a certain amount of art and are capable of an individual variety of function. Into that matter, into the whole matter, we refuse to look. Secrecy increases with each new hour. Each man is master of his own technique. If it were not for that secrecy, schools would be formed to wrangle and debate over the subject across the earth. But each man dribbles away his year with no thought of anything but concealment, and those sages who are constantly pointing out the lessons of the dogs, the bees, and the ants are silent for once.

"I have a theory by which I would criticize humanity. As long as the individual preserved the dignity of his own bowels, he retains a certain pompous isolation. But he trembles lest the thought that he owns and operates a set of viscera should occur to others, for then, even if he were a king, he would be reduced suddenly to the stature of the meanest dwarf.

"That would be my theory. Only communism or Utopia can democratize the lowly colon, for a king or a pope in a bathroom—(bathroom!)— is only a human being performing a habitual act of a most human body; a beautiful woman straining the blood-vessels of her brow (though she does it in the quest of further beauty) becomes less lovely and very evidently a woman. I would go further and say that the offal of civilization is the object for which mankind cherishes the greatest privacy—the icon, secretly celebrated, which stands between his vanity and the world—hence, the true deity of contemporary existence. In a word—"

"Never mind," Thornton interrupted him. "Here is Cynthia."

So accumulation of bigotry, and defense, superimposed upon his own intimate sorrows, frustration, and lending of a friendship never returned were, perhaps, reasons enough to send Michael walking alone on the river-front.

PART TWO

1

ONE day Michael realized that he was passionately unhappy. Surveying himself in that illuminating conviction, he was terrified. Because they had not been in the city during the summer, the majority of his influential friends had not called upon him. In that quick fright he attributed it to deliberate avoidance. The season had effected his work. Industries did not demand so many of his drawings during the summer months. With growing panic, he thought that they had seen through his device and knew as clearly as he knew that he did not work for them with any seriousness.

His more intimate if socially less important friends were ageing and growing self-sufficient. Thornton had Cynthia. Thornton was selling his stories. He stood at the incline of a career. Cynthia herself was acclimatized. Aurelius had foundered in the somber, voluptuous depths of Nadine. Even Don and Gerry were progressing amiably towards success.

While he—he, Michael, tottered on the edge of middle age, waned in spiritual prowess, and moved certainly towards a goatish solitude. It shocked him. The sturdy will that had guided a score of less vehement

mortals was paralyzed. He thought of desperate reme-
dies. His soul revolted. It was as if, in an hour, he had
read his doom.

Michael took recourse to drink. He drowned every
insinuation of his brilliant mind, every prompting of
his sensitive nature. He had been a sailor and he returned to the fringe of the sea. His friends knew only
that he was no longer at home in the evenings, that he
slept late, that he was, by turns, extraordinarily gay
and inhumanly taciturn.

Cynthia called on him alone one afternoon and
came back to Thornton with tears in her eyes. Michael
had asked her to leave. The sound of her voice, rasping
over his raw, unhealable nerves, was more than he could
bear. He became afraid of himself. He lost every vestige of his gorgeous humor, and the things he said, like
the things he drew, were lewd and meaningless.

At first his microcosm suspected him of stealing to
the boudoir of an unnamed, unknown lady for some
form of debauchery commensurate to his mighty frame
and the indignant lusts of which he seemed capable. If
they could have seen him, night after night, sitting
alone at a table in the vilest of speakeasies, his head
bowed, his fists doubled, rheum in his eyes, they would
have believed that God had died. In their compassion
they would have saved him. Michael had been deprived
of the will to paint, of his gaudy entourage, of the intimacies of his best friends.

By and by they saw him with a monstrous black
eye. He had been fighting in his water-front saloon.

Fighting was as foreign to his spirit as it is to the instincts of most men whose bodies are so huge as to make it unnecessary. But so great is the division made by a mile in New York that no rumor of the truth reached them. He became brutish and it was imagined he had commenced to take drugs. No woman could have depraved his morale to such an extent.

2

He suffered another shame. Gerry had no sooner adjusted her docile husband to her insistence on continence than she began to tamper with the idea of infidelity. Don was ineffectual. Half out of dissatisfaction with him and half out of ignorance, the theory that he was the wrong man for her physical love took possession of her. It was natural that she should think of Michael. She knew him well, and his manifold bodily supremacies suggested that he would be a likely antidote for her condition. In her banal little mind she sought to glorify the budding desire, as a woman glorifies her lust for a priest. She was successful. She was invariably able to rationalize her wishes into duties—duties, usually, by which others profited less than herself.

When she had reached that point in her thinking at which she considered herself the unfortunate victim of a wrongly chosen mate, an excuse for the rest of the proposition presented itself. However meanly she thought of her husband, she never lost sight of the importance of his material progress. She wooed the favor of the head of his firm, Mr. Dean of Dean & Payson, studiously. It was the beginning of a long intrigue.

Don came from work one afternoon with weary eyes. His head ached. Something was the matter, had been the matter for a long, unconscionable time. He recited the news of the day.

"Dean says he'll give me a month next summer, and a commission too, if I can get the Iceland Refrigerator account."

Her instant excitement depressed him. She wanted money. She was always talking about money, always spending all he could earn. "Well—you're going to get it, aren't you, honey?"

"I talked to them all afternoon. Maybe I shall and maybe I shan't. It's largely a question of finding the right artist for them."

"What sort of an artist do they want?" Gerry asked in a queer voice.

"Oh—somebody who can give them something different—but not too different. They'll pay anything all right, but they don't know just what they'll buy. Our staff artist has broken his neck and they've chucked it all out."

"Have you thought of Michael?"

"Have I! I called him up—and bang! The receiver went down like a brick into hell before I had more than said 'refrigerator.' "

"Michael has gone into a decline, I hear," she

said. "Artists do that, every so often. Temperament. Why don't you let me try?"

Don rubbed his brow wearily and laughed. "No use. He'd bite your head off."

"How do you know?"

He shrugged irritably. "He hasn't been very nice to us since our marriage. Do you know what he said?"

"What?"

Don broke a long-guarded silence. "He said that we were the most perfect propinquity couple in the world. He said that if New York was any more congested, people would have to marry other people born in the same room—or never get married at all. And a lot more."

Gerry swallowed. "That—that sounds like him."

"But it doesn't sound like a contract for the refrigerators."

"I'll bet I can get the contract."

Don regarded her gravely. "Go ahead. Try. Might do you good. Give you something to work for. But be careful—he's pretty poisonous for young married women, I hear."

"That's rubbish, and you know it." Because she could not love her husband, his jealousy only vexed her.

BABES AND SUCKLINGS

3

She found him at home, alone, sober. He had been trying, in that afternoon, to recall himself to himself. He was glad to see Gerry. He had avoided people for so many days that they were avoiding him. Her arrival gave him resilience. He saw her smooth, black, silk dress, her black hair and eyes, her sleekly curved legs, as a sign of redemption. That a woman whom he had used impolitely could still call on him at all encouraged him. It took away some of the bitterness of his disillusion, some of the force of his self-condemnation. He was flattered that she had come at such a time. She looked remarkably well and quite attractive.

On her part, she was surprised by the hospitality with which she was received. She could not know that she served only to remind him of the banished Michael to whom a countless number of women had come for friendship, defense, advice, assistance, and sometimes for his rare love.

He said: "Come in and sit down, if you have the time. I've been on a tear and I'm just coming out of it."

"So I've heard. I thought it was about time someone leaned on your shoulder long enough so that you'd forget yourself." She had invented that speech with care.

"It is. Like a drink?"

"Of course I should."

She curled in the divan with her knees against its arm. The posture was revealing to Michael, but, to her annoyance, he seemed not to notice it at all. He smiled, poured two drinks, and sat facing her. She adjusted herself with a coiled indecency. Then Michael saw. Too many women had brought themselves to him in some such fashion to permit any extended obliviousness on his part. Again he was flattered. That he would take advantage of her folly never entered his head.

"How is the new existence?" he asked.

"Marriage?" She sighed. "I don't know. You should, perhaps. Yours didn't last."

"No," Michael replied in such a tone that she discarded that subject hastily.

"Don is rather difficult to understand—and he has absolutely no conception of me, of what I want or even who I am. But I suppose husbands are always unsatisfactory in one way or another."

"So are wives, for that matter."

"Wives—are never given a chance to demonstrate —by their husbands," she said.

Most women who might have fallen in love with Michael and injudiciously pursued their whim to his dwelling would have cooled under his piercing eyes and chilly laughter. But Gerry's dreams, because they were not founded on any facts, far transcended reality. She commenced to picture him as a mingling of her savior and her destiny. Her mind at any event was always as lurid as a tabloid newspaper, by which it had actually been schooled. So the very proximity of his tremendous shoulders and tawny, leonine head made her joints weak and her cheeks pale.

He scrutinized that condition with directness and could not avoid a correct analysis. It stunned him to realize how completely she had lost control of herself. And then the inferior person he had waked within himself stirred very remotely towards her. He played with an idea.

"You probably mean that your life with Don isn't as felicitious as the life you feel you deserve?"

"Michael! You have such insight!"

The staunch Michael grappled with its brother. "You should take long walks out of doors."

"That's hard—for a young girl, isn't it?"

"Did you come to tell me that?" He spoke quickly, lest he be absurdly moved again.

"Oh, no. As a matter of fact, I came on business."

"Business?"

"Business?"

"I wanted to see if you wouldn't consider doing the—the refrigerators for Don. There. That's out."

Michael stood. "No." He turned his back. "I don't want to draw any more of that rubbish."

Then she was crying. It made him nervous. "Gee," she sobbed, "it's a tough world. And I don't seem to have any fun at all—anywhere."

"Fun!" He turned.

"We stay poor. Our friends won't help a bit. And I—well—I don't matter even to Don."

Michael in a dilemma, Michael unable to handle a simple situation, Michael confounded. His malice and his pity misfired. His motives hid themselves. She leaned against the back of the divan. Her rich black hair fell loosely over one shoulder. Her dress, which had been disarranged, became unfastened. He saw her as she was, human, appealing, tragic, a fool. He took her half-savagely, and when he let her go, he had been wholly savage.

And she, rapidly collecting the scattered and started fragments of her personality, was master of the situation. "I've got to go now. But I'll come back. You're really—quite magnificent. And sweet. And to do all those refrigerators—too good of you. I'll be back —you know why. Thanks so much. Don't tell." Then out the door, still unsatisfied in any true sense, but triumphant for that hour.

"Refrigerators!" Michael called after her. "Refrigerators!" He stabbed his fingers through the clefts in his hair that her fingers had made. "Refrigerators. Ha ha ha ha ha ha! Oh, Lord, refrigerators! Ha. Ha. Ha. He. He. He. Ho. Ho. Ho."

4

For a few brief years Michael had bloomed like a gorgeous flower and now he was withering. The light of each new day fell unfamiliarly on his haggard face. He was shaken by torrential gusts of laughter that had no source and no humor in them. When he remembered Gerry, he raged internally like a madman. That he was really going mad he did not doubt.

But his friends were slow to read alarm. Michael had been so independent of their support, he had made his place among them with such strength and energy, that the outward effect of his inner turbulence was not great upon them. They told nasty little suspicions and watched the course of his sickness with grimaces that they considered understanding.

Cynthia and Thornton were exceptions only in part. Dumfounded by the descent of a man they had loved as father and brother, they avoided him with quaking anticipation. They did not have long to wait. After their waiting was over, they were glad of their last view of Michael, their last communion with him.

The chilly breath of winter had blown down in the late autumn. They were alone on such an evening when Cynthia suggested that they call on Michael.

"He'll just throw us out. He's getting so darned petulant."

"But, Thornton, I think it's because we don't come to see him much any more that he keeps it up. He has troubles. His mind is upset. He's unhappy."

"I know it. If you want to go—we'll try."

Michael received them soberly. For an hour they talked. An uncomfortable restraint pervaded that conversation. Michael listened to them, which was unusual for Michael. Once, when they mentioned Gerry, he was animated.

"Come in the studio and I'll show you something," he said.

On his easel was a refrigerator, and beside the refrigerator stood Gerry. It was a handsome painting. But Gerry's face was painted in a morbid green and a sickly saffron. She looked like a woman whose soul had fled.

Michael smiled. "That? That's not finished. When I'm through, she'll look like the magazine-cover girl she's supposed to represent. I'm putting that underneath just for fun."

"Oh," Thornton said.

Cynthia, moving her eyes from the rancid face on the picture to Michael's countenance, instantly read a chapter that she had never guessed before. "You shouldn't be so bitter about her," she said. "It isn't her fault, and it certainly is no disgrace to you."

He was moved. His ancient friendliness unscrewed his features. "You believe that, Cynthia?"

"I know it. If that's what's on your mind, laugh it off."

"What are you talking about?" Thornton asked.

"Nothing," Michael replied. And, to Cynthia: "The wrong thing, rather."

"I'm sorry," she said. She covered the painting with a cloth.

Afterwards, when they were going, Michael held them at the door, their hands in his. "You two children are very happy, aren't you?"

"Yes." They answered together.

134

"Don't ever let anyone or anything persuade you that you are not. Love each other. You know, of all the people I've ever known, I like you two best. 'Like' is a poor word. I love you." His voice was lowered to a benediction. "Sometimes you'll think that what you feel towards one another is an illusion. Deny that feeling. It's a lie." They felt his broad hands tighten. "Goodbye. I'm glad you came over."

There was a catch in his breath. They had never seen him so moved. Wrapping themselves in their coats, they walked down the cold street. Both of them were a little frightened.

"What made him do that?" Thornton said meditatively.

"If it's what I think—" she sighed.

"What?"

"Oh, nothing. If I told you, you'd call me a fool."

"Tell me."

"I think—I think Michael is very sick. I think he is—dying."

"Dying? Michael?" The two concepts seemed mutually exclusive to Thornton.

"I told you you would. But why not? He's just a man, isn't he?"

"But what's he sick of?"

"Maybe nothing. Maybe just of himself."

"Let's ask Aurelius."

5

Aurelius bustled to his door, his eyes blinking and merry. "Hello!" he said, and continued rapidly: "Nice of you to come over. Getting cold. Nadine's here. Asked me to invite you some time. What's new?"

Nadine nodded her blond head with a distant smile that was half mysterious, half pleasurable. They drew two chairs to Aurelius's fire and talked casually. Aurelius himself brought up the subject of Michael.

"What's eating Palidini these days? Never comes around any more. Grouchy as a bear."

Cynthia shook her head. "I wish someone would take it seriously. Someone besides Thornton and me. I think Michael's a very sick man. And dreadfully lonely."

"I always thought he was lonely."

They looked at Nadine. She spoke so seldom that it gave weight to her words. Even Aurelius, who was always stimulated as if by the knowledge of a cosmic joke, was sobered. "You think that?"

"I think he's going off by himself soon and that he'll never see us again."

The fire-light flickered on her face, casting a spell, so that she seemed like an antique sibyl uttering a melancholy prophecy.

"I do, too," Cynthia said.

Aurelius glanced at Thornton. He sprawled moodily

in his chair, his eyes in the flames, his shoulders hunched, his hands dangling.

"Let's not be depressed," Aurelius said. "Michael has so much in his brain and heart that we'll never know all that lies there. You know, I knew Michael long before you did. Met him in several places. Odd corners of the world. He had a fantastic reputation."

They listened, Thornton a little resentful, while he yarned about Michael in a way they felt must be exaggerative if not wholly fictitious.

6

Four days passed. The weather remained cold, and on the fourth day it rained. All day a steady drizzle fell in the streets and on the housetops. With the slow coming of darkness it abated and was transformed into a clammy, impersonal mist. Hooded figures hurried through it like nuns on profane errands. The streets down town glittered in the morose lights of small store-fronts.

When Michael could no longer differentiate between colors, he threw down his brushes and tried to read in the aura of a shaded bridge-lamp. The book he selected was one by André Gide. Within him, crawling and gnawing, supplanting the empty hunger for food, was a desire for drink. Over and over he imagined the stages of its ingestion. The order. The little glass. The hot sting on his tongue, his throat, in his vitals. Words blurred, eddied, and tumbled on their pages until the book was alive with them, scurrying like black insects that were magically transfixed when he tensed his muscles and read a sentence.

Finally he flung down the book and donned his long overcoat. He hailed a taxi and gave an address that surprised the driver. The cab moved. He sat inside its inky stomach, pale and disinterested. Under a roaring elevated, across bumpy trolley-tracks, through an area of great illumination into one of comparative darkness. A wooden door that opened an evil eye upon the tall, cloaked figure. A voice in the night.

His silhouette was engulfed by the closing door. At his table he drank glasses of cheap whisky in rapid succession. Shuffling, strident-voiced men entered, gulped, and went out. They gazed at him in familiarity, but none of them dared speak to him. For four hours Michael sat there. Then he rose steadily and walked out of the door.

The streets were quiet. It was nearing midnight. A man with a newspaper over his head passed by and Michael heard the noise of his feet. A truck roared and clattered from the river. Michael strode in the direction of its hollow-sounding origin.

Down on the water-front it was very still. Tremendous buildings loomed through the mist. He walked to a crevice between two of them and there he sat on a beam at the river's edge. Far away were the almost imperceptible sparks of Brooklyn. Near by, the vertical nose of a steamer cut the night as if it was in hideous, unnatural progress towards him. A wraith of smoke issued from its funnel and vanished in the blacker air. The sound of a banjo and men singing came faintly from the round eyeball of a port-hole.

Whistles drifted to his ears. Some of them were high and impatient. The rest were wheezing and full of sea-fog, sea-voices, memories of distant ports. They boomed and shuddered in the night. He heard the lapping of the water, greasy water, that slipped sibilantly through the rotten timbers underneath him.

Then he stared for a long time at the golden arc of a bridge that leaped up out of the city and buried itself on the opposite side. A train crossed it like a phosphorescent worm. The smell of the sea was swept to his nostrils by a wet wind. A poignant, unforgettable smell of salt and wood and tarred rope. He passed his hand across his face and partook thirstily of that sensuous symphony.

After an hour he went back to the speakeasy and drank again. A waiter in a filthy apron put cubes of cheese and pickles on his table. The sight of them turned his stomach. He pushed them to the floor. No one spoke. The dishes broke sharply and the yellow and green food mingled in the sawdust. It reminded him of Gerry's face that he had painted underneath healthier colors. He ordered a double drink.

Someone nudged him. He looked up slowly. A man stood at his elbow—a man as large as himself. The man's eyes were little. His nose was purple. His hands were ape-like.

139

BABES AND SUCKLINGS

"I hadda idear I'd see youse some day," the man said.

"Sit down and have a drink."

The man waited for the drinks and then, aiming carefully, threw his portion into Michael's face.

Michael did not move. The liquid trickled down on his clothes. He knew the man. He had fought with him once for an hour on the deck of a ship in the Pacific. Just west of Panama. Where the glossy green islands run out into the sea as if the land were reluctant to give up to the endless blue water. Where it thundered and deluged in the middle of each steaming day. Where the sun set in vermilion, and rose palely in an opal haze.

His eyes gradually stopped stinging. He smelled the reek of the whisky. A remorseless grin overspread his dripping face. "I said, have a drink with me, not on me."

The man spat. He looked up at the other men who had surrounded the table. Their hands were ominously ready. In their rear stood the bar-tender, one arm behind his back. The man knew he was holding a blackjack. He eyed Michael with fixed hate.

"Will youse go outside wit' me?"

It was said contemptuously.

"You're drunk," Michael answered.

"Not too drunk to kick the liver out of yuh. I swore I'd tear your mouth off, an' I will."

"Get out of here," the bar-tender said impersonally.

Michael got to his feet. "Come on."

The man walked at his side, cursing and muttering lurid imprecations. After a few moments, with the cold air on his face, he realized that the person at his side was saying nothing, stalking doggedly towards the river. He was frightened.

"Lissen, guy, this is gonna be a fair fight, isn't it?"

Michael did not reply. The other halted. "Say. You gotta gang around here?"

"No."

They went on. At last, in the middle of a wide, empty street, Michael stopped. He took off his coat and folded it. His mind was a vacuum. He did not even know why he wanted to fight the other man. He had beaten him once. He could do it again. A smashing blow against the side of his face was the answer to his calm "Ready?"

In the rainy darkness, on the slippery street, they closed with each other. Michael boxed ferociously and skilfully. The other man was his equal. He saw blood, black in the darkness, on the man's face. He tasted it in his own mouth.

Straining, heaving, they were thrown apart. Michael could feel nothing. He knew that he had been hit a dozen times, that his face was dreadful to look upon, that the other man was like him. They came together again with the smack of fist on flesh. Michael's mind wandered.

He could no longer concentrate on the fight. It was not like a fight. A crashing blow that rocked him from

141

his feet brought him to. He realized that he had fallen and was on the pavement. The other man stood, waiting. Michael rose, devoid of fury, of all emotion. He fought again, as if fighting were a drunken habit. Block, slash, parry, lead. His fists landed again and again. They clinched.

Then Michael felt a singluar thing. An icicle crept into his side. He knew he had been stabbed. His rage returned. With a single, devastating swing of his arm, a swing that commenced behind his back and carried him to the tips of his toes, he lifted his antagonist off his feet, moved him in the air, so that his heels scraped across the pavement, and dropped him.

Michael put his crushed hand in his pocket. It was mangled as if it had been under a sledge. The man did not move. Coldness crept up from his feet over his ankles and through his stiffening knees. In the silence that followed, a steamer whistled, a new breath of salt air came up from the river, a horse trotted over a hard street far away.

Michael put his coat on again. A clean handkerchief touched his face and came away heavy. The pain in his side spread through his abdomen. He walked back to the speakeasy, ghastly pale. They washed his face, laughing to see that he was alone. He did not mention the deeper pain. The house set him up to a drink and then to another.

Suddenly he was sick and weak. He went out and lurched into a cab. He was surprised when it stopped and the driver knocked on his window. He looked to

see if it was the right address and then got out, to stand
on quivering legs. He paid the driver with a bill that
was blood-soaked. The two flights of stairs were inter-
minable.

He hung up his greatcoat and the coat of his suit.
He took off his shirt and undershirt. His naked torso
was Jovian. A mirror over his mantel revealed his face,
which he inspected long and curiously. There seemed
to be no need of any haste. Time had stopped. From a
bottle on his table he poured a tumbler of whisky. He
drank half of it in a single, mighty swallow.

A curious mood of whimsicality pervaded him. He
lit every lamp in his house. It did not seem quite so
dark as it had been. He poked the fire and put coal on
it. Then he moved to the tile bath and inspected the
rent in his side. He could not tell how serious it was.
Probably not serious at all. Still, he could not take
chances. He poured the contents of a bottle of Zonite
on and into the leaking wound. The thrilling pain of
that operation sent him back to his living-room, where
he finished the whisky. Again in the bath, he made a
pad of bandage and taped it over the cut. It was dyed
red instantly.

He sat down to consider calling a doctor. He didn't
know any doctors. Only an abortionist and a venereal
specialist. That, he thought, was rather funny. The fire,
given new life, warmed and consoled him. He could be
the old Michael again. Every trace of his resentment
and melancholia had vanished with the fight. It was too
bad, he reflected, that he had not realized it sooner.

143

BABES AND SUCKLINGS

That was the whole trouble. His body had been crying for the old, vigorous physical life to which it had been accustomed. There was nothing the matter with his mind. He could still paint well—brilliantly, when he cared to. He could still talk well, still entertain his friends, still remember and enjoy the dim, dead days at sea when he had been mate on a score of boats, when he had loved Hindu girls and Japanese girls and a strange ebony and ivory girl who came, she said, from Corsica and who dispensed her love for a few francs in a bawdy-house in Marseilles. He could still laugh at Gerry and her idiotic conduct, still love Thornton's serious eyes and quick, irritated wit, Cynthia's splendid beauty and her sacrificial role, Aurelius's obscure personality.

He could still remember that first night when he had walked down the Cannebière, gloriously drunk, living for the flaming joy of living. He could still dream about the islands in the South Seas that jumped conically out of the bare ocean and turned green as one approached —turned green and stretched out the bobbed-headed palm-trees towards one. The islands populated with sweaty, brown people and indolent white men in shirt-sleeves—white men always a little drunk and always on a hair-trigger of irascibility.

And the unique stench of the *djohnkis'* ratty house-boats along the rivage at Shanghai, the tinkling, monotonous music, the mincing women. The rice whisky in the paper houses in Japan. The dancing girls. The picture he had painted on the deck of a white passenger

144

liner that had fetched him to the brig. A picture painted because the lady who was its subject would not walk on deck to see the round moon and would not sip the *apéritif* he had brought on a shining silver tray. The mornings in Paris when the little motor-horns were squawking everywhere and a bustling activity was doing its best to pretend Paris was not the city it had been on the night before. He must have been very young then.

And Egypt. Horrible Egypt, with its past intruding every instant of its present. Its dissolute colonials sneaking away to the embankment to watch the native spectacle. The reproduction of a race that had been mummified five thousand years ago. All of Africa, looming over the horizon like a land of ominous secrets. Drums booming in the forest. Like the drums in *The Emperor Jones*. Boom-ba, boom-ba, boom-ba, boom-ba, boom-ba, boom-ba.

Michael realized that he was counting the beats of his heart in the imagined cadence of the drums. It was pounding heavily inside him. He put his hand over it. The room had receded from him. The faces of his paintings stared across a vasty sweep of empty air at the reclining form. Their expressions were meaningless, formless, void. He thought of himself again and of his throbbing heart, trying to determine where the center of his consciousness lay. In his head? He closed his eyes. Not there. Not in his thorax, or his belly. Nowhere.

He reviewed the dreams that had toppled into his

mind. All dreams of women and wine and motion. Answers to man's lust and his desire to transcend himself and to his migratory impulse. Simple, understandable things. Fond things.

Then he thought of his immediate friends. How quickly they had obliterated the rest. How inexplicably a few short years leading to an indeterminate present removed all the long years to the limbo of a faded pageant in which he had had a part—or someone like him had had a part. Those friends—no different from all other friends except in trivial matters of props and policies. Dear to him through use alone, strangers, silly strangers, to anyone else, although that other person felt as keenly and saw as shrewdly as he.

And that was how life went—cogently intimate, selfish, garbled, mutative, sentimental. Whether the spirit retched or reasoned, laughed or made logarithms, it went thus, on and on, till the flesh wrinkled and fell apart. Then, in the abyss of oblivion, no reward, no peace, no new struggle, but, better, infinitely better, a nothingness so profound as to be beyond imagination.

Michael slept. He fell farther down on the cushions of the divan. His face relaxed. His breath came evenly. Above and around him the lights burned remorselessly and the pictures stared down with graven eyes. Once he stirred to fitful consciousness. The pain in his side was numb and persisted only as an awareness of matter. He raised a curved hand and passed it over his brow. His eyes were glassy with the heavy narcotic of alcohol in them. A befuddled brain voiced a dozen

146

random words, understood in a harsh dream that it was reposing in a fevered skull, and fell back in sleep before it could resolve upon a course of action.

7

The morning was like a morning in London. A dubious luminescence in the canvas clouds scarcely reached to the earth beneath. Fog hung over the river. A policeman in a wet slicker caught sight of a bundle on the street. He walked over to it and, seeing what it was, tried to turn it with his toe. It did not give readily to the exertion.

"Hell," the policeman said. It meant a trip to a telephone, a wait in the fog, a delayed breakfast, a report to write.

8

Certainly it was not the light that woke Thornton. He could recall no undue sound heard in sleep. He woke thinking of Michael, woke fearfully, as from an evil dream. Cynthia lay beside him, sleeping face down, the arch of her shoulders bare. He looked at the clock. Eight-thirty. She would not wake for several hours. They had called on Aurelius and Nadine and stayed until very late.

But there was no sleep left in him. He thought

147

again of Michael and wondered if he had dreamed about him. The cold shades of the room disturbed him. He had a notion to wake Cynthia which he resisted. Better by far to go out and take breakfast alone, to bring cream and cakes for her coffee when he came back. The jumbled sound of traffic dispelled his incubus.

The air bit his lungs. He walked towards Raymond's, where he had breakfasted for the first time with Cynthia. I'll go and raise Michael to eat with me, he told himself. He did not enter the restaurant, but passed on along the street.

Michael did not answer his door-bell. "He's asleep," Thornton thought. It had happened before. Michael always slept like a dead thing. Thornton hesitated between waking his friend at that early hour and eating alone. At length he opened the front door and went upstairs. In the middle of the carpet on the landing was a dark stain. He noticed it, and climbed the second flight. The door of Michael's apartment was slightly ajar.

Thornton walked into the bedroom. Michael was not there and the bed had not been used. He shrugged and was on the point of leaving the apartment when he saw one of Michael's feet protruding over the arm of the divan. Still he was uncertain. It was evident, as he perceived the bottle and the glass, that Michael had been drinking. Better let him sleep it off. With that idea in mind, he leaned over the back of the divan merely to look at Michael.

For a long minute he held himself in that unnatural

position, leaning, looking. His face turned salt-white. No muscle of him budged. Michael was dead. He was a peculiar yellow color. His eyes were shut. His mouth was open and dry. His neck was dark blue. His bare chest was still. A clotted red smear at his side spilled across the cushions to the floor, where it lay in a puddle, half of which was absorbed by the rug.

Blood. Michael had been hurt. Thornton remembered the stain on the stairway. He had been hurt and had come home to die. It was like him. A wounded animal. And like him to die so peacefully—as if he were going to sleep.

That much Thornton thought without any stimulus except the pure activity of his mind. Then the proprieties of civilization rushed to his aid—and confused him. Could he prove he didn't do it? No one knew when he had got up in the morning. He couldn't prove it. A weapon? He might have thrown it away, hidden it, destroyed it, even. It was a dangerous predicament. One in which he would have to act coolly and sanely. Coolly and sanely. The words reiterated themselves until he could not chase them out of his mind. He wanted the space they occupied for calm thought. In a frenzy he left the room, walked into the studio, lit a cigarette, sat down and stood again. Coolly and sanely.

Perhaps Michael had committed suicide. No. Never that. Not that way. No one ever stabbed himself in the side to kill himself. Maybe it was an accident. Maybe the stain on the carpet was not blood and he had been killed in that very room. Thornton looked for signs of conflict. Like a detective, he thought. Here, at last, he was face to face with such a happening as made a hundred novels he had read. That excited him. Coolly and sanely.

He saw that his sense was running away, then, and made the proper revision of his attitude. He stood over Michael and shook his head sadly. Poor Michael! How could he, Thornton, continue to live without Michael? He would have to tell someone at once. Who? Cynthia? She would do—what? Aurelius? The police? Would they believe that he had done it? What would he say to them? He remembered that Michael had a friend on the police force. For a desperately long time he could not recall the man's name. When he succeeded, he was still dubious. He did not know Sennit very well.

At last he took up the telephone and asked for police headquarters. He was given the precinct station, but they told him how to reach Sennit. He dialed the wrong number, dialed again, and was answered by a husky voice.

"Police headquarters."

"Is Captain Sennit there?"

"Who wants him?"

"A friend."

"What name?"

Thornton hesitated. "Michael Palidini," he said.

"Wait a minute."

Sennit's greeting came in tones that belonged to another world and age. "Hello, Michael. What can I do for you?"

"This is a friend of Michael's speaking. Michael has been murdered. Killed. I'm at his apartment. I found him."

"Who are you?"

"Thornton. Remember me?"

The other gave no sign. "Michael murdered? There? What? Wait a minute. I'll be right up. At his house, you say? Stay there till I get there. Don't touch anything."

Thornton went out into the hall and sat on the stairs. He smoked another cigarette. He wondered if Cynthia was awake and what time it was and what he would say to Sennit. Sennit had seemed like an intelligent person. Jovial, fond of Michael, good fellow. And he would be favorably impressed by the fact that he found Thornton still there.

The police captain appeared in the hall, his derby making a stubby bow for the rest of his body as it plowed up the steps. "How are you?" he said to Thornton and passed by him into the apartment. Thornton followed.

Sennit examined the body, lifted up the bandage gingerly and looked at the cut, and then moved quickly here and there in the room, an expression of great abstraction on his face. He had seen every item there, no matter how small or how irrelevant, before he took cognizance of Thornton once again.

"How long have you been here?"

Thornton stiffened. The man's face was far from pleasant. "About twenty minutes, I should say."

"Good. Can you establish an alibi for yourself for
—say—three o'clock last night?"

Thornton sagged with relief. "Easily—till five.
Then I was in bed with my—with my—wife."

"Good." He nodded curtly. "Don't think it will be
necessary. But I just thought—it might be useful."

Sennit was busy again in the bathroom and afterwards on the telephone. Thornton was amazed at himself. He felt very little sorrow, no fear. He did not know
that those emotions would come later. Sennit finished
talking and looked at him.

"That's that." The vitality drained out of him.
"Dear God, what a shame! A finer man never lived.
And to get it like that. Stuck in the gut by some East
Side bum, probably. In a fight. My God, I'd like to have
seen that fight!"

"Fight?"

"Sure. Fight. He was cock-eyed. And his lips are
cut, his nose is broken, his arms are all battered to pulp,
he's been kicked on the shins, one arch of his foot has
been stamped on, and God only knows what other
things. Fight! It was a—a—a—" He stopped, at a loss
for words.

Thornton shifted his legs. Sennit spoke again. "Sit
down, kid. Take a drink, if you need it. He was your
best friend, wasn't he?"

"Yes."

"He used to talk about you often. You and that
girl of yours. I guess he was pretty keen about you.

Sorry. Here. Take a drink. Michael always had good stuff in his house."

"You see," Thornton gulped, "I came over here to get him up for breakfast and—I found him. I thought that perhaps people would think that I—"

"That you had done it?" Sennit laughed and somehow his laughter was comforting rather than shocking to Thornton. "You? Why twelve of you couldn't have done him in that way. I never saw a man worse beaten —unless he'd been brass-knuckled and clubbed. How he got here I don't know."

"There's blood on the stairs, I think."

"Yeah. Saw it coming up. And probably some independent cab-driver is washing it out of his hack this morning with one eye over his shoulder and the fear of God in his heart. Feel better?"

"A little."

The door-bell buzzed. "That's the doctor," Sennit said. "You can go any time you like. I don't think there'll be much of an inquest. We may get the man who did it and we may not. I shouldn't be surprised if he showed up in a hospital today. Or even the morgue. Leave your address with me. And—I'll keep your name out of it."

"I don't care about myself. But Cynthia—"

"Of course. Nice girl. Too bad, all this. Sometimes I almost believe in prohibition—for other people. God, but it's tough."

Thornton was going downstairs. He passed a man with a little case in his hand. The end of Michael, of all that was Michael. Like that.

153

BABES AND SUCKLINGS

9

He climbed to his room limply. The door squeaked as he pulled it open. Cynthia stirred and waved her arms. Whenever she was wakened, she was dazed for a long period. He could not shake her and say: "Dear, Michael is dead."

He stood still, looking at her, wondering why she did not wake under the impact of his thoughts. The coverlet rose and fell rhythmically and her eyes twitched beneath their pale, dark lids. He noticed that it was only five minutes past ten. Five minutes past ten, and a hundred people would be suffering, upset, distraught before six hours had passed. News of that sort traveled like prairie fire, leaping likely spots, which turned up grotesquely uniformed after the fire had swept beyond, and charring wide acres where it had no reason for burning at all. People were like grass, brittle and dry. The metaphor occupied him for a moment. Then he shook Cynthia with a pathetic and trembling hand.

She woke, drawing in a deep breath and trembling violently. She looked at him and shut her eyes again. Thornton was rousing her. The drug of heavy sleep called her back into its realm. She felt his hand again. "Don't wake me up," she said thickly. There was no reason for that waking. She heard his voice like a sound heard under water. A slight anger brought her to again.

"I don't want to get up now. If you want to work, go ahead. I can sleep. I'm tired."

"I've got bad news for you, Cynthia."

"What?" Bad news. There was no possibility of bad news between them. She lay with her face hidden, listening.

"Cynthia! Wake up, darling!"

"All right. What bad news is there?" She peered at him from beneath her touseled hair. He smiled uncertainly. She saw then that he had undergone a violent shock. She took his hand and pulled him on the bed beside her. "What's happened?"

"It's Michael."

"What's the matter with Michael?"

"He's dead, Cynthia."

"Dead." Violent agitation shook her. Dead. It was as if she had known for a long time, as if she had seen him sick with a fatal malady. A bottomless despair was her first feeling. She knew how Thornton had depended on him, and how she had depended on him. He was their outlet for emotions, their counsel. He was dead. Not because it was time for him to die, but because he had destroyed himself. "How did it happen?"

"He was killed—in a fight."

"Was—was anybody we know—"

"I don't think so, dear. It was a brawl somewhere. He used to be a sailor, you know."

He would die that way, she thought. Romantic and dramatic to the end and yet sordid. Killed in a fight— killed like Kit Marlowe—he had a delicate body.

155

Michael had a delicate soul. Oh, God, the tragic men so passionately out of key with the world, so hopelessly defenseless against their own instincts and against the demands they made on themselves. Killed like a sot. She did not speak.

"I—I found him."

She realized with an immense tenderness what that meant to Thornton, what all the horrible days ahead would mean to Thornton. A practical solicitude for him followed her philosophical requiem.

"We could have stopped him, if we had known. We could have stayed with him, drunk with him, let him get rid of his uglinesses," he said.

She cut short his recriminations. "I'll get dressed. You tell me all you know."

Thornton repeated his story with meticulous faithfulness, not omitting his worry over his possible indictment—a worry of which he was vastly ashamed.

10

After they had knocked for a long time, Aurelius came to his door in his pyjamas. He said: "My God! What's the matter? Come in."

They told him. And then they saw, for the first time, a side of his nature which was not ecstatic. He folded himself quietly into an arm-chair and did not move. They stood, shifting nervously, lighting twin cigarettes, thinking that Michael meant more to Aurelius than they had imagined and that they would go and get some coffee presently.

"I'll get Nadine," he said finally, "and we'll go over there."

He woke Nadine and she came out wide-eyed and comprehending. Cynthia was amazed at her. Nadine started a percolator after exchanging a few words with them. Cynthia tended it while she dressed.

Aurelius spoke but once during the interval. "Funny, but Nadine and I were going to get married today. We decided to after you left last night."

"Married," Thornton echoed blankly.

Cynthia took his arm and led him to the other side of the room before he could dwell upon that irony. They drank the coffee and then took a cab to Michael's apartment. It was the same cab and the same driver that had brought home the dying man on the night before. But it did not even strike the driver as strange.

11

At three o'clock they were in Raymond's partaking of a belated meal. Nadine, who had said nothing about their intended marriage, Aurelius, Cynthia, Thornton. Gerry found them there.

"I've been looking all over," she said. "Isn't it awful!" In her tone was a ring of throaty excitement not very distant from pleasure.

They did not answer her, but she was by no means

embarrassed. She sat down at the table and deliberated over the menu. "I just can't eat. I just can't eat a thing. I'm much too ex— much too horrified. But I do feel that everyone under such a strain as we shall be under for heaven only knows how long now ought to eat when they can. I'll have liver and bacon. Liver is a good nerve-builder. I don't want to break down if I can help it. Poor Michael. He was so grand a person! And to go like that. With never a word for any of us. With his work all unfinished. I know that Don will be terribly disappointed. Michael was just beginning some work for him. I was modeling it. You know, the city won't be the same any more. Hundreds of people depended on him for their—their support. Not only money, but everything. I know he paid for abortions for girls he didn't get into trouble himself and he used to do thousands of things we never dreamed of for people. He was the last of the old guard. A true gentleman. I've called up my paper already and they're sending up a man to interview me this afternoon about him. I'll do what I can for his memory—you may be sure of that—"

Up to that point they had listened in raging silence. But then Aurelius spoke. "Gerry," he said, "it isn't your business to give out interviews to the press about Michael."

"I'd like to know why not. I guess I knew Michael as well as any of the rest of you. And we can't let him sink into oblivion with the cold formality of an obituary. I'll give them a human-interest story. Tell them about his charities and how wrong the people were who thought he was wicked. I'll—"

"I forbid it." The four listeners could imagine the story Gerry would give to her scandal mongering newspaper. It was bad enough that Michael had been connected with it. But that was a part of Michael's ironic commercialization of himself. When he could not, or would not, attain the heights, no depth of artistic prostitution was too low for him.

Gerry bridled. Some kind of intellectual process was evident in the deliberate pause that she permitted herself. "Well—Michael is dead and I suppose that there is no harm in telling you now." She lowered her eyelids. "Michael loved me."

"What!" Thornton exclaimed in a thunder-stricken voice.

But Aurelius smiled coldly and remained calm. "You mean, he made love to you. There is a great deal of difference, Gerry."

"There was none in the relationship existing between him and me."

"Gerry," Aurelius said slowly, "I've known Michael for nearly ten years—which is eight more than you have known him. He never loved any woman—with the possible exception of one—in his life. That woman died when you were in panties. If Michael made love to you—which I do not doubt—it was your fault and you should be so ashamed of yourself that you will never mention it again to anyone. If you do, I'll stand in the street and denounce you publicly. And if you so much as say a word to any reporter, or any person connected with a paper, I'll come to your house, I'll follow you like a haunt until I get a chance, and then I'll take your neck in my two hands and choke every bit of life out of you. I'll kick your corpse and spit on it. And that is exactly, graphically, precisely, what I will do to you. Furthermore, if you try anything tricky, that I can trace back to you, I'll do the very same thing."

He lit a cigarette and burned his fingers with the match. No one spoke for a moment and then Gerry commenced to sob hysterically. "That's what it all means to your dirty, filthy, narrow little minds. That's the way a woman who has done the cleanest, most beautiful, most noble thing in her life is treated. That's my reward. Martyrdom. I never expected anything more. You beasts! I—I who want to sing and cry and tell the world about what I have done am threatened and bullied and—and denounced publicly. That's all that comes of your talk of freedom and being honest and good for no other reason than that it is worth while. You're worse than all the religious people put together. And you laugh at them. Ha! I laugh at you. Michael's ghost laughs at you. He's in heaven now laughing at you."

Nadine's lip curled almost indiscernibly. "Spank her, Aurelius."

"I will if she doesn't stop immediately."

"Spank me, will you! And what do you have to do with it, you two blonde boobies. Blonde!" A new inferiority smote Gerry. "You come to town with rotten reputations and *affaires* in Paris and husbands in

California. You are jealous, that's all, just because
Michael was too wise to lay his hands on your soiled
shoulders—"

Thornton, who had been repressing a desire to
laugh—a desire sprung from a well that defied his
plumbing introspection, abruptly shared Aurelius's
anger. "Shut up."

She saw his raving eyes and stopped. They pretended to eat, the cyclone of Gerry's hysterics having
abated. Finally she left the restaurant, miserable and
indignant. Aurelius's parting words stung her: "Remember what I said. I mean exactly that. If you give
out one syllable about Michael, you're a dead—" he cut
himself short.

She did not know what to do.

12

"All the women," Aurelius said, "all the sad wom-
en who will go about town for the next month in black
dresses, with carefully cultivated circles under their
eyes and a hint of suffering that can only be consoled
by nice young men—oh, God, how I hate women!"

Nadine and Cynthia exchanged glances. They, too,
hated women. More than Aurelius, more than Thornton, because they knew them better, because they found
the material for similar hypocrisies in their own na-
tures and stifled it only by an effort.

"How many do you suppose Michael knew?" Cynthia asked.

"What? Women?" Thornton cogitated. "Probably fifty who are in town."

"And they'll all lament him as if they were, each one, the reason for his dissolution," Nadine murmured. "Yes, I can understand why men hate women, and why women hate them. They are despicable."

13

The phone rang. Thornton pushed his chair away from the taboret that supported his typewriter and answered it.

"Hello," a nervous voice said. "Is this Thornton?"

"Yes."

"This is Don. Say, old man, I wonder if you can take lunch with me?"

"Why—I guess so. Want to come down here and eat with Cynthia and me?"

"I wanted to get you alone—if I could."

"Oh." Thornton reflected. "All right. Sure. Anything the matter?"

"No. Not exactly. Yes. Tell you then. Meet me at my office."

Thornton hung up and turned to Cynthia. "Don wants to take lunch with me. He's on edge about something, apparently."

"I can guess what," she said and then, with a dissociation of ideas: "I'll go over and have lunch with Michael."

"Michael?"

"Oh. I'm sorry. I'm terribly sorry."

Thornton bit his lip. "It's all right. We'll be doing things like that for weeks. Don't be sad. You couldn't help it."

"It's dreadful, isn't it? I'll go and see Aurelius and Nadine."

14

"You see," Don began, ruffling his brownish hair and quickly regretting having made such a gesture at the table, "you see, I have to go on working, even if Michael is dead. Hearing about it yesterday and going over to your house last night were all that I could do. It seems to me there must be some people in the world who can only hear about things and then go around and look—and that I'm one of them."

Thornton was sympathetic. If a lack of proper respect to Michael was all that worried Don, his dilemma was simple indeed. "Michael would laugh," he said, "if he knew that a sigh was heaved or a tear was spilled over him. He would want us to be sorry. But he hated any pageant of grief, and deliberate, premeditated ceremony, either private or public."

Don looked up from his plate with a vacant

expression. "Sure. Yes. I know. He was that sort of guy. Looked out for other people and not for himself."

"Exactly."

"But that isn't what worries me. Michael and I never were very good friends. I don't believe he saw much in me."

Thornton knew that was the truth; nevertheless he felt compelled to protest. "Nonsense. He liked you a great deal. Used to tell me so."

"Did he? Well, maybe I never figured him out the right way. He was difficult to understand. I'm not creative, as he was. I'm a business man, pretty nearly. But I wasn't thinking about that."

"What's on your mind, then?"

"Well," he hesitated, "Gerry."

It was that which Thornton and Cynthia had expected in the tacit silence that followed Don's call. "I suppose she is upset," Thornton said.

"Not only upset, she's a little bit ga-ga."

"Ga-ga? What do you mean?"

"Well, she's my wife and I love her and I know perfectly well that I shouldn't talk about her—even to you, and you've been damn decent to me, too, I must say."

Thornton knew he was referring to the night when they had called on Gerry in a state of doddering intoxication. He was touched. "That's bologny."

"It isn't, and you know it. But I'm darn near crazy myself. It's a long story. Want to hear it?" Thornton

nodded. "All right. I'll tell you. But you've got to promise you'll never tell it to a soul. Not even Cynthia."

Thornton was inclined to promise. But, instead, he
told the truth, thinking that it would have a moral effect on Don. "I couldn't promise that, because I tell
everything to Cynthia. But it amounts to the same
thing, because she's one of the least communicative
women alive."

"I wish Gerry was. All right. I'll tell you—both."
He smiled faintly and timorously. "In the first place,
Gerry isn't well."

"Not well? She seems so extraordinarily healthy,
too."

"I mean, mentally. Or, not exactly mentally. Say,
listen, you probably know as much as I do about it.
You've read more. Do you know what 'frigid' means?"
Don saw Thornton's casual nod. "Well, she's that way."

"Half the women are—more or less. But a lot of
them get over it. It's a general American condition—
like—like the belief that kids have to have mumps and
measles. Lousy thing, I admit. But you ought not to
let it ride you."

"No?" Don said with the first bitterness he had
shown. "No? I shouldn't notice. I should be ignorant
and brutal. Listen, Thornton, should you notice if Cynthia was always restive and complaining and dissatisfied? If she never had a happy moment? If she seemed
to take a peculiar desire in making you miserable?
If, no matter how many times you assured yourself
that her meanness was just a reflection of your own,

165

something new developed to show you that it came out
of her, that you had nothing to do with it, that, no matter
how decent you were, the least little thing—or nothing
at all—could make her rank mean? If she lied to you,
and lied to your friends? If she never would sit at home
in the evening and read, never go out without wishing
that she was at home? If she threatened to leave you
every two weeks, and when you became so tired of it
that you didn't resist the suggestion, she'd get so furious that she would leave? If you had to chase her out
on the street to be sure that she wasn't going to do the
crazy things she suggested? If all she wanted was
money? If she'd sit in a chair and say it over and over?
If she was always buying things she didn't want and
wouldn't use? If she'd take twenty dollars and go out in
the morning and come back with a load of junk that she
must have bought in a trance? Why, she has five apple-
corers. Of course it's funny. Go ahead and laugh if you
want to. But try to live with it. She has twenty-nine
hats. All of them new. And she wears a *béret* nine-tenths
of the time. And when I make a strike, or move up a
notch in my job, she tells me what a bum I am and how
badly I treat her and asks me when I'm going to make
a fortune for her and cries. Lately it's been getting
worse. She wants me to do things that aren't—well,
ethical. It makes me sick. For instance, an artist came
in the other day with some swell stuff that the old man
—Dean—liked right away. It was good. But the artist
like a damn fool made me a proposition. He said he'd
split fifty-fifty with me on anything he made from our

agency. If I hired him, he'd pay me, see? Just plain scurviness. I almost threw him out. And I told Gerry about it. What did she do? She said: 'You poor egg, do it.' Just like that. 'You poor egg, do it. He won't dare tell on you,' she said, 'because it will incriminate him. You can make a couple of thousand dollars without turning your hand,' she said. I walked out on her—but she's harping on it ever since until I'm scared I shall do it. Morning, noon, and night it's the same thing. 'You've got the soul of a snail,' she tells me. 'You're holding out on me,' she says. 'You have the business nerve of a guinea-pig.' I've been married less than three months—and that's the way things are. And I tell you, it all comes from that psychological business. Just phobias. Just running from one thing to another because nothing does her any good. It gets worse. Last night I thought she was going off the deep end. She talked about Michael. My God, you'd think she'd been his wife, mother, and sister, to hear her. 'My Michael,' she called him. I got sick of it. 'Looka here,' I said, 'if I didn't know you better, I'd think you'd been playing around with him.' What did she do? She screamed. She screamed until I thought we'd get kicked out. She told me exactly where I could go, and what sort of vile mind I had, and what kind of bird I was to think that way about my wife, let alone to mention it. And a lot more. When she was calmed down, I began to think, and the more I think about it, the more I believe she did have more to do with him than just sitting there as a model. He was—"

BABES AND SUCKLINGS

"He's dead."

"I know it. But what would you do, or say, or think?"

"I'd send her to a psychoanalyst."

"Sure. I thought of that. I thought of it ten days after we were married. I suggested it. That was the first big battle. 'Just because you're half a man, just because you're ignorant and don't know anything about women —or anything else—you blame it on me. You think I ought to see a doctor. How about you?' There was more of that, too. It went on for days, and every once in a while, when I forget something or get absent-minded, she says: 'Seen the psychoanalyst yet?' with a look in her eyes that makes me—well—a look in her eyes."

The memory of that expression arrested his flow of words. Thornton had never heard anything quite equal to it. "Well," he said, "why don't you divorce her?"

"I—I can't."

"Why?"

"Well, I love her, I guess."

"You mean, you've married her, and you've been brought up not to believe in divorce, and you're naturally stubborn—not to say long-suffering—which is less a virtue than a vice—and you haven't got the nerve."

"Maybe I do mean that. You have never been married. Wait till you are."

"I think I know the same things about it that you do," Thornton said with some dignity.

"Perhaps you do and perhaps you don't. I don't

know what to do. Sometimes I think that the best thing would be for her to leave me—or for me to shut my eyes and then—just hope that it will come out all right afterwards."

"It's tough."

"Sure it's tough. I admit it. I haven't any particular shame or pride left. How can I have? Every time we meet new people, another situation comes up. It takes all the diplomacy and skill I have to keep it from being serious."

Thornton hummed *sotto voce* between his teeth. "How much of that do you suppose I already knew—or guessed?"

"Then why in God's name didn't you tell me?"

"Because I just guessed most of it, for one thing. And because the majority of women are like that to a degree. But a good many of them recover." He was supererogating, somewhat, on the advantage-point of the gossip and prediction he had heard on the wedding-day of Don and Gerry. On the other hand, he had gleaned sufficient intuitive knowledge of Gerry to beware of her.

Don sighed lustily. "Well, I'm glad to get it off my chest, anyway. It was decent of you to listen."

"That's all right."

Don smiled. "I was one of those wise babies who ran around laughing at Freud, saying that sex wasn't so important as they thought and talking to girls about Platonic love. Meaning it, most of the time. So I get it in the neck full strength, undiluted. Funny, isn't it?"

"Yes, it's funny."

"I guess I'll get back to the office now."

"All right. I've got to work."

"Must be easy, working whenever you want—at whatever you want."

"Hardest thing in the world," Thornton answered, "because you don't absolutely have to work at all at any particular time. If the people who envied writers ever looked on that side of it and took a second good look at themselves, they'd see that they didn't have the stamina. No bouquet for myself. I'm a tyro. But that's the principle of it."

"Making out all right?"

"Fair. I've averaged about fifty a week on war stories and sea stories and detective stories. But I'm not in the leisure class by any means."

Don, who had advanced himself to a comfortable income that he calculated by the year instead of the week, allowed himself a moment of inner warmth. He was going to be prosperous—that he no longer doubted. And Thornton's earnings seemed percariously small to him. He had forgotten the numerals of his budget a short year before then. "Good stuff," he said tolerantly.

The reaction did not escape Thornton. He wondered if Gerry's desires were already affecting his friend. "I'll do better soon," he said quietly. "Well, so long."

"So long."

BABES AND SUCKLINGS

15

The burial "service" for Michael was held in a funeral parlor. More than two hundred persons passed the coffin and rested their eyes on his composed features. A white light poured on them. Only a few saw that the lips and cheeks were rouged, that his nose was supported inside so that the distortion would not show. Among the persons who passed in solemn silence were many whose names occupied famous niches in public opinion.

Cynthia and Thornton saw Perry Breck there and they whispered with him for a few moments. Aurelius read a poem of his own composition. Unlike the ordinary spontaneous threnody, it was masterful. Until he read it, in a clear, studied voice, the people had been calm. Afterwards, without exception, they wept. It bespoke the tragedy of Michael's life and death so simply and so powerfully that they were reminded of the man in every line.

A strange oppression permeated that group, as if Michael had taken his own life, or as if he had died of a broken heart for which they were, in part, responsible. He had been so vital as to seem immortal. He had been so reckless of himself as to make others forgetful of the fact that he was flesh and blood. They could not believe that he was dead, that he would remain dead. Then, unexpectedly, he had perished like the meanest

living thing. It was then that they perceived he had
suffered and sorrowed, that he had his own emotions
and his own soul, that his glittering armor of cynicism
was the more glittering and impenetrable because of the
delicacy of the thing within it. For the route of his
death was partially cleared. His nights of solitary drunk-
enness, his long walks by the sea and river, his moodi-
ness, had been set in relief by the matter-of-fact anno-
tations of the police department.

They dramatized those facts and sentimentalized
them. It was quite natural. The celebrities, intimate
with Michael or merely acquainted with him, felt that
a gesture would be expected from them. His friends,
stumbling through their bereavement, made gestures to
fortify themselves and, sometimes, to justify slights of
Michael and meannesses to him that they could not
forget. The motion-picture actor executed stills of himself in sorrow—but he was really sorry, in a confused
soul. A great painter bowed his red beard into his vest
and wiped his eyes with a stubby hand. A violinist
turned his back moodily on the press of people and undammed a river of grieving song to his own ear. And
the women, the women whom Aurelius had called the
sad women, silent, one by one arrived in veils and held
their heads with a proud pain, their classic heads that
Michael had kissed and painted and turned, perhaps.
But certainly he had given them no license to eternal
litany. They were appalling, Cynthia thought, appalling
mementoes for any man to leave behind, symbols of the
flesh that had perished and not, as they pretended, of

the spirit that had marched on into nothingness. Gerry
led them, choking and sobbing. *Requiescat in pace*. No.
Turn the ashes of him with a libidinous toe.

16

The cortège moved through the clamorous down-
town streets. The traffic of business mingled with it and
separated itself again. It crossed a bridge in a cold wind
and passed under the bare trees and alongside the ash-
heaps of that vast tundra beyond Brooklyn where a city
empties its entrails. The mourners talked about Michael, always Michael; low, quavering voices in remi-
niscence. It was a dun business, finished in the crema-
tory of the graveyard, with the doleful music of an
organ and the heavy scent of flowers in the chilly stone
room, and the cold, nauseating progress of the coffin
into the gate of the furnace. Thus passed the glory that
was Michael.

17

In the morning of the next day Cynthia and Thornton and Nadine and Aurelius and Don and Gerry woke
upon a world that had in some way disintegrated and
that would never again assume the same aspect of glam-
our, or of refuge, or even of purpose for some of them.

PART THREE

1

LIFE for Thornton and Cynthia was suddenly stagnant. A turbulent event often acts as a catalyst. But they were conscious of no katabolism. Interest in the death of Michael abated. The press discarded the story as soon as it had extracted every possible detail, gaudy, and tragic. His friends wearied of discussing him. They found a limit and a point of repetition even in his kaleidoscopic memoirs. Gerry no longer foamed out of her frustration.

They took inventories of themselves. Cynthia, pursuing the order of her occupations, from a late rising in the morning to a late retiring, viewed her life as a thing that would probably be stabilized. She anticipated an upward curve for it, a curve directed largely by Thornton's success. He was already embarked on a book that was ingenious without being false. In her estimation it was the sort of book that would be widely read and widely praised. She visioned, after its publication, a larger apartment, a larger if less intimate circle of friends, a trip abroad each summer, better prices for his stories from the fiction magazines, and, in consequence of those material benefits, an existence of widening interest to herself.

Of course, that was her uncomplicated wish and augury. Thornton himself was an obstacle to its attainment, in some ways. She was still his mistress and that fact might hurt his literary position. But the way in which he impeded his own progress was the more significant factor of the two because it was quite incomprehensible to her, while their social position would be arranged by an eventual marriage.

She considered herself first. To exchange comparative wealth for comparative impecuniosity was not difficult. Her family had lived in an ungallant struggle against the appearances of poverty. But her husband had been so frugal that she had not known the pleasure of prodigality. He was a little man, itching with worries and loud in a hundred contempts. His disdain was usually for things and people superior to his goods or to himself.

In all the retinue of complaints against the life from which she had revolted, her new one was an improvement. She felt that she was actually learning to know Thornton, to understand the most obscure behaviors of his mind, and that she was exerting a definite effect on him. She knew that she loved him and would always love him. His fundamental selfishness was, in its last essence, nothing more formidable than the protective cloak that hedges every individual. He had a parallel generosity that was more than adequate balance for it. His vanity—and he had been very vain at first—

175

was cured by her ridicule. Thornton's vanity was a thing peculiar to himself and offensive to very few people. Out of it grew an enormous modesty that was entirely assumed. Michael had seen it. Cynthia writhed under it. But she hid her distaste and deflated the pose slowly, so that his frank, pleasant personality emerged and dominated him.

She was almost always sure that he loved her. He exhibited every corollary of love: tenderness, thoughtfulness, friendliness, interest, approval, optimism, industry, good nature, loyalty, honesty, a dozen other estimable characteristics. He was a moody youth, but his moods were more often pleasant variety than intolerable fits of depression, anger, or distrust. On some days he would not work. He frittered away his time, he sought every form of trivial entertainment, he launched into long orations, which had neither point nor object, except perhaps the use of time. On other days a fury of energy seized him and he scarcely noticed her presence. He was liable to fits of extravagant silliness during which his conversation was almost impossible to understand. At such times he was in a high good humor and what he said corresponded to the results of effervescence in a less imaginative person. But seldom did his biological esprit show symptoms of displeasure or unhappiness. She believed at that period in their lives that she was linked to a man with a most exceptional nature. He would become quite famous and she would share his glory in every sense; she had contributed ideas and criticism to him, she had shaped his personality, she had smoothed the path of his progress. The rewards were hers as well as his. Without her he would have not improbably become the doughty and dismal idol of a small group of dilettante pretenders. With her he would belong to the world and perhaps to the ages. She was just beginning to enjoy the compensations of a woman who devotes her being to that of the man for whom she cares.

But that hopeful horizon was flecked by a single small cloud. Somewhere in his make-up Thornton carried the elements of his own destruction. Cynthia recognized them rarely. But when they presented their ugly surfaces, she was shocked and frightened. His superior, unearthly detachment was not all poise. The part of himself that he thought might really be himself, the sagacious, disillusioned spectator, was really Thornton on occasions. He had a terrific contempt. It was more than youthful dissatisfaction, more than the protest of adolescence. It was cosmic. It hated bitterly, hated people, things, emotions, thoughts, as if it had been endowed with sublime capacities and thrown thirsty on to an insufficient earth. She realized that if it was ever awakened fully, in sheer detestation it could rend Thornton apart.

It made Thornton able to see and understand with stunning clarity. She feared it. She wondered how it had developed. Not daring to believe that it was an honest growth out of his own dislike of the necessary lies and posing of life, she imagined that he had had a remote ancestor whose brooding insanity might have driven

177

him to a horrid grave. She thought of it as something dreadful in his blood. It was not human to face life so coldly and dispassionately, even at the most appropriate moments. Nevertheless, when she thought about that part of Thornton, the instances of its operations were not sufficient for great alarm.

Once, shortly after Michael's death, he had said: "I know what made Michael do that. It was a sort of suicide. How soon, or how he died, made no difference. If I had been in his place, I should have done it myself."

"Thornton!" she had replied; "don't be such a fool." For his words had been more expressive than their sense.

"How do you know, how can any woman know, what was going on in his head?"

Again, he had spoken after Gerry had left their apartment. "If I knew three people like that, I'd jump off the Woolworth Building." He had not quite intended it to be amusing.

It had been that Thornton which had struck her on the night he came home so very drunk. She knew then that, for one instant, she had meant nothing to him, Breck had meant nothing, life, death, hell, heaven, were nothing. Only his cold fury lived and leaped; that alone was to be served. It was unearthly. It was a thing she could not touch, could not know, could not love, because it was incapable of reciprocating any of those mundanities. It might rise in a savage second to be his undoing.

Thus she composed her life. Thornton was almost

perfect. His one evil quality would, in all possibility, never assert its full capacity for disaster. She was young and beautiful and good. The little refuge she reserved for herself, the refuge that all men and women reserve, lay in those facts. She could leave her lover if it ever became necessary and still live gayly, sanely, and to some purpose. She was a complete woman.

She had, in a natural and human way, emphasized certain superiorities that she possessed over him. His own particular advantage—that of his talent—was so extensive that she impressed upon him her abilities, as well as his failings, to attain a level of equality. The general effect was good except when she carried it too far. Then Thornton, shutting his eyes to the truth, which he understood generously, and out of pure temper, would be annoyed at her supererogation or depressed by criticism of him. Both sentiments were petty. But every alliance is unbalanced by such very attempts at balance, which are neither fair nor sane, but quite essential.

It is remarkable that two persons of such intricate understanding ever allowed themselves to quarrel. Intellectually and biologically they could not quarrel. But there were other aspects to their lives. Society threw into them extraneous matter, and it was socially that their bitterest struggle was waged. And it is the social aspect of the union of the sexes that is most dangerous in an intelligent civilization. For any human being, no matter how lucid, must reach points at which his very lucidity is an obstacle in his behavior.

BABES AND SUCKLINGS

They were typical. Like thousands of others, they had thrown over the medieval yoke of God and the Church. They were thoroughly acquainted with science, its achievements and its dark fields of ignorance. They were honest mentally. Their morality was utilitarian. Their ethics were simple: truth, industry, improvement, both personal and general. Such ethics were inspired by no creed and no hope of reward and consequently were vastly more valuable than any religious ethics. They understood the technique and importance of love. They knew the laws of their community and obeyed them within the conveniences of need. They familiarized themselves with progress because they represented progress. Ten million people, a hundred million people, in smaller towns and narrower environments would have risen mechanically to say that they were wicked, immoral, parasitical, and undesirable persons. Yet their effect on their friends was extremely healthy and their very lives were a charity to a not altogether unreceptive world. Fortunately, because they lived in a city as advanced and as heedless as New York, they knew no martyrdom. In fact, they were regarded as an omen and symbol of a better estate that lay ahead of humanity. They were unmarried, but their happiness was more evident than the happiness of most married people, and many times as sincere. Their knowledge of each other, gained through necessity rather than avoided because a ritual had made it unnecessary if not inadvisable, was an asset which any observer could assay at once. Their freedom to change their status was envied by such persons as Gerry, but, in reality, it was a trifling thing. The consciousness of it did not make the great difference that it is generally supposed to make. Divorce, desertion, and infidelity are too common nowadays to make freedom a vast boon. It would have required the same agony for them to part that parting requires of the legally united. They were well mated, it was said, and few who pronounced that verdict considered the intelligent effort, the restraint, the care that had gone into that adverb. They were happy.

2

Christmas moved up on the calendar and was ripped away. Thornton gave Cynthia a wrist watch set with tiny diamonds and she gave him a silk dressing-gown and afterwards, emptying their pockets of the few dollars they contained, they sat, wrapped in each other's arms, laughing at the fact that they were very nearly penniless. The condition was remedied a few days later when a check for one of his stories arrived from a newsprint magazine.

Snow fell, wrapping Manhattan in a white blanket for a brief day and then melting away at the bottoms of dirty gray piles on the street-sides. Thornton's book was nearly finished. They had made several new friends. They played bridge together very well—after Cynthia had pored over the cards with Thornton until his nimble mind, at last intrigued, had grasped the fundamental stratagems. Twice they had attended elaborate costume-balls in large hotels. Twice they had gone to the revels in Webster Hall. Once Perry Breck had taken them to the opera, and, on their own initiative, they had heard several concerts. They went to the theater when mood and money combined with leisure to direct them thither. A book-reviewer whom Thronton knew stocked his shelves with the newest novels and non-fictional literary endeavors. Cynthia read them voraciously while he wrote, and occasionally, when she found something she liked, she would arrest his work and read aloud for an hour or two. Cynthia bought some new clothes with the growing earnings of his stories. New Year's, coming after Christmas almost unexpectedly, could add nothing to the resolutions they had already made.

3

In the afternoon of a cold, gray day Cynthia came in from Raymond's bringing a warm meal in paper cartons. Thornton had been loath to leave his work. She enjoyed the errand and arranged the food on blue china plates with care so as to avoid the evidences of its transference and the implied flavor of waxed tissue. They began to eat.

"I saw Gerry there while I was waiting," she said.

"Yes?"

"You'll be amused. They're going to Bermuda in

182

two weeks. She told me, perfectly innocently, that Don had just made an extra two thousand dollars."

Thorton meditated on the length of woman's memory for detail. That he had remembered the same fact did not surprise him. "You mean that Don took it from the artist?"

"What else?"

"He might have come by it honestly."

Cynthia paused, a plate on her lap, her hand in mid-air. As she spoke, she returned it slowly to the plate. "Yes. I thought that. I hoped that he had. But I asked Gerry how the good luck arrived and she said that they never would have had it if she hadn't been a better business man than Don, and that Don was afraid to take advantage of the opportunities life offered and that the 'foundation' for the money was laid several months ago."

"Don'll lose his job if that ever gets out."

"How can it? New York is fifty worlds, all separated from each other by social oceans."

"A pretty thought, that. Maybe I'd better write it down."

"You're making fun of me," she said. "Go ahead. I'm just the little girl who runs out and gets your lunch when you're too lazy."

"You're a dear. So Gerry said that. Poor old Don. She'll have him in the Tombs yet."

"She'll have him on Park Avenue."

"Same thing."

"Goodness!" she said, in mock dismay, "but you're witty today."

"I'm writing a piece for the *New Yorker*."

"Same thing."

They laughed. It was very easy to laugh over such inanities, such faint, personal innuendo.

4

Perry Breck called on them. He brought his wife, whom they had never met. Cynthia was embarrassed. Mrs. Breck was the sort of woman calculated to embarrass Cynthia because her one idea was to put them at their ease.

"I've heard so much about you," she said, "and your interesting 'marriage.' I'm awfully glad to know you. Terribly glad." She turned to Thornton. "And I've always wanted to meet a real author."

"But I'm not."

"Not real? My dear young man, you radiate reality—and your work does, I am sure. As far as your being an author is concerned I've read your stories. In *Night Club Stories* and *Crime Tales*."

Thornton was dumfounded. He wrote for both those magazines. But he had never met anyone who read them. The idea that the wife of the wealthy Perry Breck read such drivel appalled him. He said nothing. Perry grinned uncomfortably. "How about a little bridge?" he suggested. They played for hours and won nineteen dollars. Mrs. Breck obviously played well, she obviously lost purposely. They were ashamed to take the money Perry forced on them.

"You must, my dears," Mrs. Breck said. "May we come down again? You are perfectly charming."

When they had gone, Thornton stood with the money in his hand.

"You don't know whether to laugh or cry, do you?" Cynthia said.

"I think I'll swear. I didn't believe there were women like her."

"Lots of them."

"But how did Perry get mixed up with one? He's so different."

"He married her twenty years ago," Cynthia said, as if it explained everything.

5

The day of Don's and Gerry's departure for Bermuda arrived. They had invited friends to their cabin for a *bon voyage* party. Thornton and Cynthia could hear them chattering as they climbed the steps to the deck above. The small two-room "suite" was crowded.

"Isn't it wonderful?" Gerry was saying. "Just think —to get away from the blizzards and cold for two whole weeks. To swim and sit in the sunshine. I can't believe it's really going on anywhere in the world."

"Hello."

Thornton's eyes were entirely for one of the guests. The reason was plain. That guest, a tall, middle-aged man standing against the berths, was looking at Cynthia as if he had never seen a woman in his life. His expression was so intense and so reckless of any notice that it might attract that Thornton returned a stare to which the stranger was oblivious. If Cynthia perceived it, she gave no indication.

Gerry was calling a roll of names, one hand waving, the other supporting a tall glass. Thornton and Cynthia spoke to several people. The man had not changed his gaze. He seemed unconscious of Thornton. Other men had admired Cynthia. A few, like Perry Breck, had wooed her tentatively. This man was assaulting her with his eyes. Thornton felt a powerful hostility, a touch of his impersonal madness.

"And this is Murray Dean, our boss and good provider."

That supplied the link. The incredibly rude man was the head of the advertising agency for which Don worked. The man came towards him, passed by, took Cynthia's hand. "I'm glad to meet you," he said in a deep, resonant voice. "You are marvelous."

"And this is her—" Gerry hesitated— "this is Thornton."

"Oh, yes."

They shook hands. Dean's manner was so friendly that Thornton thought he must have been mistaken. Perhaps Dean was near-sighted, or subject to fits of abstraction. He said to Thornton: "I've heard about you—from Don and from Stone. Always was sorry you left the advertising business. Wanted you in my outfit eventually. How are you making out in fiction?"

"He's doing terribly well."

Good little Cynthia! She had come to his defense. Thornton always thought of her as little when she was generous or sentimental.

"I'm glad to hear it. Very glad. Glad to meet you two. Don has told me all about you. More than he should have told."

"Here are drinks." Gerry brought them in dripping glasses that had been impressed into the congested service more than once. They drank.

Half an hour later Thornton walked out on deck. He was in a state of intoxication that he disliked. The rapid drinking of too many high-balls made him dizzy and queasy. A stinging wind blew up from the river. He had left Cynthia in animated conversation with Dean. It made him miserable, and ashamed of his misery.

Dean had noticed his departure and understood it with a feeling of satisfaction. His voice lowered and his subject changed from Don and Gerry to Cynthia.

"I never saw a woman like you," he said in low tones. "I was literally swept off my feet. I can't quite get back to normalcy. Please forgive me for mentioning it."

She sipped her drink. Such adulation was the sort for which she had come all the way to New York. Men like Murray Dean were the kind of whom she had expected it. Much as she loved Thornton, she could not

187

avoid recognition of the fact, or even a tense, trembling, and half-delicious sense of pleasure in it.

"Of course I'll forgive you," she said. "If I weren't in love, I'd even be coy. But I am—and you must always remember that."

"Always?"

He gave it such an inflection that she knew he had at once decided to see her again. She wondered if she had intended to make that insinuation.

"If you ever see me, that is."

"May I? I'd like to—very much. I'll incorporate your—your boy-friend in any bid."

She ignored the slur in "boy-friend." After all, she thought, there was a point at which niceties could become impediments to social intercourse. She was tricked into that by the haste and secrecy of their words. Gerry, casting a covert glance in their direction, brought her to her senses.

"Where's Thornton?"

"He went out on deck, I think," Dean said.

Cynthia rose. "I'm going after him."

"He'll be back. Here, better let me get your coat. It's very cold today."

"I won't stay."

She found Thornton standing at the rail and staring into the oily water with a black scowl on his face. The symptoms were plain to her. She was annoyed by the cold, by her own pleasure over a situation which displeased him, by his jealousy, by the certainty that he would behave badly for the remainder of the party.

"You come inside," she said. "You'll get pneumonia."

He knew all that was passing in her mind, all that had passed between Dean and her. He magnified it. "I'm all right. Cooling off."

"That's just what you shouldn't do. Come in, Thornton, please."

"You go back. I'll be in soon."

"Please, please, please." He approached her. "And don't be mean just because Murray Dean likes me."

He wanted to be vicious. Mr. Dean. Murray Dean. Murray. He thought of voicing that sequence sarcastically, and held his tongue. Dean, aware that he had already instituted some sort of quarrel between them, took Thornton to his corner and talked advertising to him until he was in a better humor. It would not do, Dean perceived, to set them at variance if he wished to know Cynthia better. If that happened, she would cut him off at once—because, as she had said, she loved Thornton. How much, or for how long, was another matter in Dean's mind.

When Thornton had regained his equanimity, and time and another drink had healed Cynthia's hurt, Dean suggested to the former that they take dinner together. Thornton could not refuse very well. He was inclined, in any case, to believe that he had been an awkward fool and that his jealousy was unwarranted. So he spoke to Cynthia and returned with an acceptance. The steamer whistle had blown. There was a scrimmage for wraps in the cabin. Gerry was kissing and being kissed liberally. Don shook hands again and again with the same people. The soft roar of the dining-room gong swept up from the deck below. They faced Gerry and Don, wished them well, told them to be good and not to drink too much or else to drink one extra for them, and walked with the filing throng across the gang-plank.

6

The evening presented by Murray Dean was lavish. He had had nothing to drink. He never drank liquor of which he was not sure, he said. That situation was alleviated at once. In the process Thornton reached a communicative state and one in which nothing could have impressed him greatly. Afterwards they had dinner in one of the speakeasies in the Fifties where food is served in the French manner, where a Hawaiian orchestra thrums softly, and old wine is produced in its original and ancient bottles.

By twelve o'clock, thoroughly sated with food and fairly in their cups, they progressed from the speakeasy to a night club, where they danced and sprawled over the table, watching the entertainers. Some attempt at talking was made, but topics were brought up, discussed for an instant, and forgotten in the event of the slightest interruption. At three they moved again, taking a cab to Harlem. Dean had sent his chauffeur home long before. In Harlem Cynthia fell sound asleep twice and Thornton became sufficiently conscious to remember

on the next day that they had been there. When the
whisky that Dean had brought was consumed, they
went again by cab to Reubens and there "breakfasted"
with eyes that saw double and ogled sillily and hands
that functioned abnormally.

Thornton was drunker than either of the others.
But he kept himself awake and conscious by a sort of
malicious effort. Dean scarcely showed signs of his condition; nevertheless, when he tried on the following
day, he was unable to recall much of what had happened. He took them home at last and remained in the
cab on their insistence.

Standing on the curb, swaying and tottering, Thornton said: "Nice evening. Very nice indeed. Especially
the balloons. I shall never forget the balloons as long as
I live."

Dean had no idea what he was saying. The words
were utterly inarticulate. He answered at random: "All
right I am sure and you too I hope."

"Perfect!" Cynthia said suddenly.

The cab moved off towards the address they had
given the chauffeur by combined attempt.

7

In the morning they woke slowly and uncomfortably. They had fallen asleep in their clothes. Cynthia undressed and went back to bed without exchanging words.
Thornton bathed, put on fresh clothes, went out on the

191

street and drank a bromo-seltzer, and then walked for several blocks. He brought back the same restorative to her. She was just stirring again when he came in.

They looked questioningly at each other and did not laugh. "I feel almost depraved," she said.

"I do feel depraved. There wasn't any sense in his getting us drunk."

"His getting us drunk! You didn't have to drink, did you?"

"No," Thornton answered resignedly. "How do you feel?"

"Terrible."

Then he laughed. "Me, too. I don't think I'm going to like Murray Dean."

"He probably believes we drink a great deal and did it just to please us."

It sounded like a defense of Dean and a disagreement with himself. "He probably drinks a lot, you mean," Thornton said.

"I don't believe it. He's a big business man."

"All the more reason."

"Thornton, are you going to be that way all day? Because if you are, I'm going out."

Contrition smote him. He took her head on his lap. "No, I'm not, honey. And I guess I was pretty rotten last night. Let's forget it. If he comes again, we know his measure."

8

Dean came again. He called that afternoon to see how they felt. He called the following day and invited Cynthia to lunch—an invitation she did not accept. He appeared on the next Saturday with a huge bouquet of flowers, and tickets for the newest musical show, which they attended in a state of inebriation second in their experience only to that of their first night with him. He attached himself in two weeks as their patron, drinking companion, and mentor. Thornton did not like it, but Cynthia was stimulated and entertained and it had been a long time since she had really done any extensive "bingeing"—a fact which she elaborated apologetically. Moreover, Thornton was unable to afford the glittering splendor commanded by Dean's purse. He felt that inability keenly, but he hid his displeasure as well as he could.

9

The trip Gerry and Don took to Bermuda made them intolerable—or at least made her intolerable for many days. They had met a countess and two separate millionaires. Immediately upon their return they were invited to a social function that brought their names into print in one of the New York papers. Gerry was

awed by herself. She ignored the sophistication gleaned
from her newspaper training. She disregarded the fact
that the little item in which her name was set had been
put there to fill space, chosen at hazard from the publicity and social secretarial matter at the disposal of
the editor. She carried it in her pocket-book and produced it with the pride of a small-town social climber.

She called on Cynthia, who was both dismayed and
amused. "We came back yesterday. Tomorrow we're
going to the Radley-Smith dinner." (It was before the
newspaper publicity.) "And we had a gorgeous time.
Simply gorgeous."

"I'll bet."

"You can't imagine how lovely Bermuda is. The
white chalk roads. No, they're coral. The green little
gardens. The palm-trees. The flowers everywhere." She
was reciting from a catalogue. "And the sea—on every
hand the great, thundering, eternal sea."

Cynthia closed her eyes and for an instant she was
really envious. Somehow, as she thought of the icy,
hard metropolitan streets, she could not help remembering California. Bermuda must be like California, she
thought, and wished that Thornton could afford to live
away from New York where they could have a house
and lawns and a vista of the sea. Gerry did not deserve
to come by such things, especially dishonestly. "It must
have been lovely."

"I could hardly believe it. Every day when I went
down to the beach to swim, I said to myself: 'This is
the twenty-fifth of January.' It was wonderful."

Cynthia nodded. She knew what it meant to swim on the twenty-fifth of January.

"You ought to do it," Gerry continued. "It helps you in every way. Physically, socially—especially socially—and spiritually. I'm a different woman. Even Don says so—and you know what husbands are. You and Thornton really ought to plan to go right away."

That, of course, was sheer feminine cruelty— edged, perhaps, with a desire to justify her unscrupulousness. When Gerry had gone, Cynthia was sad for a little while. She sat alone in her tiny home. Disturbing influences had been exerted on her, she thought. Murray Dean holding out pledges to her—pledges of what? Gerry talking about Bermuda. And Thornton, worried, puzzled, a little frightened. She felt sorry for him. She saw, sitting there, that she would have to be a good sport. That she would have to wait for him, to work with him, to hold herself in check, and to stave off such upsetting influences as Dean as much as she could. Poor Thornton. He was a boy trying to be a man. And she had not helped him very much.

When he came home, he found her crying. "What's the matter?" he asked in alarm.

"Oh, I don't know. I'm happy—I guess."

"Happy?"

"Yes."

"Then don't cry."

"Come here, Thornton," she said tenderly.

They kissed. Their little universe had righted itself in that moment. She wondered if the next would turn it upside-down again. Her head ached. Her nose smarted and her eyes watered even after she had stopped crying. She thought that she was catching cold. Thornton began to clatter on his typewriter. She listened to the erratic sound and wiped her reddened face. Everything had been calm for a long time. Months. And then Murray had made them drink and she had put him off and Gerry had come in, recalling California, and then Thornton, arriving from a call on an editor, had righted everything again. It was getting dark outside.

"Want some tea?" she asked.

10

Aurelius and Nadine had been away for a month. They had gone, they said, on a honeymoon. There had been little news of them. A single postcard from Washington, signed by Nadine, had said: "We got married at City Hall and now we're here. Back soon." Aurelius had always been a mysterious and vexatious person. His new wife was as mysterious, but a solid bond had been forged between her and Cynthia.

No one knew, for one thing, how Aurelius made his living. It was assumed that he had inherited a modest estate. He wrote, but his writings were esoteric, casual, and unmarketable. Nadine's parents lived in Cleveland and were known to be rich, but Thornton and Cynthia were sure that Aurelius would not accept their charity.

BABES AND SUCKLINGS

Aurelius had been in the army and the navy as well during the war. He had been wounded. After the Armistice he had lived in Paris, where he had contracted a heroin habit, the effects and cure of which he recited occasionally with harrowing detail. He had met Nadine there while she was studying to fill in the gap between adolescence and matrimony. They had loved each other, quarreled, separated, and met again at Gerry's wedding. Anecdotes of their vehement, clandestine, Paris courtship were supplied by both of them to Cynthia and Thornton.

Their return was hailed with considerable pleasure by Thornton, because they represented a certain stability, and by Cynthia because she was so fond of them. When Aurelius had broken his dope habit, he had revolted simultaneously against the other vices of humanity so that his pipe and his enthralling narratives were the only outlet of his vigorous soul. His greeting of them was typical.

"You kids look all fagged out. Especially Thornton. What the devil have you been doing?"

"Running around," Thornton said. "Met a lot of new people who wanted to show us New York." He referred, of course, to Dean. Nadine watched him as he spoke. "Drinking too much, I guess."

"Thornton has winter-sickness," Cynthia added. "We both have."

Aurelius wondered for an instant if the death of Michael was still having an effect on them. "Any trouble?" he asked.

197

"None at all."

He presumed that it was. "Well, I'd lay off liquor if I were you. Let me tell you what they did to me the second time I went to the hospital for the D.T.'s."

Thornton winked at Nadine and Cynthia as Aurelius puffed out his chest and packed his pipe for the peroration of what was certain to be a gripping story. It was good to see friendly people again—people who were not avaricious like Gerry, dull and weak like Don, desiring like Murray.

"Gee, I was glad to see them," Thornton said later that night.

"Me, too."

"They're really pretty wonderful people."

"I think so. Especially Nadine. She never says much, but she knows everything that is going on—whether you tell her or not." During the evening Nadine had taken Cynthia to one side and said: "Who is he, Cynthia? And do you care about him?"

Cynthia, surprised for the moment, made no denial. She told the story of Murray's intervention in as few words as possible. When it was finished, Nadine was tempted to advise her to be careful because of Thornton. After a moment of consideration, however, she said nothing. Cynthia would be careful, and faithful, too, if Thornton played his part.

Thornton knew, when Cynthia mentioned it, the facts to which she referred. He had known when he heard Nadine and Cynthia in whispered conversation. It rested his mind. Why he could not say.

198

BABES AND SUCKLINGS

11

Nadine was first to learn about the baby. If Michael had been alive, Cynthia would have gone to him —always because of Thornton. She felt that Michael had had the key to Thornton's nature even while she was sure that Michael would not have saved him from a long and presumptuous period of posing. She left Thornton at his typewriter, his thinnish shoulders rounded and his pale hands flowing over the letters.

Nadine was alone. All day almost every day she sat on a long, dark-red divan, dreaming, turning the leaves of magazines, waiting for her round of time to end. She was Asiatic in that. She might have been set up as the antipode of Geraldine Shaw in every respect. She remained very nearly in the same position when Cynthia came in. Only her eyes showed friendliness. She said: "Hello" and did not ask any questions.

Cynthia said: "Where's Aurelius?"

"Walking." Nadine laughed with an inward amusement. "Walking. When we got up this morning, he told me that he was going for a walk. 'I'm going for a walk!'" She mimicked Aurelius's chopped accent. "Out he went. Five minutes later he returned and said he would not be here for lunch."

Cynthia wondered why she thought that was a joke. "Was he angry?"

"I guess so. But he'll come back. I like him to do that once in a while. It shows he is not growing old."

"How old is he?"

"Thirty-three."

"Were you going out?"

"No. I was waiting for him."

"But he won't be back until tonight."

"Probably not," Nadine answered. "But I wasn't very hungry."

Cynthia wished that she had as simple and satisfying a philosophy of life. She wished she had Nadine's patience and repose. They looked at each other for a moment and Nadine smile. She was like Lilith. Nothing could surprise her, no wrong, no sin, no ugly sight, no bliss. But she was not cold. A warm eternal passion made her very alive and desirable. Cynthia could understand then why men killed themselves for women, why they considered women an eternal enigma, why they broke themselves for women. Her admiration for Nadine was almost worship. She thought that Nadine would make a perfect wife for Thornton—or for any man. It never occurred to her that she was very much like Nadine. They were both generous women—and there are few such women in the world.

"Will you take lunch with me?"

Nadine looked down at her scarlet lounging pyjamas, her high-heeled mules. "Why not?"

In a few minutes she was dressed. And by the manner of her dressing, a woman's character may be understood. Wrapped in a fur coat she resembled an expensive doll. They went to Raymond's.

During lunch Cynthia said: "I'm going to have a baby."

"That's wonderful," Nadine answered. Not surprised, not flimsily ecstatic. "There are three ways of saying that. One is, 'I'm pregnant.' The next, 'I'm going to have a baby.' Most people I know say: 'By the way, do you know of a good surgeon—who is reliable and inexpensive?'"

Cynthia smiled. "That's right. But I'm going to have mine."

Nadine pondered. "I guess it's all right. Thornton has always been healthy hasn't he?"

"Just the usual thing. Mumps, measles, chickenpox. You know."

"How about his family and your family?"

That, Cynthia reflected, was what Nadine would consider first. "All right. No insanity. No disease. He looks frail, but he has a tough constitution. And lots of intelligence there, too. His father was a librarian and a student. His mother taught school and wrote—until she had too many babies. Mine are healthy peasants."

"Money?"

"He's making more every month. By summertime we ought to be quite well off."

"It's to be summer?"

"August."

"Seen a doctor?"

"Yes."

"Does he know? Of course he doesn't. You wanted to ask me how to tell him."

Cynthia blushed faintly. "I suppose I did. It isn't easy. I'm afraid he might not like it. Once before I—"

"I remember. How about this Murray person?"

Cynthia shook her head slowly. "I was a little bit silly at first. You know how you feel. But he's nobody. It was all in Thornton's mind anyway, wasn't it? I think so. This—this ought to end that."

Nadine wondered how much Cynthia desired the baby and how much she desired to keep Thornton's mind unperturbed. The baby would surely do that. "Going to marry him?"

"Maybe. Some day. After the baby's born. There isn't any hurry."

Then Nadine felt the timeless, vital pulse of Cynthia that was like her own. She also understood Cynthia's love, her modesty, her restraints. "I'd just say: 'Thornton, I want to have a child.' Then I'd make up my mind how to tell him when he answered."

"I will."

"A lot of my friends have had babies," Nadine continued. "And they've all done it badly. Everybody gets born. It's common. But they make such a mummery out of it. Sobbing and making clothes and being nauseated and swelling—all in public. If I ever have one, I won't make any clothes. If I get sick, I'll stay at home and refuse visitors. When I'm well along, I'll stay home entirely. I'll let Aurelius see me, and wait on me, and I won't talk about it. A husband who is going to be

a father can stand all that. What's the use of pretend-
ing? Or of drama? It isn't a miracle, it's a bore. It
doesn't take courage—it takes patience. They talk about
suffering and how much women suffer. Suppose they
do. When I was in Paris I worked in a hospital in the
last year of the war. I was fourteen—but I looked a
lot older. I don't believe the women suffer so much as
those men suffered. Not nearly. And the men were hurt
for no reason or purpose. That must make a difference.
Anyway, suffering never amounts to anything except
while it lasts—and when it's happening, I always feel
sort of dead and distant."

"I wasn't worrying about that, in any case."

"Of course you weren't. I don't know. They talk
a lot about the nine long months. Did you ever have to
earn your living? To support yourself? Entirely? Every
day? Did you ever have to support two people—working at a job you pretended to like in order to bear it,
for people you felt were your inferiors, and never daring to stop? Making money—just making money—is
something that most women don't understand. There
are exceptions. Prunish women that earn money. Lots
of it. But their sex makes them conspicuous and gives
the thing interest. I'll bet men would trade pregnancy,
pains and all, sometimes, just for the pleasure of staying out of the office—except for the fact that they're
men and have a great deal of natural courage—as well
as bravado. I'm not talking about thick-skinned, insen-
sitive people, mind you. They don't count. They're
workers, and not at all interesting or important to

humanity. The great masses. There are always great masses and there always will be. It's the few who can feel things enough to want to change them that are interesting. Did you ever cry because the gas-man was mean? A man wouldn't do that. Never. But I've seen Aurelius getting his nerve up to bawl out our gas-man, and it took so much honest grit that I hurt inside. Sometimes I'll bet they have little aches and nuisances just as we do—only they're not soft. They never say anything about it. I've seen Aurelius get cross and wondered what was the matter and found out eventually that he had a fever of three degrees—and that he hadn't given himself enough attention even to know it! Can you imagine a woman with three degrees of fever and not knowing it? Whenever I've seen the feminists out campaigning and all dressed up in male clothes, with jutty chins and hard eyes, I laugh. Little things make the difference. Last night a centipede got into our house. I was positively hysterical. I couldn't move. And don't imagine I'm going to stop talking about things like that just because you're pregnant. Aurelius hopped up and squashed it. There wasn't any paper and it was near me, so he used his bare hand. Afterwards he went out in the bathroom and was sick. Awfully sick. I couldn't help hearing him. He came back and said: 'Damn it, I got soap in my mouth and choked. Did you hear me?' I could have cried. But what could I say? Just 'Did you?' or something like that. He'd have been furious if I'd intimated the truth. I think that's why he went out this morning. He had to work it off some way, and he knew

I knew. Women'll do things like that—sometimes, some women. But that's what I mean about them. Nine months three or four times in a life is getting off pretty easily."

Cynthia thought about that. She could imagine Thornton in the same circumstance. He, too, would jump up and kill the centipede with his bare hand. He, too, would probably be sick. And he, too, would be angry at her afterwards. Men were like that. Good men. She walked back to Nadine's house. The peace that Murray had disrupted was restored.

12

That evening, acting on Nadine's suggestion, she approached Thornton indirectly. He was sitting in the deep chair in the corner, where he always sat. The room was strewn with the pages that he had written. She came from the outdoors, cold and red-cheeked. He kissed her. His lips felt feverish. His eyes were bright. A day of steady concentration had made him taut and nervous. His let-down was slow. He strummed his guitar to assist the process. She took off her wraps. The blue coat that they had bought together. The hat to match, which had been an extravagance.

"I've been with Nadine all day," she said. "I'm crazy about her."

"Nice girl." Um-boom-boom. Um-boom-boom.

"She has a faculty for putting you at ease with the whole world."

"Yes." Um-boom-boom.

"Say, Thornton—?"

Um-boom-boom. Um-boom-boom. "What?"

"I want to have a child."

The playing stopped. "A baby?"

"Yes." She watched him. He snuggled the guitar as if to begin again, hesitated, and said: "Go ahead."

Then she wished that she had told him she was going to have a child. His answer meant nothing. It was a polite phrase, a casual indulgence. He had not considered, emotionally, that she had any intention of having a child. He was playing again contentedly.

"That's not quite what I mean."

He stopped a second time. "What do you mean, then?"

"I mean—please listen, Thornton. This is terribly important." He smiled. "I mean that I'm already having one and that I want it."

"Oh."

He made his face impermeable to his reaction. It was unkind, she thought. He sat there, tired and dimly flushed. At last he laid his guitar on the floor. Every moment seemed long and tremendously important to her. She watched him constantly. He stood, turned his back, thrust his hands into his pockets. She was afraid that he would be sentimental. And Thornton, facing the darkened street, was inclined to be sentimental until he remembered how Cynthia distrusted sentimentality.

He recognized a crisis. If Cynthia had a child, she would probably be his forever, as long as he lived. That was the thing towards which he had been patently struggling. Faced with it, he was astonished by the rush of doubts that accompanied it. No other women for him afterwards. No other life. Cynthia always near him, knowing his secrets, piercing the veil of his subterfuges, directing his life and demanding it. And the child. The child would grow and become a person and sap his energy. He would have to stay sober and work hard. He could never be the Lothario, Don Juan, carefree, desirable, and handsome bachelor he had set out to become when he entered college, he had so nearly become in New York. The familiar form of Cynthia would be more and more familiar. No erotic adventure would be possible to him. Those were all selfish thoughts, of course. But a human being should insist on some selfish rights. Perhaps. With a start he realized that his back had been turned for several minutes and that Cynthia was still waiting for his answer. He perceived the trouble he had made for her and him by not answering spontaneously. He turned. She was lying on the bed with her face covered.

"I had to think," he said lamely. "It never occurred to me before."

Cynthia was trying to imagine Nadine, what she would say and do and how she would behave. She was sure Thornton did not want the baby. She felt him sit beside her, felt his hands.

"I wanted to think about you and me—about our

207

whole life together. Having a baby will change it, make it permanent."

"Not necessarily—if that's what you want."

"Listen, Cynthia." His voice was so deep and tender that she sat up, wondering. "That's just what I don't want. I love you, Cynthia."

"Let's not talk about that. It's your answer to everything, good and bad."

"Rightly my answer, perhaps. But I don't want us bound together just because of a child. Do you see? I'm not afraid you're doing it to keep me. I wish I could think that. If we have a child, I want it because we want a child—and for no other reason. As for me, I never thought of children very much. But there is nothing in life that I'd sooner be than the father of your and my child. That's all I have to say."

In those few sentences the very best of Thornton had emerged. She held him tightly. Her mind was confused, but in that riot of thought and feeling she recognized the capacity for a great happiness. She clung to him and kissed him and they did not speak. He had offered the very best that was in him simply, unassumingly, and without the pretensions he usually gave to his deeds. She knew that nothing more could be asked of a human being.

BABES AND SUCKLINGS

13

Soon after that the fact was common property. They felt no urge to conceal it. Time would make it evident, even if they had. The reactions of their friends were surprisingly violent to them. They had imagined that they would be congratulated, or treated with a sort of diffidence. But they became the center of all conversation and attention.

Later in that same evening Aurelius dashed up their stairway. In the excitement of the news, he had forgotten his oddly motivated pique at Nadine. "Heard about the child," he said at once. "Great! Splendid! Wonderful! Going to have one myself as soon as possible. Congratulations! Haven't been more surprised or pleased since I came to town. Makes me young. Makes me believe in humanity. Nadine wants you over there tonight. Couldn't come. Too cold. Get your things on. She's making supper. Magnificent!"

Perry Breck, who had become an occasional and staunch friend of both of them, called a few days later to apologize for bringing his wife to their house.

"I had to take her," he said. "Knew you wouldn't get along well together. But I thought you'd stand it as a favor to me."

"I think she was nice," Cynthia said loyally. "She tried to be just as nice as she knew how."

"She is good at heart." Perry looked at Cynthia

209

approvingly. "Just—isn't aware, that's all. You were mighty nice to her. She doesn't see people like you often. Still talks about it."

"Bring her again." Cynthia felt well disposed towards all the world. She told Perry about herself.

He took a chair and played indolently with his stick. "Well, you two, I wish you luck. I'm glad you're doing it, in a lot of ways. And I'd like to say something. If you get stuck later on—any way at all—money—doctors—anything—don't hesitate to let me know. Who is your doctor, by the way?"

"Well—" Cynthia glanced embarrassedly at Thornton—"we have a friend. Just out of medical school. Awfully nice boy. Went to high school with Thornton. He's starting in—and we go to him."

"May I make you a present?"

"Why—yes," she said.

"I'm going to send you to a man I know. Specialist. Maternity doctor. You've got to promise to let him take care of you."

Cynthia's eyes shone. Her baby—the baby for which she had desired the very best chances. What would Thornton say? He was looking at Breck wistfully. "If you'll promise to let me pay back every cent," he mumbled.

"Sure." He ignored their exchange of glances and, more touched than he cared to show, pounced on a telephone book. "Here's his address. Best man in the country. You can pay me, Thornton—but not a cent until the baby's a year old. Gotta go. See you soon."

"God Almighty!" Thornton said, when the door had closed. "And I socked that bird on the jaw."

"It ought to teach you a lesson."

"It does," Thornton said, and left the room percipitately.

14

Gerry was scandalized. "You mean you're going through with it, and you aren't married? I'm surprised. The poor child! It isn't fair to him. Why he'll be a—" The enormity of the notion silenced her.

Nadine, who was present at the telling, came as close to a grin as her dignity permitted. "It won't be able to protest—at that age."

"At what age?"

"Oh—one, or six months."

"I think it ought to be stopped. I think the S.P.C.C. ought to do it if no one else will. It's against the law. Why, it's unthinkable. I don't understand you, Cynthia."

"My, my," Thornton said. That shifted her invective.

"How about you? Aren't you a man? Can't you do anything at all?"

"I've done what little I can."

She rose, speechless. Nadine observed her departure as one watches the going of an ant. "Well," she

211

said. It made an end to the business. The trio laughed uproariously.

But Gerry was by no means through. A committee of ladies called on Cynthia "to investigate her living-conditions." They were very curious, but very indirect. Cynthia let them in. Thornton was at work. "And are you the young lady's husband?" the leader inquired, after they had passed Cynthia, leaving her speechless, and examined the apartment with cordial criticism. Thornton had watched them like a panther, ready to spring, his eyes moving from the startled Cynthia to the meddlesome women.

"I don't see what business it is of yours," he said in a tone that would have warned anyone who knew him.

"We are the field committee of the Society for Moral and Social Betterment," the woman said.

Thornton, numb with outrage, could not conceive of anything sufficiently fearsome to express himself. He gulped. They were all in the room, peering and moving about. Four of them. He counted.

"We understand," the woman said, "that you two are—ah—are—not properly united."

"Who told you?"

"Ah—we were informed—through a newspaper."

Then Thornton rose. His face was livid. He stood in front of the aggressive, simpering female. "Get out. Go. Leave." His tongue found itself. "If a crowd of lewd, filthy maggots crawled into my house I should be gladder to see them. I should rather live in hell forever

212

than see one of you again. I hate you. I spit on you.
You stink. Get out of my house before I tear the clothes
from you and grind you up. You make me crazy. You
insult my wife and me. You are dirtier than pigs, more
loathsome than slugs. You, with your louse-ridden,
queasy, prurient minds, your itching fingers and itching bellies, you flabby old fools. Get out of my house,
I tell you."

"We'll call the police," one of them shrieked.
"We'll have you locked away."

"I never heard such language."

"I haven't used a word that isn't in the dictionary," Thornton responded with a fanatical wrath. "But
I will. By God, I'll call you such names as you really
are. Smut-mungering, low-living termagants, shrews,
busy-bodies, vixens. Get the hell out of here!"

They left. Thornton would have followed them into the street, but Cynthia restrained him. They closed
the door. Cynthia called Nadine with a nervous voice
and told her what had happened. Aurelius came over
at once. He found them laughing weakly. They were
worried about the possible aftermath of the intrusion.
The courts could be ugly in such matters, even to the
violated.

"I'll fix that," Aurelius promised. He was, apparently, as good as his word. They never heard from the
Society for Moral and Social Betterment again, and
they were disturbed by no other public-minded or pub-
lic-functioning body.

Of course there was no way of proving that Gerry

had been responsible for the interference. It was even possible that she had not. There are women in every community eager to make others miserable, to threaten and cajole and reprimand and manage, to leave ruin and dispose of the blame by charging it to those who had been devastated. Nevertheless, Thornton was convinced that the four horrid apparitions were due to her indignant agency. He never hated anyone more than he hated Gerry. But when she heard the story, she acted so naïvely about it that he could not be sufficiently certain for the wreaking of an awful but undetermined vengeance.

15

In the ensuing weeks Gerry passed through a gamut of psychological derangements that made her wholly pestiferous. After a few days she ceased to be scandalized, at least superficially, and called on Cynthia regularly. The first item in her mental processional was a morbid interest in birth and the stages related to it. She poured midwives' tales into Cynthia's ears. While Thornton wrote more earnestly and with more incentive than he had ever had, Gerry came and went, babbling the undammed deluge of her monstrous misinformation.

No subject lends itself to greater distortion. And Gerry had accumulated a full measure. She dilated upon pain and anguish, upon the obscure and untractable maladies of the mother, upon fevers, rashes, sores, boils, cankers, varicosis, upon hospitals and lying-in, upon the bizarre malformations that overtake the unborn, and the monotony of the entire procedure. Occasionally Thornton overheard morsels of her gossip.

"I don't see," he would say to Cynthia, "why you listen to such rubbish."

"If anything makes me calm, it is to see her in such a state. You would think she was having the child."

The climax of Gerry's state arrived when she called on them in frenzied fear. "I'm going to have a child, too," she said.

Cynthia looked at her with amazement. "You?"

"I. I am going to be a mother."

Thornton slammed a dictionary on the floor. "See here, Gerry," he said, "don't you think this assininity has gone far enough?"

"Why—what do you mean?"

"I mean, I think you're a sap and a moron and—" but Cynthia held her finger over her lips.

"Have you seen a doctor, Gerry?" she asked.

"No. But I'm going to."

"I would."

Gerry went to see the doctor, but the doctor did not know. Three days passed. Then Gerry came with other and more personal details. Things had happened to her. Dreadful things that happen to unlucky women. She was not going to have her child after all. She discussed that misfortune as loudly as she had prated on the ills and tribulations of maternity. But she was careful not to let Thornton be a part of her audience. At last even

Cynthia's patience was exhausted and whatever spring of satisfaction she had found in Gerry's hysteria dried up. She sent Gerry home.

"I don't wonder," she said to Thornton, "that women go a little mad when they're in this state."

"You shouldn't have listened to her at all, darling."

"It did me good—until I got sick of it."

16

The last, and logically the last, for they had not heard from him for some time, was Murray Dean. He learned of Cynthia's condition through an aside of Don's. It was Murray's idea to stay away from Cynthia and Thornton and that idea was rooted in two reasons. He wanted to test his own feeling for Cynthia and he wanted to give the leaven he had set to work an opportunity to increase and grow. When he had last seen them, they were dissatisfied with each other and their condition. Murray Dean would have denied promptly that he was either subtle or scheming. And yet he was both and diabolically ingenious at both subtlety and intrigue.

Murray Dean was tall, and acid-thin and hawk-nosed. His manner was highly civilized. He had never been married. He talked well. His education was broad. He had spent a number of years in Europe and in Asia. His basic attitude towards women was one of contempt, seizure, and flattery. He was interested in his business only because it made him a great deal of money. He was known to be rapacious, suspected of being unscrupulous, and was obviously clever. There were few better advertising agencies than Dean and Payson. Payson was his foil. A genial, innocent, plodding Babbitt. Dean's only vice and relaxation was woman. And, in his case, it was vicious. He had never entertained any conception of love. His first experience was sophisticated and deliberate.

It would be wrong to describe him, or any other member of contemporary New York society, as sinister. Poisonous would not do. Nor would dangerous, because women no longer believe that any men are dangerous. Many people think that is because they are not beaten any more. He had cold, blue eyes, long hands, and an affability that disguised him. He was a man of singular vitality and stamina. He considered depravity an intimate art. And he had decided to want Cynthia. No other expression would describe his attitude.

As a commercial superior he was stern and impersonal except when sentiment or emotional display served his ends to better advantage. He was the sort of man who would have a mistress, require everything of her, pay her well, and leave her with the feeling that she was detestable—unless she had a stronger personality, which was unlikely. He read widely, was an amateur athlete, and considered himself a unique and very nearly perfect human being, both mentally and biologically. Perhaps he was.

When four weeks had elapsed, during which he had refrained from communicating with Cynthia, he said to Don: "By the way, how's Cynthia?"

Don considered that he had been negligent not to tell Murray about her. He was not a talebearer. "Why —I suppose you know that she is going to have a baby."

Dean's eyebrows lifted a fraction of an inch. "I hadn't heard. Must look her up." His fingers drummed on his desk-top. "Thornton's, I suppose."

"Oh—of course."

"Well, well. Say—never mind."

Don left the inner office without noticing that his words had made a profound effect. A surprise such as he had never had in his life was already fomenting in Dean's mind.

17

On the day after, Dean strolled towards his desk. "I say, Don," he began, "if you aren't doing anything for lunch, should you like to take it with me?"

"I surely should." Don was excited. Dean had taken him to lunch but twice—once when he was going to get a raise; again when a very difficult business situation required a tactful duplicity on Don's part. Lunch with Dean was always full of moment.

At one o'clock they sat facing each other across the table of a very exclusive club. Dean ordered cocktails.

218

They had never taken a drink together before. Dean did not believe in drinking—except on rare occasions. At least, that was the impression he had created in the office. Don thought of his party with Cynthia and Thornton as such a rare occasion. They consumed three cocktails before the soup was served.

Then Dean began. "I brought you here today, Don, because I have some rather important things to say to you."

Don murmured and he went on. "How long have you been here now?"

"Three years."

"Exactly. And you've done well. You handled several things as well as I could have handled them myself."

Don made a disparaging gesture. "Don't belittle yourself," Dean said. "You have and you know it. The only worth-while man is the one who is aware of his own value. Well, as I've watched you work, I've made plans for you. Some day—and the day is not far away—" he spun his empty glass on the table-cloth—"I am going to get out of the advertising business."

"Get out?" Don echoed.

"Why, yes. It has made a comfortable fortune for me. I'd keep the company and draw profit—nominally —of course. But it needs a head, a manager, a new executive. Payson is good at routine. But he has no ideas. He lacks your insight in business."

Don perceived what Dean was suggesting. He became confused and stammered. "Why—I'm—"

219

BABES AND SUCKLINGS

"I know. You're young and you've never had any experience elsewhere. But you have remedied that. I think you could step into my shoes today and fill them competently. As a matter of fact, the business runs itself. You know that. It needs the appearance of an iron hand, rather than the iron hand itself. And, in the next few months, I'm going to boost you through. It may be a bit bewildering. But you'll make it. You'll have to change your friends—slowly, of course. In the end you will be in the position where I am now."

"But do you think I'm capable?" Don was overwhelmed. The idea of such a dizzy accession was one he could not incorporate at once. "I'm not even thirty yet. I—"

"That is immaterial. I say you can—and I am seldom wrong."

Then Don wanted to thank him. "I don't see why you chose me. You owe me nothing. I can never repay you. I've done nothing to deserve it. I'm not a—a—relative, a friend. Why, I'm a stranger. At least, I was until you came here with me today."

Dean eyed him narrowly. The time and the opportunity for which he had played were at hand. "Don't think about that. I'd rather have you in my place than anyone I know. Your salary, of course, will be made commensurate at once. You will need it for your new life. I'll see about getting you into the right clubs. Oh, Pierson!" He raised his voice slightly. "Let's have a bottle of that 1911 Chablis. Or is it 1909?"

There was a pause while the wine was brought

reverently and poured, a pause while Don's fuddled mind tried to collect itself. "That's about all," Dean resumed. "I know you'll succeed."

"I don't know how to—"

"Don't mention it, dear boy." Dear boy. What was he driving at? Don thought with sudden suspicion. "There is—" he hesitated and did not speak.

Politeness demanded that Don say: "Yes?"

"There is one trivial matter—and very delicate—in which you might help me. But perhaps not. You may think me a fool."

"Of course not. Anything I can do—"

Dean smiled. "Well, I'm afraid it will sound like an absurd and unethical confession. I scarcely know how to broach it. But the fact of the matter is, bluntly, that I'm rather keen—very keen about—" He paused while Don's heart leaped in the expectancy that the next words would be "your wife." They were: "Cynthia, lovely, blonde Cynthia."

Don was shocked—more shocked than the mention of his wife would have made him. "Cynthia?" he repeated.

"Yes."

Don's mind fumbled and groped. "But—but she's already—allied. And she is going to have a child. And—"

"I know." Dean was sad for a moment. "Just the whim of a slightly shop-worn gentleman." Then he was savage. The wine stirred him. "But I tell you, Shaw, I'm crazier about that girl than about life itself. I want her. I must have her. I'd give anything I possess—everything I possess for her. She's beautiful. She's tall and blonde and slender and composed and wise and cool. Cool, Don. Do you know what it is to have a cool woman who is fire inside? That is the sort of women they brought prisoner for thousands of miles and threw at the feet of haughty Persian kings. Helen was like that. Cleopatra was like that. And she is wasting herself on that preposterous dreamer." He became calmer. "Oh, I'm not a poet and I'm not an artist, yet I know what they must feel. You know it, Don. A woman comes into the lives of all of us. The woman. And we will go over mountains, through rivers, through hell to get that woman. I feel that way about her. She is the priceless gem that has been tossed into my life. Our saner self cautions us, reminds us of the proprieties of society. But what are obstacles, what are other men, babies, alliances, except whets to make our appetites keen and our purposes sharp and strong? I can make no brief to justify that. I put myself in your hands with the confidence. Thinking about her drives me mad. She was built for the finest things of life. She contents herself with the meanest. I'd give her a castle, the cities of the earth, diamonds—I'd be the sort of lord her heart requires. I'd save her from strife and penury and the disfigurements of old age. It is a man like me that such a woman needs. But what? She does not love me. She is held by youthful infatuation. That is all. Go to their home and watch them. The merest intrusion of outside influences sets them quarreling. That is not romance.

That is not love. That is not the life for which she was destined." The tempo of his voice died then. "I know that I have outraged you, bored you, perhaps. But I could not refrain from confiding in the man who would be closest to me in the years to come."

Don did not know what or how to think, what to expect. He lit a cigarette and extinguished it at once. "It was not outrageous—it was rather—magnificent," he said.

Dean slumped back in his chair. He had won the first victory. The rest would be easy, particularly because it would require no emotional acting, but only the subtleties in which he dealt so effectively. "Perhaps. Perhaps. It is as true and clean a passion as I have known. For a long month I have fought against it. But I am sure to lose. Against the spell of the one woman, you invariably lose. But what shall I do?"

"I don't know," Don answered with the precise truth.

"Should you despise me—suppose I am interested only in your respect—should you despise me if I courted her?"

"Why—no. I suppose not."

"All's fair—" Dean said lightly.

"It must be."

"To take any worth-while girl, one must take her away from another."

"That's right," Don admitted, heartened. He drank his glass dry and it was refilled promptly.

"Would you help me?"

"I—I—I don't see much I can do."

"Suppose—suppose you talk to your wife. She'd be a help with Cynthia and with Thornton, too."

Don saw the direction of his mind and swallowed hard. "I'm afraid—"

"I could, of course, talk directly to Gerry," Dean said casually.

Don's mouth was compressed. "I'll talk to her. I—we'll see what we can do."

"It will be best for Cynthia in the end."

"Yes."

"It would be easier—for me and for them—if the elements for disquietude which every alliance contains were allowed to mature. In my eyes, it is only a question of time before that will take place normally. That is where I counted on you. It sounds unfair superficially. But it is not, when you consider the end rather than any particular means."

Don realized that he was drunk. The image of Dean receded and drew near. "Yes," he said again. "I've got to get back to the office."

Dean smiled. "You need not return today." He rose and extended his hand. "Nothing about this, of course, except to Gerry. I'm mighty glad to have poured myself out in such a way. It relieves me. And I am more than glad to see that you understand."

He was gone. The waiter was helping Don into his coat. He found himself in the street. Snow was falling. Faces turned whitely towards him in the dingy light. Strange faces. "Poor Thornton," he said. He found a

224

speakeasy. Drank. Walked again. Dean had wanted to talk to Gerry himself. He shuddered. What task would he insinuate for her? Don could imagine. Warmed by his last drink, he walked rapidly. The best thing to do would be to throw up his job, to tell Dean what he really thought of him, and then to make a clean confession of it to Thornton and Cynthia. If it were not for Gerry, he would do precisely that. Better make no rash decisions while the alcohol fired him. The morrow would still be time enough.

"Poor old Thornton," he repeated to himself. He spent some time trying to persuade himself that the feat was impossible. Cynthia would never go away for Dean. She was too much in love. It was absurd, fantastic, vainglorious on the part of Dean. Silly, libidinous old man. Notional. Cracked. But it might work.

Gerry would be glad. Don knew that she had always been vexed by Thornton's love for Cynthia. Gerry called her blonde and dumb. Gerry hated her, hated her looks, her peace, her ease of gesture, everything about her. Gerry would be glad. The thought made Don want to swear. But he could not swear aloud on the street among those people. Never. They'd lock him up in Bellevue. He went home and told Gerry.

"I think that's wonderful," she said. "Thornton could never do any real creative work tied to her. Cynthia wants money—you can see that. Otherwise she wouldn't drive him so hard. Now she can get it. Dean is a genius. And a philanthropist. We'll help all we can."

Don allowed himself to be persuaded.

BABES AND SUCKLINGS

18

Spring triumphed at last over the relapses of winter. The air was warm and kindly. All day Thornton worked and Cynthia sat near by, watching, waiting. In the evening they would walk, slowly, through the park, down to the river, back again, and to bed. The meanest pedestrian recognized her condition and its exigencies of night strolling. They did not mind the smiles, malicious or friendly. It was spring.

Their financial state was their only worry. Thornton's book had been finished, but he could find no publisher for it. His stories had sold fairly well, but they had been under heavy expense. And, in the spring, they were going to move to a larger apartment. That would mean more money. Perry Breck had kept his promise and paid for the best doctor that could be found. But their slender savings account had not undergone the healthy growth that they had anticipated. Thornton redoubled his efforts when, in March, they realized that more than half of their time had been dissipated.

The result was to make him irritable and petulant from sheer overwork. But it did not increase their earnings appreciably. In fact, when March had fled gustily and April was in its place, letters from and interviews with editors made it clear that Thornton would profit by a vacation, a rest, a complete forgetfulness. Cynthia's courage, about which he troubled himself more than his own, did not flag during the weary months. She kept up his confidence in himself. And, although he grew to hate the formulas of love and danger and victory that brought checks for the transcribing, he did not falter.

Aurelius and Nadine, discussing it privately, expressed amazement at his tenacity and Cynthia's indomitable goodwill. Gerry and Don, on the other hand, were very discouraging. More discouraging even than Dean, who had said openly that the only safe step for them to take in his opinion was to return to advertising and obliterate even the wish to write for five years or ten years. But Thornton's independence, once asserted, was the strongest factor in his life. He would not go back to a desk and an exhausting routine until every other hope had been swept away.

Dean troubled him, and Dean troubled Cynthia because of his effect on Thornton. He would drive down town to their apartment two and three times each week with flowers and huge boxes of candy, with light chatter of the world in which he lived—to all intents out of pure unselfishness and a desire to be helpful. But when Thornton caught him off guard with his gaze on Cynthia (a thing Dean was careful to let him do), he tugged nervously at his pale hair, and his mind knew an oppression that lasted long after Dean departed.

After his visits Cynthia would be particularly lively. That was natural. Since the first of the year she had scarcely moved from the house for anything but the most essential errand. Talk of hockey games and fêtes and coming-out parties reminded her that some day her confinement would end and she could come and go as she pleased. But it made Thornton feel that he had foisted upon her a situation which she sometimes regretted. Whenever either of them tried to right those circumstances, it always buried them deeper in a quicksand of small doubts.

"Wasn't it grand of Murray to bring these things?" she would say.

"Yes. It was. He didn't make you restless, did he?"

Cynthia would turn sharply towards him. "What makes you ask that?"

"Nothing. Only—you must be unhappy."

She would resent that. Why couldn't he assume that she was really happy, happy with a deep, internal, perpetual bliss? "Does that mean you're unhappy?"

"Of course not."

"Sometimes," she would say moodily, "I wish we hadn't decided to go ahead. When you are like that, I wish it."

"Like what?"

"Oh—never mind."

"Don't be angry with me."

"I'm not angry."

Silence. Then the gradual beginning of a new typewritten line and the chatter of the little keys as they tried to make money for the baby that was coming so inexorably. He would write, then, ready to weep, tired, harried, until she would stand beside him and kiss his head. Then they would be reconciled. But there would

be minute, gnawing memories. Often they sat separately and wished that Michael had not died. He would have
prevented those misunderstandings. In such a situation
he would have been constant and magnificent. But he
was nothing. Ashes in a jug.

19

May. When his back was turned, she would wonder
for hours just how much she loved him, just why she
was doing such a thing for him. He had retreated to a
sphere that was quite his own. He complained no more,
he railed against nothing. He wrote from habit, with
mechanical fingers and mechanical ideas. Sometimes
they sold and more often they did not. He had given
up trying to place his book himself and turned it over
to an agent. He talked no more about a second book.
He was always serious, sober. She had not heard him
laugh for a long time. Was he envisioning already the
suffering that would be hers? Did he regret the responsibility he had undertaken? She could not tell. They
had given up trying to probe each other's minds. It resulted only in misunderstanding. Her one refuge lay in
the thought that, on the day she brought back the baby,
he would discard his tribulations and preoccupations.
There was in that return an old necromancy which had
always had an effect on men, whether they were sentimental or cold and reasoning. Oddily, she could not be
sure to which class he belonged. Yet she felt that she
knew him thoroughly.

BABES AND SUCKLINGS

20

In July she began to count the probable number of days and nights. Two weeks passed. It could not be much longer. Everything was ready, planned, prepared. They had gone through it like a rehearsal. Then, one morning, she could stand the typewriter no more. Thornton's first intimation of that was the crash of a dish upon the floor. It lay there, spilling salad and tomato juice on the carpet. Cynthia stood over the mess. Her hands were clenched. Her eyes flamed. He blenched.

"What's the matter, honey?" he whispered.

For a long time she did not answer. Then her voice came, icy, direct. "I can't stand it any longer, Thornton."

"Stand what?"

"You. Not you. The writing. The typewriter. For two weeks I've thought I was going crazy. For months all I've heard is the clicking of those keys. On and on and on until I thought I'd go crazy. Now I guess I have gone a little crazy. But I can't bear it. I'm sorry. If you could only know what I mean. I get so that, when you hesitate, I want to scream—and when you go on writing again, I can scarcely keep from bursting out in hysterics. You can't imagine how I've fought against it. But it's no use. If you write another line in this place—one word—on that machine, I'll throw myself out the window."

BABES AND SUCKLINGS

It was unreasonable. That very typewriter was the only thing that stood between them and ruin. He had no other place to go. He could not stop. And he did not want to write any more. It would have given him more pleasure than anything else in the world to leave that machine. It would have been like taking a victim from the rack, undoing the cords, setting him in a soft bed; or like the withdrawal of the splints from beneath tortured finger-nails.

"I have to write," he said softly, unargumentatively.

"Not any more. Go somewhere else. I can't stand it." She was still on the verge of madness.

Thornton rubbed his brow. He could understand that, after all, and it was not an unreasonable request. For a pregnant woman she had been remarkably controlled and calm. "I guess that can be arranged. I'm sorry. I wish you had told me before."

Then Cynthia unloosed a torrent of tears. She sobbed irreconcilably. She took herself to task for being so mean. He held her and caressed her. She looked at herself and wept afresh. They were quite sad for an hour, and, after it had passed, gayer than they had been for a long time. Thornton did not write any more that day.

BABES AND SUCKLINGS

21

Gerry came to see them after supper. Thornton hated her for her intrusion, but Cynthia had tolerated her, and he humored Cynthia. It would have been still worse if they had had no friends at all. And they had given up all their casual acquaintances because of Cynthia's innate modesty and because she felt that such friends would not care to see her at that time. It was hypersensitive of her to be so drastic, but that, too, Thornton understood.

He asked Gerry if she knew anyone who had an apartment vacant during the day-time. After she had gone, he interrogated himself and decided that the question had been wholly naïve. But Cynthia was hurt by the request. She knew instantly what the answer would be. Still, she could not stand the typewriter any longer, and Gerry was something of a friend, and she would never win Thornton permanently from her. Perhaps Thornton had a right to ask it of Gerry. In a more barbaric civilization, in an Eastern civilization, she could have expected nothing else. Cynthia was broad-minded. While she was hurt, she shrugged and entered into what followed. Things were muddled, at best, and only time would redeem and straighten them. The interval could take care of itself. Better Gerry, she thought, than someone she did not know.

Gerry said: "You poor morons! Why didn't you

bring that up long ago? For that matter, why didn't I think of it? It must be miserable for you two to be cooped up in one room together all day and night. And—oh dear—I'm ashamed of myself." She smiled at them. "I have five rooms and not one of them in use at all for the whole day long. All you have to do is to move your typewriter. We'll do it tomorrow."

Thornton was surprised. He looked guiltily at Cynthia. But she had already conquered her emotions and was inscrutable. "That's very nice of you," she said. And, when Gerry was going home, flushed, excited, full of invitation and kindness, Cynthia added: "Be good to my boy-friend. He doesn't like to be disturbed."

Thornton tried to protest. "I don't believe I can stand working in her house. Can't we think of someone else?"

"It will be good for you. And I shan't mind. I'm not jealous of you, Thornton."

"I wish to God you were."

That was the nearest approach to a promise and an explanation that she would permit him.

"You don't have much fun any more, do you?" she said quietly. He wondered if her meaning was more than its literal sense conveyed.

22

Thornton brought his typewriter in a taxi-cab and rang her bell with considerable misgiving. She opened the door. It was what he had expected. Gerry's black hair ran down her shoulders in rivulets. She wore a crimson dressing-gown and mules that matched it. He was given a glimpse of nakedness beneath. She said that she was sorry not to be dressed. She cleared a table for him. He wanted to laugh and he was also frightened.

He interested himself immediately in the business of preparing the tools of his labor. She stood close by, watching him. She explained that Don had gone to work, that Don approved of the arrangement. She laughed. He made a grunting sound that might have been laughter.

An hour passed. He commenced to be conscious of what he was writing, to be interested in it, even. His preliminary fear was ebbing. He forgot Gerry. Then, suddenly, he felt her hands over his eyes. She had slipped close behind him. He realized that she had been watching him silently during that hour.

"Don't you ever stop?" she said.

"No." He tried to write again.

"Well, you'll stop when you're under my supervision. Stop—and relax, too."

It was useless to try to go on. She held his hands. "One hour at a stretch is enough—even for a genius," she proclaimed.

Thornton smiled. He was trying to pass off the situation. A very uncomfortable dread of himself worked in his mind. "All right. What do I do?"

"Talk to me."

"Then sit down."

She sat—but in his lap. He was embarrassed. It had been so many months since another woman had been in his lap. More than a year, he thought. And, in that position, women were much the same. She was redolent of perfume. She was thinking of him as she had thought of Michael. Thornton might help her, might conquer her. She felt that what she required was conquest—but she was not averse to assisting such a maneuver. And she thought, too, of the fortune that would descend on her through her husband, through Murray Dean, if Thornton and Cynthia were estranged. She had ample motive for her actions, however shameless they may have been.

"You're a nice boy, Thornton," she said.

"I hope so."

"I think I like you—too much. Don't you like me —even a little bit?"

"Of course I do. You've been very nice to Cynthia —and me."

"I was just thinking—"

"What?" His voice was toneless. His hands were inert.

"Just thinking how hard it must be for a man when his wife is—is the way Cynthia is. And how hard you've worked. And wondering how you suddenly transformed yourself from a libertine to the most restrained gentleman in town. It isn't natural, Thornton. It isn't even good for you."

Thornton realized that it was a powerful potion which her cloying syllables had brewed. He felt like the

rich man who was almost persuaded to enter the king-
dom of heaven. The simile gave him further resistance.
She still sat on his knees, balancing herself. "It wasn't
as hard as I thought. And it was worth the trouble."

"I don't know. We're both—married. The things of
which you and I—or I, at least—were so careful don't
matter any more. They are not of any importance. It
seems to me that human beings should be kinder to
themselves—biologically—than then were before—well,
before such things lost their terror. Taking the peril
from sex will eventually make society different. And
you and I are man and woman—which is a primitive,
simple thing, basically."

Thornton thought rapidly. He had an impulse to
yield. There was no tangible reason for not yielding.
Morally, physically, socially it could make no difference, as Gerry had said. One by one she had attacked
the arguments he would form—attacked them intellectually, so that the voluptuousness behind her suggestion
was veiled. And he would relax. It was not easy for a
man in his predicament. And Cynthia had practically
consented. She had said: "Be good to my boy-friend"
with an inflection that meant much, that could be in-
terpreted. She knew what he had withstood and what
he had borne. Perhaps she had surrendered her "claim"
to a comprehension of necessities. He put his arm around
Gerry. He had forgotten that she revolted him. He did
not recall the hatred he had held for her. That familiarity was commonplace, pacific, pleasant. "You're a
wily girl, aren't you?" he said.

"You do care about me, then?"

"I don't know. Let's be honest. A man who didn't recognize your bodily lure would be stupid, wouldn't he? I can't quite find the words for my meaning—they all sound silly—"

"Why stoop to words, then, when a better expression is so easy?" She bent down and kissed him on the mouth. It was a lewd kiss and one calculated to provoke him instantly. He thought later that if she had not kissed him, the outcome might have been different. But he remembered himself, as if he had awakened when he felt that kiss. The difference would not appear. But Cynthia would know that he had made love to Gerry. He realized that abruptly. And he would never be able to think of Cynthia in quite the same way. He would feel that Cynthia had exposed him to that temptation —he already was aware that she had—but he would feel also that he had not quite measured up to her belief in him. He struggled with that premise, trying to tell himself that it was puritanical, an infantile remainder, a schoolroom inhibition, a moral delusion. Probably Cynthia would not care—or would pretend not to care. They would forget it. As his vision cleared, he saw a new obstacle to misbehavior. Gerry. Always, afterwards, she would fawn on him, she would make public expressions of their intimacy, she would seek to show ownership of him. It was a wretched and revolting thought. Perfume no longer hung in the air. His mind, stumbling towards an earnest solution of the problem, had come upon a practical solution. He picked her up, crossed the room with her, laid her gently on a couch. She closed her eyes. He lit a cigarette. The sound of the match opened her eyes again.

"Are you frightened?" she said.

"No."

"What's the matter?" Gerry's tone rose in the scale. She saw that she was going to be defeated. She thought of her own outraged person, of Murray and his intrigue. The world was treating her evilly. She wept.

23

He wrote every day at Gerry's house. She never solicited his attention again. He told Cynthia what had happened. She said very little and what she said did not make him proud of himself. He had been proud. But Cynthia, when he had gone to work on the second day, was happy, although she felt ill and lay in bed alone through the bright, hot hours.

24

At last it was August. There was suspense in the motionless heat of each sultry day. Sun belched itself from a brassy sky. The streets shimmered in it. Screen doors slammed, flies buzzed, electric fans whirred. Thornton quit work. He tended Cynthia, who stayed in bed, a hot, damp sheet pushed in fretful rolls to her feet, a picture of the ceiling burned in her eye-sockets.

Monday. Wednesday. Friday. Each day the tension increased. No one called on them. It was as if their friends were waiting for news. Aurelius and Nadine were at the beach. Cynthia wanted to see them and could not. Dean and Perry Breck were unresponsive to phone calls and messages. They did not talk. They scarcely ate.

Saturday morning. The heat was still relentless. The night had been like a night spent in an oven. Cynthia woke first. She glanced around the small world of their bedroom. Thornton, beside her, was statuesque in sleep. No lines, no vices, no sorrow in his face. Only the stickiness of the humid air. Youth and—almost—delicacy. High brow, pale hair, dark streaks under his veined eyelids, red mouth, long chin. He moved, roused himself, frowned involuntarily, and looked at her.

"Morning. How do you feel?"

"The same."

One of his feet loosed itself from the snarled sheet and found a worn carpet-slipper. He trod heavily towards the kitchenette, yawning. The smell of coffee reached her nostrils with growing insistence.

"Any cream in the ice-box?" he asked.

"Suppose you look." She heard the familiar squeak of the refrigerator door. Thornton began to whistle and stopped while he poured the coffee. At ten o'clock the boy came for the laundry. Cynthia directed Thornton's collection of soiled garments. Finally they were assembled, counted, and dispatched.

"Want to play cards?"

"No, thanks. I'll just lie here."

"Sure you're all right?"

She answered in even tones, without annoyance or rebuke: "If it weren't, I'd tell you, Thornton."

"Of course."

"Play your guitar."

It was difficult to play. Impossible to sing. "What's the matter with us this morning?"

"Nothing. Does my staying in bed upset the order of the universe?"

"No. What'll I play next?"

Eleven. "I think—" Cynthia began.

"What?"

"Never mind."

His hands were slippery on the frets. Shortly before twelve Cynthia turned on one side, stopped in the middle of the motion, and called to Thornton in a voice that was nearly normal: "Probably you'd better send for them soon."

"The—the—it's—"

"Yes. One a long time ago. Now I've had two more. I couldn't be mistaken."

Demons of fear and sympathy stabbed and jeered him. Time passed. He stared at Cynthia with an expression so agonized and intense that she begged him not to look at her at all.

They came for her, making her dress and walk

240

downstairs. She stood in the door, unalarmed, smiling. He came near her, trying to copy her valiancy. The men from the ambulance waited impersonally. He kissed her; he attempted to hold her in his arms. She shook her head. There were spectators. She was gone. The room was so empty that he could not recognize it. He wanted to fling himself on his face, he wanted to pray and weep. He recalled all the favorable reports that the doctor had made, concentrating on each one deliberately. He did not dare leave the house because they had promised to let him know by phone.

Cynthia, lying in the almost unbearable heat of the ambulance, considered the possibility of death for one frightened instant. She was swept by a wave of compassion when her mind presented the haggard features of Thornton. She wondered what difference the baby would make when she brought it to their new house. They had deferred moving until she went to the hospital. It saved rent. They had six hundred dollars. Plenty of money. Thornton might get a stroke moving alone in that hot weather. He was so careless of himself. Childbirth was just what Nadine had said. She forced herself to think about Nadine. Thinking of Thornton at that moment was too poignant. The ambulance surgeon was talking to her. His face was round, like a pumpkin. It hung over her. The ambulance blew its horn. She could feel the vibration.

Thornton sat in a chair, analyzing his sensations with meticulous precision. He had never felt more alone. He wondered if it would be morally right to take a drink. After an hour he decided that he could have one. He mixed it and poured it into a tall glass. A heat like hell filled the room. People were falling on the street. Their names would be in the next day's newspaper. And his child: Born to Mr. and Mrs.—but that could not be. His child was illegitimate. A nice slander from a nice-minded world. He took the dregs of his drink.

25

At four o'clock he put the glass on the table. He had held it for three hours. Innumerable thoughts had plagued his mind. It was a vigil calculated to strain him to the utmost—after he had already been weakened by the winter and spring and summer of waiting. He underwent a procession of abnormal emotions and daydreams. He pictured himself beating the consciousness from Murray Dean. He made love to Gerry in the same trauma. When he thought of the former, the muscles of his arms and shoulders tensed. The light was softer. He knew that he was a little crazy. He made a second drink. The first had had ample time to wear off, he explained to himself. He shut his eyes and dozed after it had been consumed. The telephone woke him. He snatched it from its dimunitive table.

"Hello?"

"Is this Grimes's studio?"

Thornton wanted to curse at the person on the

other end of the wire. He did not even reply, but shot the receiver into the hook.

Cynthia opened her eyes on a pain-maddened world, ground her teeth, and shut them again, because she did not like what she saw. She whispered Thornton's name and heard the whisper answered by the cheery tongues of her tormentors. Sweat trickled from every pore.

Thornton turned on a light. No use sitting in the dark. If Michael were only there! He saw the broad body, the relaxed arms, the red hair, the friendly black eyes. Michael! He spoke the name. Not even the hollowest response came from the ashes that were somewhere, somewhere holding a hundred dead loves forever. Thornton could see Cynthia clearly. So pellucid was his imagination that he knew the very expression her face would wear and the joints she would flex in her travail. He spat on the floor and cried.

26

An end came with the plushy darkness of midsummer evening. The phone rang again. A nurse exchanged orientations with Thornton in factual, metallic tones. He was compelled to answer correctly, carefully.

"I am afraid that I have bad news for you."

Bad news—you're what I'm waiting for. Bad news. He gave vent to a hideous, laughing sound. He was spent.

"Your baby," the voice went on arithmetically, "was born dead. Some nervous condition of your wife's. The doctor does not know precisely. It never lived at all."

Sense burst through the anarchistic chant in his mind. Bad news—you're what I'm waiting for. "Stop. To hell with the baby! What about Cynthia?"

"Oh. She's quite all right. Quite all right. Quite all right. Quite all right. Quite all right."

"When can I see her?"

"Tomorrow afternoon."

"Not tonight?"

"No."

Bang.

Thornton toppled on the bed. The telephone, which he had relinquished in mid-air, crashed on the rug, and the sound of its dial tone hummed in the room like a hornet in flight.

27

He parted the doors of the saloon and blinked in the discord of illumination.

"Double Scotch," he ordered. He drank three.

"What's the matter?" the bar-tender asked.

"Baby born dead today."

"Didn't know you had one."

"Yeah. Give me another."

"Take it easy, kid. I've lost a couple myself."

Thornton was reluctantly interested. "Have you? What did your wife do afterwards? How did she take it? That's what's making hash of me."

"Women's funny. First time she set around a whole week and wouldn't do no housework or nothin'. Finally I hands her a broom an' says: 'Sarah, you clean up this pig-pen or out you go.' Next time she says: 'God blast the luck!' Gets up in a day or so and goes out an' tanks up. Never says another word about it. The next five lives—worse luck."

Thornton nodded. His mind was very clear. "Mine's different."

"They all are."

"Yeah. Give me another."

"Best thing—I says. Tomorrow it won't look the same."

"Never does—tomorrow—does it?"

"Nope. Remember how I cleaned up one grand at the races an' lost it the next day. Went out an' drank thirty Scotches in a row. Mebbe forty. Woke up the next morning an' took three more. From that day on I didn't give a hoot in hell about the money."

"Yeah." Thornton ruminated. "Say. How long does it take a bird—bird like me—to drink himself out of the picture for good?"

"Well—" the bar-tender studied the wall—"it depends. If you tried it on beer, it would take a long time. Years. If you drank gin—an' guzzled it—you might do it in five, if you was drunk every night. This Scotch I'm sellin' would take more. If you could get

cognac—a slender bird like you—you might get somewhere in a couple. Then again you might get—soaked."

"Immune?"

The man in the dirty apron blinked. "Somethin'
like that. Ain't thinkin' of it, are you?"

"Nope. Curious."

"It ain't a healthy kind of curiosity, not by a
damn sight. I always figured a little drinkin' was good
for a man. Eases him up. But if you want to do a fade-
out, jump. Yes, sir, I always said jump. Surest and
quickest. You don't get hurt none an' God Almighty
can't stop you after you get goin.' Everything else is
risky. You might get a bad break an' come out deaf
or blind or somethin'."

Thornton's thirst commanded him again. "What's
the matter with drink? Just stay drunk until you don't
wake up."

"It's the last stages. The last stages." He paused and
reflected. "I've seen 'em yellin' an' screamin' an' hol-
lerin.' Things chasin' 'em. Climbin' up on tables to get
away from lizards an' tearin' the hide off their bellies
to get the spiders out. Never nothin' there." The solemn awfulness of that transfixed the speaker.

"I think I'm a little morbid tonight," Thornton
said.

"You probably are," the bar-tender replied vacantly.

Thornton was tired. His legs ached and trembled.
"Guess I'll sit down."

"Help yourself."

"Bring me a beer."

Business was slack. The fleshy, aproned man stood at the table. "Hear that guy you used to come in here with was murdered."

"Yeah."

"Good friend of yourn, wasn't he?"

"Yeah."

"That's the way it is. Here today an' gone tomorrow. But not many of 'em's murdered. Not many."

"Comparatively few."

"You ain't drunk, are you?"

"Not very."

"Should have stuck to Scotch. Beer's too watery. Throws up on you."

"Well, bring me Scotch and shoot the beer."

Thornton swallowed the Scotch with closed eyes. It no longer burned his throat. He was numb. His mind and consciousness were like a point of fire in a vasty void.

Cynthia awoke from a drugged sleep. She thought at once of Thornton, and with the thought of him her pain returned. She wondered what he was doing. Perhaps he had fallen asleep by that time. Did he know about the baby? Probably. She hoped that he wouldn't get drunk. Sleep came again and she dreamed of Thornton sitting before a monstrous schooner of beer, which grew and grew until it engulfed him. She moved her arms with fitful swimmings and surgings.

BABES AND SUCKLINGS

28

Thornton sat on a curb-stone. He said to himself with a thorough exaction that was in itself an emotion: "There are two possibilities which I must face. Cynthia is a delicately balanced creature. On the one hand, she will react powerfully to this tragedy. She will want to drink and dance and see other men besides me. I shall always remind her of it. That is natural. On the other, she may slowly recover. She has a strong and generous character. She may forget. She may even try again."

He spoke hundreds of inanities to himself, but through them he seemed to have a certain perception. He did not consider or even recollect the baby except as the instrument of a situation. The baby had never lived, had never been a person. It was nothing—a condition of Cynthia's health, no more, no less. And he did not consider the attitude which Cynthia would actually have. She would worry about him and what he was going to think and do, rather than about herself. If he had known that, it would have saved him all that followed her return from the hospital. But, in the struggle to be unselfish, he had forgotten that she was trying to be his, to be like him, to be equally unselfish.

Instead of meeting her with a calm smile on the next day, instead of saying that he was sorry, and they would forget and have another baby, he came to her trembling, sympathetic, a pitiful figure of a man. There was no other interpretation for her to make. She saw that the death of the baby had broken him. Each had believed that the constancy of the other depended on the baby, for the baby had meant such sacrifice, such titanic endeavor, that they could not have the faith to believe it merely an incident in a relationship of intrinsic strength and abstract immortality.

29

After he had gone, Cynthia spun the curtain-pull which she could reach through the bars of her bed. She wondered what was going to happen to her. Thornton's nervousness and alarm were a sign that he had been irretrievably shocked. He had found her insufficient. His hyper-sympathy was a token of it. His confession of drinking on the night before was evidence. It did not occur to her that he was tortured only by the same fear for her that she had for him. They had survived the death of Michael, however, and they might outgrow the estrangement brought by the death of the baby. Her hope was based on that. Michael's funeral had ushered in the same sick dreads—dreads that the blow would separate them. Thornton's actions were obliquely motivated always, and at times he could cover the motives even from her. Suppose he loved her no more. Suppose his behavior was already a pretense that covered a stark horror. He had a capacity for horror that was like Poe's. He seemed always susceptible of dissipation into madness, always looking madness in the eye. His abnormal control on the day he found Michael's body was an exhibition of that. Now she would see it again in his every kindness, his every effort to lead conversation away from herself, from the baby, from death. Death. It stared at them. And they had started out a long year ago with such ecstatic life. Perhaps she would have to leave him. He might hate her.

Cynthia sobbed weakly when she reached that conclusion. A nurse, provokingly unaware of the cause of her sobs, tried to calm her. Cynthia was driven to desparate rudeness, and the nurse thought that she was badly behaved. She gave Cynthia two white pills so that she would sleep again. A bushel of flowers from Murray Dean was tiptoed to her bedside.

30

Gerry found Thornton at Raymond's, where he was listlessly trying to keep his promise to Cynthia to eat three times a day. He was dangerously thin and his eyes were like bruises.

"I heard about it," she said with quavering tones. "We are all so sorry."

"You did?"

"I called the hospital. I called Nadine first, and she didn't know, so I called them."

250

"My God," Thornton said shortly. He had told no one. All his friends had probably called the hospital or each other. He had left the curb-stone on the night before and gone to bed. Thereafter he had lain in a trance that lasted until time to go to the hospital.

"It's too bad. We were all afraid that Cynthia was too nervous—and that it wasn't an auspicious time for you to have one. We—"

"I'd rather not have any afterbirth of ideas on this," he said. It revived him to have thought of so patent an answer. "Did you tell Nadine?"

"She called the hospital, too. We've been looking for you all day. You shouldn't be alone at such a time."

"No?"

"It makes you morose."

"Well, I don't want to be cheered up. I want to think. Think, see? That is the only thing of which I am capable in solitude. And I need solitude."

"I'll run along, then?"

"Don't jump. I'm nearly through thinking."

Gerry watched him narrowly, trying to discern the effect of his bereavement so that she could have facts to report to Dean by way of Don. All she saw was a young man fearfully distraught. That could mean nothing in so far as it reflected the relations between him and Cynthia. She dared another question. "Cynthia ought to have a change after this. You should send her away. Do you believe she'll feel the same about anything, now?"

251

A dull pain hurt Thornton. He rubbed his chest with a doubled fist. "What do you mean?"

"Only that. Losing a baby changes a woman. And she needs a vacation—even from you, Thornton."

When Gerry departed, he called on Aurelius and Nadine. They let him talk as he wished, and after he had gone home, Nadine sighed. "I hope he's over that before she gets back from the hospital."

"It's too bad," Aurelius said, "that you can't manage people by strings sometimes. He certainly is near the deep end."

"Poor Cynthia. I want to talk to her."

31

They brought Cynthia from the hospital. Already she could walk again. She exhibited her ability pridefully before they wheeled her out to the taxi-cab. He gave their familiar address. Cynthia paled.

"I thought we were going to our new apartment?"

Every nerve in his body ached. "No, honey. I didn't sign the lease. After the baby was born—I—well, I thought you'd need a vacation. So I kept the old house. With the difference, you can spend a couple of weeks in the country. I know that's what you need."

Tears came to her eyes. She wanted to lean on him, to whisper that she wouldn't leave him for anything in the world, especially then, when he was feeling so badly. But she could not. Perhaps he had arranged her involuntary vacation because he was not ready to take her back, because he wanted a vacation, because he wanted to be alone.

"You've seen too much of me," he said, after a while.

Did he mean that he had seen too much of her? She was forced into that conclusion. Couldn't he see that two weeks in the hospital had been enough of absence for her? That all she wanted was him and peace?

The cab halted at the familiar chipped brownstone steps. They got out. Thornton paid the driver. He went off without grumbling his thanks. They were poor, then. She ascended the stairs, each step hurting her vaguely.

"How nice it is to be home!" she said.

Thornton trembled. She did not think it was nice. She had said that to put him at ease. She went to bed.

"If I'm very good, may I get up after supper and go to the movies?" she asked. She thought that going to the movies together would help to re-establish their old contact.

But to him it was the indication of the scramble for forgetfulness that was overtaking her even then. "I—I don't think so. Well—if you want to."

Her eyes were like a child's. "You may kiss me the way you used to. The doctor said I was all right." It was a lie—a pleading lie.

The notion revolted him. "You couldn't, Cynthia."
Then he wanted to kiss her, but he held himself back.

Everything had gone wrong. They were like
strangers, sad strangers. Nadine came up the stairs.
But even Nadine could not prevail in that mist of
misunderstandings.

32

In the morning, after dreaming through a night of
ill-assorted mockeries, he began the business of their
awakening. The sound, the light and shadow, the scent
that came into their room were gray and chilly. The
world was like some mournful tundra of Hades that
is depressing through its sheer extent of barrenness.
He prodded into his senses the intention of cheerful-
ness.

Cynthia woke and rose. She went into the bathroom without speaking. He watched her when she
came out and took off her night-dress. The gold had
gone from her hair, and it was the hue of ashes. Her
beautiful body was wrinkled and flabby from her ill-
ness. Her hands touched her garments furtively.

"You look swell," he said.

She lifted a foot, lost her balance, and regained
it with a little stagger of pain. "Do I?"

"To me you do."

"Don't we pity ourselves too much?"

He did not answer. He untwisted the cord of the

telephone and ordered a bottle of cream from the delicatessen. The wind soughed dismally. When he came
out of the kitchen, he said: "We've gone Russian, I
guess."

A feeble hope moved her to laugher. It was a
gleam of Thornton defiant. The coffee was warm. "We
ought to write about it. 'Stay home and get morbid.
Play while you slay.'"

He glanced at her sharply, and, with a feeling that
every syllable was perilous, she broke off abruptly and
drank the coffee.

"Where shall I go?" she asked.

"Go?"

"You're going to write, aren't you?"

"I guess so."

"Don't if you don't want to."

"Oh—I want to, all right."

"I'm sick of Gerry. I guess I'll call on Nadine."

"Don't you think you'd better stay in bed?" He
shuffled the sheets of his latest story absently and
fitted a page into his machine. She called Nadine and
left the house.

Thornton, sitting alone, bent forward like an athlete ready to run and then relaxed. He repeated the
effort a dozen times. Nothing happened. His thoughts
swarmed with troubles. Out of them he tried to invent
the ending of a detective story. He hated the world and
he felt that he was a failure.

33

They were together at supper in Raymond's. Ghosts lurked in the place and she felt tired to the veins. She could not move without a bitter effort. The sight of Thornton's calf-grieving eyes and his nervous hands was as much as she could bear.

"Want to see a movie?"

"Not tonight. Let's go home and read."

"You're just trying to be nice to me."

"Thornton!"

"All right. Let's read."

She fell asleep with the first paragraph and woke up conscious that he was looking sadly at her.

34

"I guess I'd better get another job. This racket of mine won't get us anywhere." The very idea of moving from one office to another, of summoning courage and enthusiasm about himself, nauseated Thornton.

Cynthia shook her head stubbornly. "What do you say? We'll fight it out along these lines—"

"But we aren't fighting and our lines are all shot up."

"I'd like to use a very unladylike word," she said.

256

BABES AND SUCKLINGS

35

"You know" (it was late and they were sitting on the bed together; Thornton had brought sandwiches from the delicatessen), "I keep thinking about Don and Gerry. He made out well—and I swear he's not so good at it as I was. We were the same at the start —education and goodwill and nothing else. Look at him. Money—a grand home—snooty friends—"

"And Gerry."

He kissed her. "And Gerry. But you can never tell about her. She may not be so bad as he and you and I think."

"I hope you don't believe that."

"I don't. But it makes no difference. You're vastly better than she. But—look at us."

"Well?"

"Where are we?"

Cynthia shook her head. "I don't know, Thornton. I thought we were on the road to something much better than advertising and a neat apartment. Aren't we?"

"I guess you're more patient than I."

"And what is there to want on earth? Food, clothes, shelter, each other. All the rest is—just vanity."

"Each other," he repeated.

"You're sentimental tonight."

"Dotage, I guess. And fatigue."
"You do get tired, don't you?"
"Not very."

36

The wind blew freezingly over the melodious chimneys. Thornton played on his guitar. She lay very still and listened to him. "I wish we could get up a good game of bridge—but nobody comes around any more."

"It's my fault, I guess."

"Don't be so self-condemning. It's nobody's fault. We just haven't been able to be social lately. That's all."

"If we had more money—"

"Don't speak about money." She began to cry softly.

He took her hand. "I know it's boring—"

"If you apologize any more, I'll scream. Don't you realize that when you apologize, it puts the blame partly on me?"

"But I meant to take it."

"There you go. I tell you—it's nobody's fault. There isn't any blame. But what's the use—"

The chilly fingers of fear touched him and he became immobile. His tenseness was unbearable to her. If he would only relax—laugh—swear—cry! What Spartan ancestor made him in that fashion, made him believe that, at best, life was inferior? Even if that

258

view-point was correct, an illusion would be necessary. And he had stripped everything away. The very abstraction of those thoughts fretted her.

"Don't you ever get mad, Thornton? Can't you get mad?"

He was perplexed. It seemed unfair of her. She had seen him angry, and she had not liked it. What did she wish? That he should rave at the world because he was born into it impotent? "I can get mad," he said solemnly. "But not now. Not when I—"

"When you are to blame." She rocked herself.

"That isn't what I was going to say," he lied.

"Don't say it, anyway. We talk too much."

The fingers pushed and squeezed and his muscles tautened to the pressure. God! What road for deliverance?

37

Cynthia was propelled to her vacation by Thornton's insistence. She went to Atlantic City and was miserable, sitting in the sand with the noisy people on every side. At night she locked herself in her room and tried to read. If she had not met Murray Dean, who had gone there alone for a week-end, she would have been utterly wretched. But he was like a father and a brother to her. He made her laugh. He entertained her and instituted a new dominion for her regal beauty. She could almost forget Thornton when he led her into a shimmering restaurant where music played and cutlery tinkled and waiters trotted over deep carpets. His sense of propriety was all and more than she could have decreed. He sent small, amusing presents, culled from the board walk in the early morning. He allowed her one cocktail and one high-ball every evening. He stayed into the middle of the first week and returned for the second. She wrote letters to Thornton telling him how much good her vacation was doing and how glad she would be to return to him. Thornton read them and ached for her. He did not imagine that she scanned each passing face, hoping that he had relented and come for her. Gerry and Don, who had informed Dean of Cynthia's destination, went about with anticipatory smiles. Once Don drank too much and threatened to tell the truth to Thornton. Gerry missed having a fit by a narrow margin. She quivered for two days after that experience. He never attempted it again.

38

Cynthia returned. Thornton was writing in the house again. She tried through the long autumn to amuse herself. He never left his work. His love for her seemed to grow more perfunctory each day. She depended on Murray Dean for entertainment. Perry Breck was in Europe. On the first of October Don and Gerry moved up town. Their new home had six rooms, and the rent they paid was four times the rent paid by

BABES AND SUCKLINGS

Thornton. Cynthia inspected the house and came to him singing its praise. He felt it was a criticism of his ability. Then a day arrived when Thornton could write no more. He sat before the typewriter and stared. Cynthia blamed herself. She could not stay in the house while the typewriter "jittered," as she expressed it. And he, longing for her even when she was in his arms, had reached a point of nervous exhaustion beyond which he did not or could not force himself.

She found him sitting there with a blank sheet in his machine and half a story lying on the floor near by.

"What's the matter?" she asked. "Stuck?"

"All of a sudden," he said, in a melancholy, resigned voice, "I realized that there was nothing more in me to write."

She realized it was a crisis. "Don't worry, dear. It'll be all right. We've taken a beating, but we'll pull through."

His head shook on his bended neck. "I don't know what's the matter. All I want to do is to go out and get drunk."

Fear seized her then. But she said: "Go ahead, if you feel like it."

"Want to come with me?"

She wanted to go with him. "No."

"Well. I hate to be such a bum. Maybe I better not."

"Do as you please."

He went out, sure that she did not care what he did, where he went, or why. He returned at three in

the morning. She was not at home. At five Murray
Dean brought her up the stairs. They were laughing.
She laughed on and on over a trifling jest he had made
in the cab. She wanted Thornton to hear her laughing.
She could not let him know how she was suffering.
If he did not want her any more, it would be too much
to let him know that. She laughed. He beat himself
drunkenly when he heard her.

39

On Christmas Day they possessed four dollars in
the world. It bought their dinner. Lunch had consisted
of coffee. The gas was shut off because they had not
paid the gas bill. They brought two boxes from the
street and made a little fire in their grate. There were
no presents, no cards. They had made their friends
promise to do nothing for them because they could do
nothing in return. Even Murray Dean had withdrawn
a bounty that was hateful to Thornton. He knew, perhaps, what it meant to be poor on Christmas. Cynthia
wore her warm woolly dress. It was light brown and
dark brown. After dinner she took it off and went to
bed. There was nothing to do. Aurelius and Nadine
had a tree. They could not go there—with the tree
lighted and tissue and string on the floor. Thornton
read a book. He read fragments of it aloud. Cynthia
chuckled over them.

40

On the day after Christmas, and every day, Thornton looked for work. He had given up writing. He did not want to write, to be a writer. He told that to Cynthia a hundred times. She always said: "Yes, darling." But the advertising for the winter had been done. No one seemed to want him. References? Samples? He had none. He passed the eternal knot of men that watch the employment-bulletins on Sixth Avenue. He stopped and he, too, looked. Eighteen dollars a week. Eighteen dollars was a good deal of money. He commenced to think what he could do with it.

"Maybe I can wash dishes," he said to Cynthia.

She smiled. "Sure. We won't be broke for long. I sent out all your rejected stories today."

"You did? Where—" He was going to ask where she got the money for the postage.

"Borrowed it from Murray at lunch yesterday. If any of them sell, we can pay him at once. Otherwise —he can wait."

They looked away from each other. He wondered how much she had borrowed. The twenty dollars he had asked of Aurelius was half spent.

"If we sell a story, we'll be out of the woods." She had mailed each one with a short, fervent prayer.

"For the time being. But I can't do any more. I can't."

BABES AND SUCKLINGS

41

In the twilight, after a day spent searching for work, Thornton found the note. He had to light a candle to read it: "Thornton. I've gone away. I know I've been a handicap. I couldn't work or help you. Please forget all the nasty things I've done. C."

Neither of them had mentioned it. Both had foreseen it, dreaded it. He held the little paper—the only reality left of Cynthia, beautiful Cynthia, his Cynthia. He called her. The candle guttered with the issue of his voice. He began to sob plaintively.

42

Sitting on the floor of his room, in the dark, he could feel the universe beat and shudder underneath him. It had a pulse. The floor tilted and undulated.

He said: "Cynthia!"

Then he lit the candle again. He walked to the closet. Her clothes were not there. He lifted the cover of the bed. She had taken her mules. He looked into the hall. It was dimly lighted by a brown electric globe. He fainted.

When he came to, he was lying across the threshold of his own door in the spot where he had fallen. He remembered that Cynthia had gone, and tried to guess with a vacant irrelevance how long he had been in that position. The floor boards were warm where his body had been lying and cold on both sides, so he deduced that it had been some time. It surprised him to see that his mind was functioning so well. He did not consider that such an examination of minutiæ might be a symptom of mental disturbance.

He tried to light a lamp and remembered that the electricity had been turned off two days after the gas. Some stubborn impulse made him push the button, nevertheless, and he was remotely surprised when the light did not come. The bare fact that there was a bottle of gin in the kitchenette occupied him. He took the candle and carried it into that chamber. Cynthia had left an apron on the back of the door. She had forgotten it, he thought. Or else she had decided that she would not need it wherever she was going. That made him sit on the floor again. He had never been quite so weak as he was. He brought to mind a time when he had drunk so much port wine that he could not stand up. He had been forced to lie prone, spinning dizzily, and feeling as if there were a weight on his chest. His body was in the identical condition—except that he had had no port.

He tipped up the gin bottle. It was empty. Then Cynthia had been drinking before she left. A smell of gin reeked from the sink. She had poured it into the sink. She did not want his first reaction to be one of desperate, all-consuming thirst for alcohol. Well, it had not been. Not the very first reaction, at least.

BABES AND SUCKLINGS

He emerged from the kitchenette and observed the time. Six-twenty. She would be going to dinner somewhere. With Murray Dean. She would have called Murray Dean first. He walked over to the telephone. Of all the mechanical devices in the house, the phone alone still functioned. He called Dean's home. Before his call was answered, he began to smash the instrument methodically. When it was in splinters, he walked out.

43

The notion of time obsessed him. He looked at clocks. He walked for blocks at a feverish pace in order to see clocks. He imagined that they made faces at him. The hands were mouths that turned up or down, not according to any sentiment, but because they were governed by an inexorable law. The four-faced, illuminated clock on top of Jefferson Market was particularly interesting to him.

Ultimately he decided that he had seen enough clocks and that a drink was indicated. He had forgotten his coat, but he did not mind the cold. He went into the saloon and stated his decision: "A drink is indicated."

The bar-tender said something about his wife. Thornton blew his nose into his handkerchief with a tremendous noise. He drank gin. A long time afterwards two newspaper reporters whom he knew slightly

entered the saloon. They were laughing. He looked at
them with bizarre eyes. They sat at his table without
invitation. Thornton wanted to shock them. He laid
his plans meticulously. They would ask him what the
matter was. He saw the question forming.

"What's the matter with you?" one of them
asked.

"It's not today, it's tomorrow."

"Tomorrow?"

"Yes. I have to get drunk tonight, because tomorrow I have a fearful task to undertake."

The reporters looked at each other. "What is it?"

"I have to climb an ulcer. An ulcer fifteen hundred feet high. An ulcer so gigantic that the microbes
are as large as maggots. But they have eyes. And as
I climb, they fasten their toothless mouths on me everywhere. The mountain is red and white—yellow, brown,
purple. Avalanches of pus and putrefaction pour down
upon me, make my clothes sticky and nauseous and
my hands slippery with rottenness. The boulders on
it are chunks of melting, dripping flesh. Separate pus-
tules, tall as a man, burst and spread their creamy,
opaque suppuration over the hideous landscape. It can
be smelt for hundreds of miles, and for a thousand it
exerts a gangrenous influence. The abscess itself is
alive. My skidding shoes hurt it and it writhes and
palpitates with a monstrous separate existence of its
own. Blood and exudate leak through its valleys. I
must climb that mountain until I reach its awful cone
and look down in the volcanic tube where the stinking,

267

infectious essence of its malignance sucks and bubbles. Then—"

"Good God!" one of the men said. They left the table together.

Thornton chuckled.

44

As the nature and character of Cynthia had remained obscure to Thornton, so it had remained to others of their acquaintance. Michael alone had understood it, but he had communicated his intelligence to no one. Gerry knew that Cynthia was unhappy. Don saw merely that she was desirable and trustworthy, in sad contrast to his mate. Dean perceived both that she was unhappy and that she was desirable. He probed deeper than the others and discovered the seat of her discontent. He also found a courageous, practical sense of living in her. He capitalized those elements to his advantage.

On the day of her desertion Cynthia felt that a course had been forced upon her. For a week she had been reviewing her life with Thornton and she could see no alternative. It was a course she detested. One in which she anticipated each destruction, each agony. She sat before the inadequate fire in their apartment until she was compelled to retreat to her bed for warmth. There she summed up the arguments.

She knew that Thornton was wretched. Her presence deterred him from working. It had been so for many months. Without admitting it he blamed her for it. She was sure that he loved her and also sure that he loved himself more. It followed that he could never close the gap that was widening between them. They had built the bonds of their union on things rather than on each other. She wanted an equality of giving, a mutuality of being. Instead, nothing was shared, everything was suspected, and everything was handled until it lost its savor. Separately they would have had a thousand friends. Together they had scarcely a dozen whom they might call more than acquaintances. Thornton was poor and becoming poorer.

She thought about their poverty—an insidious, reckless thing. If Thornton had been in a normal state, she might have enjoyed it as another adventure, a real but romantic condition the conquest of which would be in itself beneficial and stimulating. But Thornton could not believe that she had faith and fondness enough for that. On the contrary, he raised dissension by listening for complaint where none was made. He did not trust her.

So they sat, month after month, drawing further apart, frittering away their money, their emotions, their days. Circumstances that should have brought them closer together had the opposite result. Michael's death. The dead baby. Out of such tragedy they could have forged a strong friendship. But fear of hurting each other, misinterpretation, reticence, balked every approach. It was time to give up the struggle. Sympathy was worn to tatters. Understanding was nil.

Reconciliation impossible. Cynthia would leave. She knew that Thornton would never leave her.

What would she do? She had often thought about that. Under Thornton's long-suffering, gentle (and now odious and insincere) kindness was a restive, tactile spirit. (One that could be made immortal if it could be touched at all.) He might commit suicide. Slow death in such a present was as bad. He might go mad. It might ruin his career. Finally she judged that the vanity which his humbleness concealed would override any storm. He would undergo a fearful wrench. It would leave a mark of some sort. But he would survive and those parts of him that were most essential would be left whole. She had no right to judge him, but she was compelled to judge.

Murray Dean was nothing—a figure, a piece of material. That was the thing Thornton could not fathom. She would satisfy her obligation to Dean, refusing to count the cost to herself, and she would leave him. Neither of them would be worse for the exchange. It was in the loss of Thornton that she would pay dearly. Cynthia knew something of that price even before she left. Fleeing a husband whom she did not love had been a painful business. This would be infinitely more agonizing. The pain would never abate entirely, and she could picture her old age dotted with reminiscences of Thornton. She allowed herself that much sentiment.

As she studied her dilemma, she dwelt on the possibility of work. Then to her came a fragment of the emotion that must have kept Thornton from writing when he felt his hold on her was weakening. Work would be difficult and depressing. She was fitted for nothing that would elevate her above drudgery. In time she might rise in a department store or a small shop to be a business woman. The word was loathing in her ears. That rise, too, would be accompanied by the knowledge that it was attained because her lover was deficient. Dean would be preferable in that respect. The value of being a pure woman was not great—especially if one has lost one's mate. She had been married before. She was not pure when her first husband led her to the altar. She had lived with Thornton, unmarried, and taken money from him. She could see that it would be different morally to accept support from Dean. But so-called honest toil in the machine of civilization was as degrading to the soul, the body, and the heart as the occupation of mistress. Moral codes would have to admit that before they were purged of silliness.

She made lists in her mind, deriving them from alternate conditions as one derives many short words from a long word. Luxury, health, comfort, position, wealth, travel, friends, entertainment, opportunity to live and observe, leisure to read and play and exercise, protection, freedom, a retreat for sorrow—those things were better than further misery, squalor, slavery, poverty. The adages lied. They had been made by unintelligent men. Certainly intelligent women had not invented them. She had added that wisdom to her store in the past year.

45

On the day of her departure Cynthia bade Thornton good-bye in a natural voice, but she knew it would be her last sight of him. During the long, cold mornings and afternoons while he had sought vainly for a job, those thoughts and arguments had scurried through her mind until each became fixed in its channel. She did not hesitate or question after her decision was made.

Thornton kissed her and left. She watched him and saw his heel flicked out of view through the door. An impulse to rush to the window and call him back died still-born. She lay for fifteen minutes, until she was sure that he had forgotten nothing, that he was not returning to kiss her, as he had in their earlier life together. Then she telephoned Dean.

"I'm leaving Thornton."

He feigned astonishment. "When?"

"Now."

"Where are you?"

"At our—his house. Will you come for me?"

"Of course. Right away. I think you are very wise, Cynthia."

She packed her clothes in two bags. Of the three they possessed she left the best one for Thornton. She worked expeditiously. She wiped out every evidence of herself that she could find, realizing how he would feel if he came upon a reminder afterwards. She wrote the note. Then she put on her coat and hat and sat in a chair, waiting for Dean.

He came quickly. He had driven in his car from the office. "Are you all ready?"

"Yes."

He carried her suit-cases to the automobile. He gave her no chance to linger. They started.

"Funny," Cynthia said, "but I packed everything I own in the world in a few minutes."

"It's pathetic."

"I'm not sorry for myself."

He did not answer directly. "Where do you want to go?"

"Can you take a day off?"

"Certainly. Twenty, if you like. I told Don I should not return."

Her thoughts veered in various directions. "Is Don as competent as that?"

"As what?"

"Can he run the office in your absence?"

"I am making him my junior partner this month. He'll take my place whenever I wish to retire."

The car was progressing steadily up town. It was as if Dean wished to leave her life down town behind, by symbol and fact. "Any orders?" he said after a pause.

"Is it too early for cocktails? I'd like a drink. In an elegant speakeasy where there will be no one but us."

They stopped in the upper Fifties. He followed her

273

into a building that had once been the home of an ambassador—brownstone outside, with the elaborate carving of the eighties ornamenting the interior. In spite of the hour they were served with speed and ostentation.

"It's nice," Cynthia said.

He understood her desire for a drink. Without some assistance she could not sustain that unnatural composure for long. Her gold hair curved out under the brim of her hat and disappeared again. Her deep-blue eyes held a suggestion of pain. She was more beautiful than he had imagined. Women seldom affected him in that way when their possession was near.

He turned his hand over in an easy gesture. "Fairly nice. A hole in the wall. But the stuff is bona fide. Do you like baccardi?"

"Yes."

He leaned forward and drank in her features. She suffered it quietly. "Cynthia," he said, with a quick agitation, "I want to congratulate you. You are not only the most beautiful, but also the wisest and bravest woman I have ever known."

"I'm not in a good mood for flattery."

"So I haven't flattered," he said, regaining his usual poise.

She sighed. He began again with the second cocktail. "You had to leave. He is a nice boy—but he is only a boy. He is clever—but cleverness is bad company for loyalty. You were too good to him. He was never good to you. I have heard you criticized for your treatment of him—for going out with me, and other things. You and I know who should have been criticized."

Her interruption was decisive. "I know my mind and my reasons for my actions. Whatever happens, Murray, will you please never talk about him to me."

"Sorry. Have another cocktail?"

"Yes."

He smiled. "I'll move heaven and earth for you. I don't expect you to like me immediately. Just accept what you can and let me woo for the rest."

Her shoulders hunched imperceptibly. "I was going to speak to you about that. I'm terribly upset. I'm in no mood—for an amour—yet. I want to be alone for a while. To think. I don't mean you can't see me. But you must expect nothing for a while but my company. Is that clear?"

No emotion showed on his face, but he conquered a bitter disappointment. "Of course I see. You're perfectly right. We'll find a suite in a hotel, install you there, and you can think all you wish."

She wished that Thornton had shown such mature control. But she said: "All right. But nothing lavish. I have no clothes at all."

Again Dean smiled. "Fine! It gives us something to do this afternoon. We'll shop. Every store in town and everything you want. Dresses and evening dresses. *Lingerie* and coats. Fifty pairs of stockings. Twenty pairs of shoes. Whatever you desire. When we finish, we'll find a hotel."

It was a startling notion. She was on the verge of

acceptance. But she answered: "No. I don't even want that yet. I just want to be alone, without excitement or prejudice until I've adjusted myself. You needn't be afraid."

"I'm beginning to gather some conception of your real worth," he said.

They had luncheon together and attended the matinée of a musical comedy. It was the best suggestion she could make. Her life was aimless then. After the theater, more cocktails. Dinner. They chose a quiet restaurant near Central Park. He followed her every wish. At ten he called a hotel. The car drew up at its canopy.

"Have you any money?"

"A dollar and a quarter," she said.

He put a bill in her hand, which she stuffed into her pocket-book. A uniformed Negro took her two suit-cases.

"Good-bye and thank you," she said. "Call me at lunch-time—if you want to."

"If I want to!"

The car started. His hand waved. She registered and went to her room. He had been kind. Easy to manage. Thoughtful. Controlled. A rueful expression clouded her face. How long would it be before he tired of playing? Before his vigorous and penetrating nature was beyond management? Before he was drunk, perhaps, and disgusting?

"This is the room, ma'am."

"Thank you." She gave a quarter to the voice.

"Really a suite, ma'am."

In that point he was already the victor. He had reserved a suite, not a room.

"A suite—" the voice continued, tentatively.

She added her dollar to the quarter.

"Thank you, ma'am. Thank you kindly."

She entered. The other bill, the bill Dean had
given her, was a hundred dollars. She laughed.

46

She lay on the wide bed with closed eyes. Her slippers were kicked to the floor. Some time before dawn
she woke and undressed. The cocktails had made her
sluggish. She slept again.

47

Thornton stumbled into his house. His body was
black and blue. His face was cut. He had been in two
fights and acquitted himself well, but he had been
thrown out of the place where the last combat had been
staged. On his face on the sidewalk. He could not see
or feel. He fell on the bed.

Day came like a worn article that had been used
by countries round the world and was full of the dead
sorrows discarded into it. Thornton lifted his head. A
flask in his pocket pressed against him. He drew it out

and drank noisily. He shook his fist at the room. Seeing that it was clotted with blood, he laughed in a slow, hiccuping way. He went downstairs. In the mail box was a check for one of his stories. One hundred and fifty dollars. He put it in his pocket. The bar-tender refused to give him a drink, so he went to another speakeasy.

Half an hour afterwards Aurelius ran lightly up the stone steps of Thornton's home. He did not ring the bell, but hastened to the apartment. The door was sagging open. He walked in. No sign of Cynthia or Thornton. Blood on the pillow. An empty flask on the floor. A quick search of the room made some of the story intelligible. Cynthia had gone and Thornton was drinking. Had been hurt.

"Oh, Lord," Aurelius said.

It did not take much time to find Thornton. He was sitting at a table drinking. He looked scarcely human. His hair was matted. His face was filthy. His clothes were torn. One sleeve dangled at the elbow. Except to cringe, he gave no sign of recognizing Aurelius.

Aurelius said: "Come on, Thornton."

No response. He shook the drunken boy. "Snap out of it."

"Go away. This is my day on the ulcer."

"What?"

"Go away, demon. Go." His eyes were sightless.

Aurelius lifted him to his feet and carried him to the door of the speakeasy. From there Thornton walked mechanically. People stared at them. Aurelius wanted to stop at a drug-store and telephone to Nadine to explain that he was bringing Thornton, but he did not dare. She opened the door when he knocked.

"What's the matter?"

Aurelius was almost crying. "Cynthia's left him and he's drunk." He relinquished Thornton for an instant and he toppled to the floor.

"Oh."

Nadine and Aurelius undressed Thornton. He roused himself to protest intermittently. They put him in a tub of warm water. He seemed unconscious, but once, while they bathed him, he said quite lucidly: "Damn nice of you people." They were startled. They put him in their bed between clean sheets. He slept.

They found the check in his pocket before they threw away his clothes. Nadine took it, looked at the date, and under her breath muttered a curse that dumbfounded Aurelius.

48

When Thornton saw daylight again, there was a fire burning in the grate in the next room. A morning sun reflected in the mirror of Nadine's dressing-table flecked the wall with rainbows. He had been unconscious for twenty hours. His head hurt, he was weak, but he felt immeasurably better than he had felt for a long time. He walked into the living-room and sat before the fire. Nadine and Aurelius waited for him to speak.

After a long time, during which he remained motionless, with his hands extended towards the fire, **he** said: "Thanks."

The word broke a spell of silence. Nadine went to the kitchen and he heard the sizzle of bacon and eggs. They ate breakfast. He realized that both of them were watching him furtively. He tried to remember what had happened and how he had been brought there, but he could not. The name of Cynthia in his mind was like a stab. After breakfast they smoked. No one appeared to have any interest in talking, any intention of deserting the company.

Thornton took the cue of that tranquillity. "Well, I've lost, haven't I? And I didn't do it well. What happened?"

Nadine said: "Circumstance."

Thornton waited. "She didn't want to go."

"Of course not. And she'll come back."

He stood up and walked over to the hearth. "No. That I do not even hope. Cynthia—Cynthia could cut things cleanly. Just as she left her husband in California and never mentioned him again. I will be the same. Yesterday that thought would have given me the heebie-geebies. I feel firmer today."

"Too bad you couldn't have married each other."

"She wouldn't marry me." He turned towards them easily, the fire-light searching out deep planes and shadows on his pale cheeks. "She was right, in her own way. We never became acquainted. For two years we lived as intimately as anyone ever did. But we reached no understanding. We scarcely touched the edges. I know how she looks and how she talks. Nothing else. I haven't even the remotest notion of what she thinks about me now." He stopped abruptly.

"Wouldn't that be reason enough for her to go away?" Nadine asked. "What do you think women are, animals?"

Thornton started. He had said precisely that long ago, before he knew Cynthia. Aurelius spoke. "I noticed it sometimes. You were kind and tender and thoughtful, you were even stubborn and unruly sometimes—which is part of the system—but you were always conscious of what you did, conscious that it was a system."

"What could I do?" Thornton answered. "Every time I talked to her, touched her, smiled at her, there was a meaning behind it that I knew."

"Didn't you ever do anything spontaneously?"

"Of course. I did nice things for no reason—but that was the reason—if you understand me. Once in a while when I did a thing like that, she would cry. I couldn't tell whether it was because she liked it or because she was disappointed."

"You starved her."

Thornton's body became tense. "How in the name of heaven could I help myself? Day and night I tried to get away from it. Day and night I tried to stop screwing up my thoughts to the point where they would miss nothing, fail in nothing, guess everything. And I missed it all, failed everywhere, guessed nothing. I knew such elaborate concentration was unnecessary. I knew it was what almost every man goes through for a while—he tries, fails less drastically than I failed, becomes discouraged, believes woman an outrageous creature, relegates her to a small corner of his mind; and thereafter marriage becomes the parallel enterprise of two separate lives faintly interested in each other because of the protection they give and receive. I knew it. Look at Gerry and Don. They started about when we started. In the same way, very nearly. Now they don't care. I didn't want Cynthia and myself to wake up and find our lives a replica of theirs. I wanted understanding. But, great God! I couldn't stop thinking, could I? I couldn't shut off my mind and leap into our lives without judging, analyzing, observing, could I? I couldn't fail to see the expression on other men's faces when they looked at her, or the little mannerisms she adopted in their presence, could I? I couldn't help knowing what I felt and what she felt when other women rubbed their eyes against mine like cats, could I? On went the brain. Down went the heart. Gerry tried to make love to me. She failed. I told Cynthia. But she wouldn't tell me about herself. I stopped working. I didn't know what to believe. I saw De— this business beginning. I was terrified. I didn't know what to believe. I knew I was jealous. I felt like a man in one of Poe's tales—on the brink of a horrible deed which I was doing purely because I dreaded its commission. Every kindness of the man became a slap in my face. Every failure of my own another insurmountable wall to wrap me in. Every intrusion of circumstance a piece of irony over which I was powerless. I was gay, and it sounded like tumbril wheels to me. I seemed to be driving her towards the thing from which I wanted to extricate her. I pleaded. I begged. I held my peace. I grew angry. I wept. I worshipped. I suggested. I petted her. I laughed. I loved and refused to love. I invented a thousand games and stories. I—"

"It is she who must have gone nearly crazy, not you. Did you ever try to think how she felt?"

"I never tried anything else."

Nadine watched the fire with unreadable eyes. "What do you suppose Cynthia was saying to herself then?"

"I wish I knew."

"I think I can tell you. She was saying, 'He doesn't love me. He doesn't trust me'. "

Thornton shook his head. "She knew I loved her."

"She knew you did all those hysterical things you say you did. But not a single one of them showed you loved her. They were all performed for one purpose: to keep her from doing anything that would hurt you."

It was an icy judgment. "In other words—" Thornton began.

"In other words, you loved her, but you loved yourself more." Nadine smiled. "Oh, you're complicated, Thornton. Like Aurelius. He's equally difficult and recondite in another way. But so much you do is insincere. You haven't any idea what goes on inside you and why. If you found out, you'd hide it under another layer, and so on, until you had to go through forty layers to reach the one above the last burial. You would have died for Cynthia in a minute. Gone to the stake for her. Everybody knows that. But you considered it so important. I'm not going to be trite and say that you were unwilling to live for her. But I will say that she didn't want a dead hero for a lover. You actually wanted to die for her. You hung yourself on the handiest cross—your and her troubles—so you could say: 'Here I am, Cynthia, suffering for you. But see! I'm gay. Brave! The blood drips out, but it's for you, so I don't even notice it.' That's masochism, I suppose. And I don't have to tell you that I hate to say this. I know how hard it is."

"Never mind," Thornton answered. "Go on."

"There you are again!" Nadine rose. "Listening to the cruel truth and showing poor, simple Aurelius and me what a soldier you can be. You've found out one thing in life and it's a great discovery. Half—three fifths of all that man believes is founded on that discovery. And it's only a silly little natural law, not important at all. You've learned that, between the pleasant emotions and the disagreeable, the ecstatic and the agonistic, there is no comparison. The lesson is written on you like stone-chiseling. You discovered that you can suffer fifty times as much as you can enjoy. Despair is an emotion that pales bliss. Grief is greater than delight. Woe is mightier than happiness. That fact makes the lives of most people nothing but avoidances. It stands in the way of progress. You know, too, that thought comes from emotion. You think. So, with pretty accurate intuition, you seek the most poignant emotions. But that has nothing to do with love. Love is a state of being. It isn't an emotion. It isn't an idea. It isn't a system of living. It's founded on certainties. You were certain of nothing. Your own words show that you were not even certain of Cynthia. Naturally, she could not be certain of you. You foundered when you considered yourself. You were shaky in your attitude towards the world. In the end—"

"What shall I do?"

"Just—live. Be. Do anything. You've built your world around yourself to coddle your brain. To stimulate it. The earth was your tonic, and you asked for it bitter. Now you've drunk the bottleful."

"I think you're wrong," Thornton said quietly.

"Of course I'm wrong. You're too damn clever about living. I'm perfectly wrong about you. Nobody knows better than I that, at bottom, you loved Cynthia, and loved her in the right way. But the layers I spoke about are so thick that she wore herself to nothing trying to penetrate them. Tiers and tiers of rationalizations and concealments and subterfuges and dissimulations and excuses and props and explanations. If I knew Cynthia a little better, I'd do one of two things—I'd tell you to go out and get drunk again and pick up the first pretty girl you could find to console yourself, or else I'd give you more encouragement than you deserve."

"Which leaves me nowhere."

"Which is where you were before, and where you always will be until you get on to yourself." She raised her voice slightly. "I could enlarge that theme. The theme of love. You talk about it and write about it and you used to look for people to tell you that you and Cynthia were the perfect couple. She did, too. I suppose it reassured her. When I think about that, I'm almost ready to persuade you to drink and the pretty girl. Cynthia just wouldn't quit until she was sure. She was that sort. She left you because it was absolutely useless to hope that she would attain in you the calm, loving mate she desired. Did you ever think what she must feel now? Two years—or nearly two years—thrown away. Two years that began eagerly and ended in ruin because of you. Did you ever think of that?"

"Yes. And it doesn't make me feel any better."

"There you are! Thinking about your own feelings again. It's a trick you have. Well, she's brave, anyway. She knew what to do. She'll live for herself now—just as you always did. She'll accumulate an assurance of permanent financial stability. I'll bet she knows the exact sum right now. And then let any other man look at her except for fun. She'll still be able to play. Only —you'd probably call it disintegration or sorrow-drowning. But two failures don't indicate touching the fire again. She's braver and cleaner than all you people who go around talking about love as an illusion, and love as something physical. It is physical. But you haven't scrutinized the body yet. You study only the morbid nerves. The diseased ones."

"I wish you'd stop," Thornton said.

"It won't do you any good. I'll stop. For every fifty people like you, there's a genius. You're just a machine. You have exploited feeling and emotion until all that is left is backwash. If you can produce a work of art, you won't be a complete social anomaly. Biology." Her voice modulated. "You can stay here—and sleep on the couch, if you like. We'd be glad to have you. There are limits to my rudeness when it considers your body—even if there are few for your soul."

"Well—"

49

The same bright daylight, untempered by anything so comfortable and homely as a wood fire, waked Cynthia. She telephoned to the desk and asked the time. Then she ordered breakfast. She remembered her appointment for lunch with Murray Dean. She drank coffee and ate an orange.

Water boomed into the great tub. Cynthia lay in it. Her face was blank. Perhaps Thornton would be dead. She sat up suddenly and stepped from the bath, dripping. The room service furnished her with a file of morning papers. The water seemed very hot when she stepped into it again. There was a suicide in Hoboken. A maniac on a trolley car. A fall from a high window. But all the persons had been identified and none of them was Thornton. She examined every item in the papers. No news. Once she looked at the telephone longingly. She had only to go to it, lift the receiver, recite a word and some numbers, to hear his voice. But would he be at home? Maybe it would ring long and vainly. That would be horrible.

A knock at the door. Flowers. Flowers to fill the two rooms and flowers to throw on the street, if she wished. Twenty minutes later a second knock announced a bandbox filled with silk and laces. She accepted it, frowning. He was not keeping his promise. She sat undecided, eying first her own tattered underthings, paled by many washings, and then the confections in the bandbox. Finally she selected the plainest combination and the severest slip. Even they were gorgeous. She put them on and surveyed the effect in a long mirror. Her eyes were dark and odd, so that she believed she had aged. She went again to the bathroom and commenced a process that was complete when Dean sent his card to her. He looked younger. Almost handsome in his austere clothes. His eyes outshone the suggestion of a characteristic she hesitated to identify. "I cheated," he said.

50

At luncheon he told her he wanted to make a confession. A confession of something shameful and despicable. He said that he would tell her because he intended always to tell her the truth. It was sagacious policy. She gave him permission to speak.

"There are certain—things—I'm not allowed to mention. I'll try not to do it. But long, long ago I saw that you were making a terrible mistake. It seemed so wrong to me that I dared interfere—"

"I'd rather not—"

"Interfere in more ways than you know. Did you ever observe, for example, that the attitude of Don and Gerry towards you and—towards you two changed?"

Cynthia swallowed hastily. "You mean that you—?"

"I did. I simply pointed out the error of your ways to them—"

"—and made it perfectly clear what you wanted."

"It was fair, wasn't it? Your own actions have vindicated me. I couldn't have told you then how much I cared for you—even though I saw you were doomed. It would have turned you against me at once."

She made a pattern on the table-cloth with her finger. "Murray, you certainly don't leave any stones unturned. But what was it you said to me about cleverness and loyalty the other day?"

"*Touche!*"

"Yes, that was a touch. I'm going to have some extraordinary fencing on my hands. I'd hate to be your rival in business."

"The exertion of such diplomacy springs from a desire deeper than any commercial want."

"I expect so. Don and Gerry. The dirty—"

Dean frowned. "You don't mean that, I hope? That was why I told you. Means to ends are justified—such means."

"Sorry," she said. "But are we going to have to pretend about them to each other?"

He laughed. "I give up. Refuse to play. You're much better today. Have you finished your thinking?"

She ignored the question. "It was Gerry—not Don."

"Yes. Don confines his intrigues to advertising."

She thought suddenly that Don and Gerry would know about Thornton. They had probably been detailed by Dean to watch him. So that there would be no scandal. The truth was that Dean had underestimated Thornton's affection for Cynthia. She said: "After all, I have no quarrel with them. It was typical of her. Sometimes I even feel sorry for Gerry. But it came out the way it was certain to come out. Suppose we four play bridge at my hotel tonight?"

Dean stared at her quizzically. He could not resolve such a decision. "Good. You need company, friends, a few familiar things."

"Yes, I do."

51

She had gambled, of course, that Don and Gerry would arrive first. They did. They were embarrassed. Cynthia could not wait upon their rather peculiar sensitivities. "Hello! Take your things off. I want to ask you something before Murray comes."

"Swell place."

"Lovely."

She was not to be refused. "Have you seen or heard of Thornton?"

"No."

"No."

She tried not to show her leadenness of heart. "Not that I'm going back. But I worried. He's so irresponsible."

Don nodded. "I'll look him up and let you know— some time when I'm out of the office."

"Tomorrow?"

"Tomorrow."

"Why not call Nadine?" Gerry asked.

Cynthia reddened. "Pride." She played bridge badly.

52

On the second morning of her new life Cynthia took stock of herself. She had a slight hang-over. Thoughts of Thornton troubled her. A surprising illumination had flooded the actions of Don and Gerry— an illumination that came too late to be useful, but not too late to be interesting. The removal of such a small factor might have made a difference in Thornton. She assured herself that nothing could have made a difference.

But he had known, he must have known. He had even tried to tell her in his devious way. She had a small headache that was susceptible to abolition or that could be nurtured into real pain. The idea was kept-womanish. Already! How Thornton would spit that word, making it cruel and nasty! New *lingerie* and a thousand flowers. A rich man ready to spill his fortune at her feet. A suite in a hotel. She ordered a paper. Nothing. Thornton had not committed a spectacular suicide. She told herself that she was foolish to expect such a thing.

Gerry called up. "Hello, darling."

"Hello, Gerry. Any news?"

"None. Are you very, very happy?"

Cynthia lay back on her pillows. "Why?"

"You must be. I'm pretty jealous of you."

"Oh."

They wasted banalities, made an engagement, hung up. At noon Don telephoned.

"Have you seen him?" Cynthia could scarcely recognize her voice.

"No."

"Oh."

"But I ran into Aurelius, and he's seen him."

"Yes—?"

"Met him on the way to the office. Aurelius, that is. 'Did you know that Cynthia has left Thornton?' he asked."

Cynthia cut in impatiently. "Then what? What about Thornton?"

"If you'd called Nadine, you could have found out. Thornton has been there for two days."

"Has he? Does he look all right?"

"I guess so. Aurelius didn't say anything about that. Yes, he did. Said he was busted up."

"Busted up!"

"Oh, it wasn't anything. The night you—the night —he went off his nut a little. Beat up some people and got beaten up—"

"Oh, my God."

"But he was pretty batty, I guess—I guess it was tough—for him. Everybody down town is talking about it. The way he went around."

"How did he go around?"

"Just kind of vague. You know how crazy people are. Talking. All about abscesses—"

"About what?"

"Oh, abscesses and things. I don't think he said anything about you. I asked particularly. You needn't worry about that, I guess." Don's voice halted.

"Is that all Aurelius said?"

"Just asked me if I knew. I said I did. Then he told me about Thornton going blooey. He's better now. Then he asked me what I thought."

"Then?"

"I said I thought it was a good thing."

"What did he say?"

"Aurelius? He gave me a funny look and said: 'Good thing? For whom? Dean?'"

"Is that all he said?"

"That's all."

"Nothing more about Thornton?"

"No."

"All right, Don. Thanks for calling."

"Oh, you're welcome. I'm afraid it wasn't very good news. I'm in two minds about the whole thing."

"I'd rather you left opinions to me."

"Of course. Want me to talk to Thornton?"

"Well—yes. No. I'm glad to hear that—that nothing happened to him."

"Naturally. You would worry about him when you weren't there."

"Don, are you deceiving me?"

That discomfited Don. He felt that he should have consulted with someone before calling Cynthia. He had done it spontaneously—possibly as a weak attempt at regeneration and reprieve. Don's conscience was different from Gerry's. "Oh," he said, "Thornton is really all right. Aurelius was upset. That's all."

"All right," Cynthia replied. "I'm glad you told me about Thornton."

"He didn't do anything, understand. Just walked and talked and sat on curbs and things like that."

"But he's improved?"

"Oh, yes. Aurelius took care of him. Aurelius and a doctor. Gave him dope and today he was perfectly O.K."

"Sure?"

"Positive."

"Well, good-bye."

BABES AND SUCKLINGS

Cynthia picked at the quilt. If Aurelius had let them give dope to Thornton, he must have been in bad shape. She did not know and Thornton did not know—they never knew—what had passed during the twenty hours through which he had lain unconscious at Aurelius's house. Fantastic, impossible things, shapes and screamings, and two forms holding a fierce and profane body to a quivering bed for hours while its mouth babbled the heinous, bloody business of living in such terms as would move stars from their orbits. But Cynthia felt the oppression of those hours. Her eyes brooded, her hands clenched, her legs twisted themselves like flesh in fire.

53

Five days passed. Thornton was living in his own house again. He crawled out of bed, not knowing whether it was morning or afternoon. He attached a percolator, waited, and drank his first cup of coffee. Hunger suggested itself. He opened the ice-box, closed it, and pulled the door a second time. His head was set at an angle as if he was trying to sow the creak of the door deep in his mind so that it could never be forgotten.

There were three eggs. He took two. Someone else could have the third. They fried and he watched them while they fried. Afterwards he ate them. Then he drank his second cup of coffee.

BABES AND SUCKLINGS

Sun filled the air. Brilliant winter sun. It was not so cold as it had been. He washed the dishes. Each one was set in the water laboriously, rounded with the mop, and set in the rack—the plate first, the saucer, the cup, the two spoons. Then the frying-pan. He took the percolator apart, dumped the coffee grounds into the garbage pail, and replaced its noisy lid. He washed the percolator and set it upside-down on the draining-board. Then he dried the dishes and put them in the closet.

Nothing could describe the precision, the care, the sadness with which he performed each of the little tasks.

He stretched out in the over-stuffed chair. His eyes were abstract. His face was white. He looked like a man who had been wasted in sickness and recovered only after a long and intimate inspection of death. A man who did not yet realize his recovery.

A faucet dripped in the kitchenette. He rose and shut it firmly. He sat down again. By and by he picked up an envelope from a small table and fumbled in his pocket. He produced a stubby pencil. He copied a column of figures from his check-book. Then he added them and subtracted other figures. His last total was ninety-one dollars and fifty-three cents. He put everything back in its place.

An hour stalked through the room and he did not notice its passing.

Finally he stood up and crossed the apartment. He took the suit-case from the closet shelf. It was his

296

best and now his only suit-case. Drawers were opened and their contents transferred. Good suit. Day suit. Old suit. Tuxedo? It gave him pause. It was returned to its hanger. Dust would collect upon it.

Ties. Shirts. How many? Eight. Plenty. Pyjamas. Three union suits. Three pairs of pyjamas. Razor. Shaving-cream. Mirror. Tooth-brush. Paste. The other paste was gone, but the old tube would suffice. He remembered telling her once that he preferred the brand of the old tube.

His lip bled.

Handkerchiefs. A towel. New shoes. Old shoes. He made an inventory with studied calm. In one of the drawers he found a *brassière*. He held it stupidly in his hand and at last replaced it. He closed the empty drawers and the closet door. The lid of the suit-case fell of its own accord.

He sat on the bed. It would be better to have a destination in mind. Of course, it was warm—but still cold. He sniffed and pondered. His eye lighted on the guitar. He would not be wanting it. Where to go? Away. Where? Away from New York. From the city. Michael had been on the sea. Perhaps he would go out on the sea. The sea.

Then he froze with a dreadful terror. His scalp pricked. A key was being inserted in the door! He stood, trembling from head to foot. His aloneness engulfed him. He thumped his head with the heel of his hand. The door was opening. He braced himself.

Cynthia!

He fell at her feet. Real feet. She was on the floor beside him. Kissing. Their lips were cold as snow.

"One of us had to do it," she said, a long time afterwards. "You thought you were. I thought I was."

"What?"

She quoted a verse he had written:

> "For you who come at length to me
> May love enough to set us free."

"I don't see what you mean, dear. But it doesn't matter."

"It doesn't matter."

She unpacked his suit-case while he lay on the day-bed. He could hear her weeping.

Then she was matter-of-fact. "I suppose we're broke?"

"Ninety-one dollars and fifty-three cents."

"What!"

"A check came. The next day. Or the day after. The stories you sent out."

"Poor Thornton!"

"I'm the—"

"Never mind. Ninety-one dollars. That will pay my hotel bill. And enough left over to get married—"

His voice was like an echo across a wide lake. "Married?"

"Of course. This afternoon, if I can arrange it. Michael got a divorce for me—long ago. Right away. Because I'm going to work."

"But I'll earn thousands. Start tomorrow—"

"I'll stop when you do."

Her clothes were in their right places. "Now, be a dear and call the hotel. Find out how much I owe. It's charged, but tell them I'm going to pay."

"Hotel? You stayed at a—"

"Yes." She waited for his questions. The insinuating or falsely comforting things he always said. They did not come. Instead he gave her a single glimpse of wide, shining eyes and went to the telephone.

54

Evening. Cynthia sat so close to him that it was difficult to play his guitar. But he strummed with felted finger-tips, and melody went out through the lamplight. Then the key changed. He sang.

> Ten thousand God-damned cattle,
> They left my ranch and rambled away,
> Sons of bitches
> Is what I say.
> Now I'm lone man,
> Dead broke—today.
> My girl she left me strayin,'
> She left my ranch and rambled away
> With a son of a bitch
> From Ioway.
> Now I'm lone man,
> Dead broke—today.

299

BABES AND SUCKLINGS

Lone man!
Ten thousand cattle strayin'—
Lone man.
In gamblin' hell delayin'—
My girl she left me, ramblin,'
And I'm lone man, dead broke—today.

He looked down at her and smiled.

www.ingramcontent.com/pod-product-compliance
Lightning Source LLC
Chambersburg PA
CBHW021953010726
47494CB00003B/714